CONTENTS

CRIME
UNSOLVED

A BUCK TAYLOR NOVEL

BY

CHUCK MORGAN

ISBN 978-0-9988730-6-0 Paperback

ISBN 978-0-9988730-7-7 eBook

ISBN 978-1-7337960-2-6 Large Print

LIBRARY OF CONGRESS CONTROL NUMBER

2018910461

Dedication

To wildland and structure firefighters who battle the monster every day.

CHAPTER ONE

The hike through the valley had been long and arduous, especially since they were carrying four five-gallon jerry cans full of gas. They had stopped earlier in the day at the local twenty-four-hour convenience store and filled the four cans. The trailer they were towing held two four-wheel ATVs, so no one at the store gave them a second look when they filled the cans up with gas. They filled them with the cheapest gas—no sense using high test gas and paying more just to burn it up.

They started down the trail just after full dark. They'd chosen this night because there was no moon, and they almost missed the old game trail they had spotted a couple of weeks before, but after doubling back a couple of times, they finally located the trail. Access to where they were heading was limited.

When the wealthy developer had traded the parcel he owned on the back side of the new Elk Mountain Ski Resort, with the Forest Service for this piece of isolated land, the property did not have any access easements. There was so much controversy when the land swap was made public that, due to the enormous amount of local pressure, the Forest Service agreed as part of the deal not to allow an access easement through the remaining public land.

The opposition figured that would be the end of the lodge project, but the developer was not going to be deterred so easily. He fought through the courts and was faced with countersuits all along the way by local outdoor associations, fishing groups, and conservation groups. In the end, none of this mattered. The fishing lodge the wealthy developer intended to build would be exclusive. A play place for his rich and famous friends, so the less access, the better. All of these wealthy snobs would be flown in by helicopter, so they would never have to deal with the local riffraff.

There was an old fire road that led to the property line, so as part of the compromise, the court allowed the developer to use this for construction access only. Once construction was completed, the developer would be required to close the road at the edge of his property. Local law enforcement and the local fire department were allowed access to the road.

This part of the compromise didn't make anyone happy. In the end, the locals blockaded the road, and no one had access. The developer chose to fly in all his labor and materials. He wasn't going to let a bunch of local yokels stand in his way.

As the two guys carried their gas cans down the old game trail, they believed that tonight, this would all end. They would take care of the problem when the courts and the locals could not. The environment would once again rule the day.

The game trail skirted the security shack that had been built inside the property line along the old forest service road. They'd spotted six armed security guards on their last excursion, and they had no interest in messing with them. Stealth was the name of their game, and they were good at what they did.

On their last trip, they scouted out a great hiding spot on the edge of the forest, and they were now sitting quietly and observing the guards as they made their rounds. Almost all the construction workers had been airlifted off the site over the past couple of days. The lodge was finished, and soon the staff would arrive to make sure it was clean for the first group of guests. If all went according to plan, there should be no collateral damage.

They worked their way to the service door at the rear of the kitchen and prepared to pick the lock. Phase one of their plan would happen once they were inside the lodge: essentially, pouring out the contents of their gas cans. They had little doubt that all this wood would burn like a bonfire. Once they were satisfied they had covered everything with the gas, they would pull a couple of cellular igniters out of their backpacks and position them in the middle of piles of rags they would have taken from the supply closet and doused with gas.

Phase two of their plan involved opening all the valves for the propane equipment in the kitchen. They also had to access the mechanical room and shut the valve that controlled the water for the fire sprinkler system. The mechanical room was in a large closet behind the kitchen. The door was kept unlocked, but they knew there was a chain and padlock around the sprinkler system valve, which was there to prevent someone from closing the valve and preventing the water from reaching the sprinklers in the event of a fire. They would make quick work of the lock with the bolt cutters they brought with them.

They had gone over the plan several times over the last couple of days, and each man knew his part. They had used this same plan several times in multiple locations, and it had always worked as planned. They had been working together long enough; they could almost read each other's thoughts. Tonight would be no different. The issue that concerned them the most, at this point, was the weather. The winds were always unpredictable, and the last thing they wanted was to find themselves amid a sudden wind shift and set more than the lodge on fire. So far, the weather report—when they'd last checked, as they started their hike through the woods—was on their side. The front wasn't expected for several hours yet.

They knew from experience something wasn't right as soon as they pushed open the kitchen door. There was a sudden rush of air into the building, and they heard the unmistakable sound of the back draft as the inrush of fresh air fed the unseen fire smoldering somewhere in the building.

They both looked at each other and simultaneously yelled, "FUCK, RUN!"

They made it a couple of steps before the explosion from inside the lodge blew out all the windows, and the concussive blast sent them flying head over heels. They picked themselves up off the ground and made a mad dash to the forest, leaving the gas cans where they landed near the back door. When they looked back, the entire lodge was engulfed in flames, and the heat was intense.

They both knew it was time to leave. They had no idea what had happened, but they wanted to get as far away as possible from the fire before the authorities arrived. Whatever happened was not part of their plan, and they needed to get the hell out of there. Someone had gotten there ahead of them and set a smoldering fire, but who could that be? And why?

CHAPTER TWO

Buck Taylor stood behind the fire command center that had been set up in the parking lot of the Vaughan Lake campground just off Rio Blanco Route 8.

Buck was six feet tall and weighed in at 185 pounds, very little of it flab for a fifty-eight-year-old man. Buck's hair was salt-and-pepper, with what seemed like a lot more salt than pepper, and he wore it slightly longer than was typically the fashion of the day. He was always pleased when he looked in the mirror, since other than getting older, he was in as good a shape as he had been when he played defensive linebacker for the Gunnison High School Cowboys, a long time ago. He still tried to jog five miles every day when he could, and he tried to ride his mountain bike every weekend, weather permitting. The bike was always hanging off the back of his state-provided Jeep Grand Cherokee. Except for a couple of sore knees, coming mostly from age, Buck was in good shape, which was necessary in his line of work.

Buck was an investigative agent with the

Colorado Bureau of Investigation. He was currently assigned to the CBI field office in Grand Junction, Colorado, but he hadn't been in the office much during the past year. Somehow, he'd become the favorite go-to guy for the governor of Colorado, Richard J. Kennedy, who was, in fact, one of "those" Kennedys. The governor had been in office about eight months, and Buck had been instrumental in closing several high-profile investigations during that period that made the governor look good. As a result, when a situation came up that might get a little hairy, the governor always asked to have Buck assigned.

The sun was still a few hours away from rising over the mountains to the east, but the glow from the fire a few miles away lit up the sky. Buck stood there almost mesmerized by the flames he could see in the distance.

The Williams Fork fire, as it was being called, started a week before and had consumed nearly a thousand acres of some of the most pristine forest in Colorado. The Forest Service brought in a Level One incident commander and several hotshot teams from around the region. The air and ground battle had been relentless, and once the winds died down, the air tankers and hotshot crews had been able to achieve 25 percent containment.

The fire may have been 25 percent contained, but there was still a lot of fire out there, and Buck wasn't sure if he would be able to get to the crime scene anytime soon. He took a sip from the bottle of Coke he had brought with him.

The call came while Buck was in the middle of cleaning out the closet in his home in Gunnison. Buck's wife, Lucy, had been diagnosed with metastatic breast cancer five years earlier and lost her battle a couple of months back. It had been a valiant fight, and Buck missed his wife of thirty-five years every day. The pain of the loss had lessened, and he knew it was time to face the task of clearing out the memories. That started with donating all of Lucy's clothes to her church. Some volunteers would be by the next day to pick up all the donated clothes, so Buck had set his mind to finally getting it done.

He soon realized this was going to be one of the hardest jobs he had ever taken on. Each piece of clothing brought a memory, and Buck felt like he spent most of the day fighting back the tears. He was not winning the fight. His daughter-in-law Judy, who was married to his oldest son, David, had already cleaned out a lot of the house, with the help of Buck's grandchildren, but Buck wanted to tackle their room and closet by himself.

He decided that going through each piece of clothing was going to make the process even more difficult, so he started pulling everything off the hangers and putting it all in big black contractor trash bags. He then carried the bags out to the living room and piled them up in the front corner.

He was cleaning out all her personal items —toothbrush, combs, and medicines—when his phone rang. He looked at the number on the screen and considered not answering it. He was back at work following Lucy's death, but his bosses kept his schedule reasonably light. It looked like it was time to get back in the game.

CHAPTER THREE

"Yes, sir."

"Hi, Buck. Hope I didn't catch you at a bad time. You doing okay?" asked Kevin Jackson.

Kevin Jackson was the director of the Colorado Bureau of Investigation. He'd had a stellar career with the Colorado Springs Police Department before being tapped for the top post at CBI. He was more bureaucrat than cop, having spent most of his career on the administrative side of things, but he was well respected in law enforcement, and so far, Buck was impressed with him. He was also the youngest person ever to be picked for the director's position.

"Doing good, sir. Ready to get back into the trenches. What have you got?"

"Got a call from the governor this morning. There is a wildland fire underway in Rio Blanco County that started with the destruction of a huge, controversial fishing lodge. The lodge belongs to a couple of big opposition donors, and they are making a big stink about the governor not being able to handle the issue. There have been several fires over the last couple of years, and a group calling itself the National Environmental Task Force is claiming responsibility for this fire as well as several others."

"Excuse me for interrupting, sir, but did you say that a group that is at the forefront of fighting for the environment set fire to a forest while burning down a fishing lodge? I've heard about these guys over the years, and this seems like kind of a rookie mistake. Are we sure the group claiming credit is legit? Seems a little odd, sir."

"You picked up on that, huh?"

"Yes, sir."

The director continued. "We don't know for sure; that's where you come in. It appears they set this brand-new lodge on fire and didn't pay attention to the latest weather report, because a front blew through and the winds jumped up to thirty-five miles an hour with gusts up to seventy. Anyway, the governor wants us to get all over this, and he asked for you, personally. But before you start to feel flattered, one of the guys making the most noise is Hardy Braxton. He is even threatening to run against the governor when he comes up for reelection in a couple of years. You got any kind of conflict you can't work through with that?"

Buck didn't hesitate. "No conflict, sir. I can deal with Hardy and his friends."

The director went on to fill Buck in on the rest of the crimes the NETF had taken responsibility for. Over the years, there had been several mysterious fires involving controversial projects around the state, including the destruction of a new lodge and restaurant at the top of Vail Mountain. The NETF was considered, by many in law enforcement, to be the special forces unit in the war to protect the environment. They were fearless and deadly, and no one had been able to get close to this group.

He told Buck to use whatever resources he needed and to check in with the Rio Blanco County sheriff. The sheriff had already been briefed, and he knew Buck was coming. The director told Buck to be careful and stay in touch.

Even though the Colorado Bureau of Investigation had the authority to work anywhere in the state, it had always been customary to wait to be invited into an investigation by the local authorities, be it police or sheriff's office. This time would be a little different since this investigation would cover several locations throughout the state, and it was at the request of the governor. Buck would have full authority to handle the investigation as he saw fit.

Buck hung up the phone, walked into his home office and sat down at his laptop. True to his word, the director had sent Buck several files on the various crimes connected to the NETF. There wasn't much information in the files, and there was a severe lack of any cohesive investigation into their activities. Buck vowed he would fix that.

Buck pulled out his phone and dialed a number. The phone rang three times, and Bax answered.

"Hey, Buck. What's up?" asked Bax.

"Hey, Bax. You working on anything that can't wait?"

Bax was CBI Agent Ashley Baxter. Bax was five foot six with long blond hair she usually wore in a ponytail. She'd joined CBI four years before, right out of the University of Wisconsin. A Denver native, she had no issues moving to Grand Junction and thrived in her new environment. She was also one of the best internet and social media researchers Buck had ever worked with.

Buck went on to explain the conversation he had with the director. He asked Bax if she could pull together everything she could find on the National Environmental Task Force and any environmental groups that might be associated with it. He told her he was looking for a really deep dive. As he'd expected, Bax told him not to worry, and she was all over it.

Buck hung up, jumped in the shower, toweled off, got dressed and packed a bag with a couple of days of clean clothes. He clipped his gun and badge to his belt, grabbed his CBI windbreaker out of the front closet and headed for his car. Once in the car, he dialed his daughter-in-law Judy and let her know where he was headed. She promised to keep an eye on the house and make sure the church volunteers picked up all the donated clothes from the living room.

Buck started the car and pulled out of the driveway. He felt good about getting back in the game. He headed for Meeker, Colorado, and the Rio Blanco County sheriff.

CHAPTER FOUR

There is no easy way to get from Gunnison to Meeker. No matter which of the two options you take, it still takes almost four hours to make the drive. Buck left Gunnison on Highway 50 and headed west. Knowing he had a while to kill, he decided to call his daughter.

Cassie was the middle child, and she was every bit a middle child. In high school, she played soccer, ran track and played volleyball. She lettered in all three sports. She was also the one who got in trouble for violating curfew, drinking and whatever other mischief she could find to get into. Buck was surprised when she was accepted to the University of Arizona with a full scholarship for volleyball. He was even more surprised when she was accepted into law school. Cassie was never much for regimented education.

A year and a half ago, she dropped out of law school, and her career path took a different track. She joined the Forest Service and was now working as a wildland firefighter with the Helena Hotshots, an elite firefighting team based out of Helena, Montana. Buck was not surprised. He never saw her sitting behind a desk as a lawyer. She loved the outdoors, and she was as tough as they came. Lucy wasn't pleased she'd quit school without any discussion, and she worried whenever Cassie was called out to a fire, but she also knew her daughter, and if this was where she was happy, then so was her mom.

The director had mentioned that several hotshot teams had been called in to fight the Williams Fork fire, and he wanted to see if her team was one of those called in. Her phone went straight to voice mail, which Buck knew meant she was in the field. He left a message that he was heading for Meeker and to call when she got in from the field.

The rest of the drive was quiet, and Buck spent a lot of the time thinking about all the family drives he and Lucy used to take when the kids were younger. Those memories brought tears to his eyes, knowing there would no longer be road trips with Lucy at his side. Several times he had to pass through songs on his iPod that brought back memories of their time together until he turned it off and drove along in silence. He missed Lucy so much. She had always been there for him, and he worried about going through life without his constant companion.

Buck arrived in Meeker just before dark, and as he turned off Highway 13 onto Fourth Street, he let the memories clear from his mind as he focused on the job at hand. He crossed Main Street and pulled into the parking lot behind the Rio Blanco County Sheriff's Office.

Buck walked through the front door of the sheriff's office, presented his ID to the deputy on duty at the front desk and was buzzed into the back. Sheriff Caleb McCabe was sitting at his desk reading a report when Buck walked in.

"Buck Taylor, as I live and breathe. It's great to see you." The sheriff stood up, walked around his desk and gave Buck's hand a hearty shake.

Rio Blanco County was named for the White River, which flows through the county. The county borders the state of Utah on its western edge and is predominantly an agricultural area. Covering more than 3,200 square miles, the county had a population of around 6,600 people, of which 95 percent were white, and it was a Republican stronghold. In 1936, Rio Blanco County, along with two other counties west of the Mississippi River, had voted for Alf Landon over Franklin Delano Roosevelt for president.

Meeker, Colorado, is the county seat and was founded in 1880. With a population of just over 2,500 people, the city sat in the east-central portion of the county and, although largely agricultural, was also a mecca for outdoorsmen and women. The county was named for Nathan

Meeker, an Indian agent, and was rich with the history of the Old West. Nathan Meeker was killed with eleven other people during the Meeker Massacre of 1879. The massacre eventually led to the expulsion of the White River Utes from the area.

"Sheriff, good to see you. It's been a long time," replied Buck. "Sounds like we have a problem we need to deal with."

"Yeah. I spoke with Director Jackson this morning, and he said he was sending you up here at the request of the governor. You know the governor is not well thought of around these parts, so you may want to downplay that part a little."

"Thanks for the advice. You want to fill me in on what's going on?"

The sheriff pointed to the empty visitor's chair in the corner and walked back around his desk and sat down. Buck sat down and took the file the sheriff handed him.

Caleb McCabe had just started his second term as sheriff. Born and raised on a hardscrabble ranch near Rangely, he had served in the military for four years and had seen action in both Afghanistan and Iraq. With a Silver Star and Purple Heart, Caleb was a shoo-in for the sheriff's job when the former sheriff, Clint Powell, was arrested in Craig, Colorado, on sexual assault charges stemming from a drunken party.

Caleb stood five foot eight, but he was 155 pounds of pure muscle. Being a local who was well respected gave him an advantage, which came in handy in such a large county, where most of the residents would rather solve any problem themselves instead of calling in the authorities. Life was hard in this windswept county, and the people were even harder.

CHAPTER FIVE

The sheriff gave Buck the Reader's Digest version of the events leading up to the fire at the lodge.

"By the way. Sorry to hear about your loss. My condolences. Your wife was one tough lady."

Buck nodded and choked back a tear.

"No one was happy when Mark Richards, the hedge fund guy, and his buddies decided to build their lodge. Anywhere else in the county would have been fine. You know we have a bunch of private lodges here, but this one was on a piece of pristine forest, and no one liked the idea of the Forest Service doing a land swap with this guy for a chunk of land at a ski resort."

Buck looked at the pictures of the property in the file the sheriff handed him. The sheriff continued. "Worst part was they closed almost a mile of both rivers for their private use. That was some of the best fishing on the river. I will say they did a nice job improving the trout habitat along that stretch, and I've heard tales of some huge fish coming out of there now, but the locals were not happy."

The sheriff and Buck discussed the terms of the land swap and the access issues that had been the catalyst for a bunch of local rallies against the project. Buck sat back and looked through the thin file.

"How do we know the National Environmental Task Force was responsible for the fire?" Buck asked.

The sheriff handed Buck a separate piece of paper. "Bastards sent a press release to the local paper. Can you believe that?"

Buck read the press release. It was full of environmental buzzwords, vague accusations and innuendos, which Buck would need to follow up on. There was a lot of legalese that hinted at corruption and payoffs on a broad scale. It did not paint a nice picture of Mark Richards or his partners, but it stopped short of making any specific accusations towards them.

"Mark Richards and his friends are not happy, and they are making serious threats towards the county, the federal government and the governor. I bet I get three or four calls a day looking for a progress report, and I keep telling them we can't even get to the crime scene until the fire is out. They don't want to hear it. They even sent a private investigator by yesterday. Not a very pleasant fellow, so watch your ass."

The press release was signed by NETF, but that alone was not an admission of responsibility. The sheriff noted the look of uncertainty in Buck's eyes.

"I know, Buck. This could have been written by anyone. Truth is we won't know who set the fire until we can get in there and take a look. The incident commander says we might be able to get into what's left of the building sometime tomorrow."

"Okay," replied Buck. "I spoke with Jack Spencer, the state fire investigator, on my way up here, and he will be here sometime tomorrow morning along with a couple of forensic techs from the State Crime Lab. In the meantime, I am going to check into a hotel and crash. I will see you on-site tomorrow morning."

Buck and the sheriff both stood and shook hands, and Buck walked out of the sheriff's office and headed for his car. Once in his car, he realized he hadn't eaten in a while, and he needed nourishment. He left his car in the parking lot and walked across the street to the Cozy Up Bar and Grill.

Buck hadn't been in the Cozy Up in years, but he knew nothing had changed since the last time he was there as soon as he opened the door. The bar had operated under several names over the previous hundred years and was listed on the

National Register of Historic Places as one of the oldest continually operating bars in the country.

The original building had been a log cabin, and parts of it were still visible, although the low light made it hard to see anything. As Buck's eyes adjusted to the lack of light, he saw that the old vinyl chairs and laminate tables were still in place. A few old ranchers were sitting at the massive wood bar having a heated discussion about something that had them all riled up. They stopped their debate as Buck stepped up to the bar, and they all looked at him and nodded before going back to their discussion.

Buck grabbed a seat at the end of the bar and looked around. Nope, nothing had changed since the last time he was there, including the bartender, who made her way down the bar towards Buck with a big smile on her face.

"Oh my god. Buck Taylor. It's been a long time," said Sam. She grabbed a can of Coke out of the cooler as she passed.

Samantha Reynolds set the Coke on the bar, walked through the opening at the end of the bar and gave Buck a huge hug. Buck thought she might have held on a little too long, but he didn't mind, and he felt his pulse quicken. Sam did that to people.

Sam had grown up on a working horse ranch outside Meeker and had taken over the bar when her mom decided to retire about ten years back. Now somewhere in her mid-fifties, Sam had gone through three husbands and raised four kids. She was also drop-dead gorgeous. At five foot eight, 130 pounds with long red hair pulled back in a ponytail and incredible hazel eyes, Sam stopped the conversation in any room she walked into. It might also have been that there was no way she would ever be able to close the top three buttons of any shirt she wore. Sam was what most men would have commonly called "stacked," and she was proud of it.

Sam let go, walked back around the bar, grabbed a clean glass off the huge Montana backbar and poured the Coke into the glass before sliding it over to Buck.

"I heard your wife passed away a couple of months back. I was sorry to hear that. You doin' okay?" she asked.

Buck thanked her for the Coke and filled her in on the last couple of months. Sam listened, only stepping away to fill a couple of beers down the bar. He told her about how the chemo and radiation had stopped working on the brain tumors, and they made the decision, as hard as it was, to stop treatment.

He also mentioned how the family had all gathered at a small handicapped fishing dock in a park along the Gunnison River, in Gunnison, one Sunday morning to scatter Lucy's ashes. It was supposed to be a quiet family affair, but somehow, word had gotten out, and three hundred people had quietly gathered behind them on the grass. The private affair turned into a huge picnic in Lucy's honor. Even though Lucy didn't want any kind of service, Buck thought she would have loved the idea of a spontaneous party.

When Buck was finished, Sam handed him a stack of napkins and wiped the tears from her own eyes. She handed Buck a menu, and he ordered the cowboy rib eye steak and a baked potato.

After calling Buck's order to the cook, she leaned across the bar, which required Buck to force himself to look into her eyes, and she whispered, "Don't take this the wrong way, but if you need anything while you're in town, and I do mean anything, give me a call."

She smiled and walked back down the bar. Buck knew Sam was sincere since she flirted with him every time he walked into the bar. He hadn't thought about dating yet, but if he did, she would be his first call.

CHAPTER SIX

B uck finished his steak, kissed Sam on the cheek and stepped through the front door into the cool night air. He was going to head to his hotel when he looked to the east and could see the fire lighting up the night sky. He climbed into his car and headed back out to the highway, turned left and headed for Route 8. After turning onto County Route 8, it took a little more than an hour to get to the Vaughan Lake Campground parking lot, where the Forest Service had set up their incident command center.

Buck pulled into the parking lot and parked his car next to the huge white tent that was serving as the command center. He climbed out and zipped up his CBI windbreaker against the chill in the air. Stepping into the tent, he was amazed there was hardly anyone on duty. Except for a couple of young folks looking at weather patterns on their computer screens, the only other person stood in front of a large topographic map of the area.

Buck stepped up to the map. "Lookin' for the

incident commander."

Without turning, the tall guy in the yellow firefighter shirt responded, "That'd be me. Can I help you?"

"Buck Taylor, with the Colorado Bureau of Investigation."

The tall firefighter turned and extended his hand. "Pat Sutton. I was told to expect you. Nice to meet you." They shook hands.

"Can I ask you how it's going?" Buck asked.

"Well, the good news is the winds have died down, and tonight the humidity has started climbing, which is helping lay down the fire. Right now, I've got four hotshot teams working the front edge, and with any luck, by tomorrow morning, we should have this beast about sixty percent contained."

Buck looked at the map on the wall. "How about the area around the lodge? Can we get in there tomorrow to start looking around?"

"Probably, as long as the weather holds. We knocked down all the remaining hotspots this morning, and I have a mop-up crew working that area tonight to make sure nothing flares back up."

He looked at Buck, and Buck could see the seriousness in his eyes. "I know you have an investigation to get started, but I need you to understand that this is a very erratic fire, and once you get in that area, I cannot guarantee your safety. If the winds whip up again as they did three days ago, that fire could run over you in a heartbeat. Understand?"

Buck nodded. "Got it. We won't move unless you tell us we are good. I would like to have one of your radios if you can spare one, and if you tell us to get out of there, we are gone. Fair enough?"

Pat nodded. "I'll do better than that. If I can break away, I will escort you up there myself. When they told me I was gonna be babysitting a state cop, I expected you to come in here and start ordering everyone around. Thanks for not doing that. This job's hard enough as it is."

"No problem. You'll find I'm pretty easy to work with. By the way, have you got the Helena Hotshots working this fire?"

Pat pointed to a spot at the center of the fire line on the map. "They are working this point. Pretty tough terrain. You know them?"

"My daughter, Cassie Taylor, is on that team. Wasn't sure they were out here."

"Your daughter is Cassie? She is one tough girl. Damn good at reading the fire, and she works harder than most of the guys on her team. I'm always glad to have someone like her around."

Buck thanked Pat and told him the team would

assemble sometime late morning. They shook hands, and Buck walked out through the tent flap. He stepped around behind the tent, found a spot at the edge of the parking lot and watched the flames.

Hardy Braxton walked through the lot and stood next to Buck, who didn't seem to react at all to his presence, but Hardy knew better. He knew Buck heard him coming, and even though Buck didn't acknowledge him, he was well aware that Buck had his hand on the backstrap of his pistol and had unsnapped the thumb break.

Hardy stood there for a few minutes in silence and watched the flames. From behind, they could have been twins, except Hardy had gained a few pounds since high school and now wore a wide-brimmed Stetson to cover his receding hairline. Buck and Hardy played football for Gunnison High School. They were the team's defensive backfield and were called the "Wrecking Crew" during senior year. Between them, they broke every defensive high school football record in the state, many of which stood to this day. They had also been friends, on and off, since first grade.

Buck passed up several full-ride scholarships and instead joined the army and later the Gunnison County Sheriff's Department. Hardy, on the other hand, accepted a full-ride scholarship to Stanford and spent the next four years as an All-American football player and later went on to play in the National Football League until a knee injury sidelined him for good.

Hardy left the NFL and took over the reins of his father's small livestock company. Over the years, he turned that small company, based out of Gunnison County, into the premier bucking stock and livestock company in the world. A rodeo didn't happen anywhere that didn't have numerous animals from Braxton Bucking Stock in its corrals. He also invested heavily in energy exploration companies and owned the largest private fracking company in the country. By all measures, Hardy Braxton was hugely successful. He was also Buck's brother-in-law.

Hardy married Lucy's younger sister, Rachel, the year after Lucy and Buck got married. Their marriage was blessed with four children, all of whom were now involved in the numerous family businesses. Businesses that now numbered at least a dozen and stretched from Gunnison to California and even dipped down into South America. Hardy was the big dog in Gunnison County, and he was not afraid to use that power to his family's advantage.

Buck knew Hardy was somehow involved with the controversial fishing lodge project, but he didn't know to what extent. He knew one thing about Hardy Braxton. He never walked away from a fight, and he wasn't afraid of a little controversy.

CHAPTER SEVEN

B uck took a sideways glance and went back to looking at the fire. After a few minutes of silence, he said, "Hardy."

"Buck," replied Hardy.

They both stood looking at the flames for a few more minutes until Hardy broke the silence.

"Rachel and I wanted to be at Lucy's service. We were on a livestock buying trip through South America and couldn't get back. Rachel was devastated."

"Not a problem," replied Buck. "We knew you were tied up."

"I want you to know," Hardy continued, "we are working with the county to buy a one-mile strip of land on the west side of the river where you scattered Lucy's ashes. We want to turn it into a riverwalk in honor of Lucy. She meant a lot to us. I asked Jason if he had a landscape architect at his firm that could do the design work."

Jason was Buck's youngest son, and he worked as an architect in Boulder. Buck was surprised to hear Jason was involved in the riverwalk project. He'd seen Jason and the family a couple of weeks back, and he never mentioned it. He figured they must have been trying to keep it a secret, which wouldn't have lasted long. Little happened in the county that Buck wasn't aware of.

Buck turned and looked at Hardy. "Thanks. You don't have to do that."

Hardy started to explain, but Buck cut him off. "What's your interest in this lodge? Heard you were making a lot of noise. Got a bunch of people fired up."

"Mark Richards and I are partners in this venture and several others, and you are damn right I raised a stink. This is the third fire in the past year that has impacted a project like this, and we are getting tired of it. I have also had four fracking sites vandalized. Two last month alone, and that weasel of a governor doesn't have a damn bit of interest in figuring out who is doing this. So yeah, if I have to make a little noise and threaten to run against him, then so be it. It got you here, didn't it?"

Buck was silent for a minute while he continued to watch the fire. He turned and looked at Hardy.

"Okay, Hardy. I will figure out who's doing this, and I will shut them down, but I need you to back off and let me do my job."

"You just make sure you do," replied Hardy. "Because if you don't, we will take care of those fucking environmentalists ourselves."

Buck knew it wasn't worth fighting with Hardy when he got all riled up. He would talk to Hardy when he calmed down. He turned back to the fire.

"By the way," said Hardy. "Your son designed this lodge. He was very proud of it."

Buck had had no idea his son Jason was the architect for the lodge. He also wondered why he'd found out two things tonight he wasn't aware of. Jason and Hardy had always been close, but it seemed strange that Jason failed to mention either project.

Hardy stood for a few minutes and then turned to leave. "Stop by the house when you get time, and I will give you what we have on the NETF."

Hardy started to walk off and stopped. "Is Cassie and her team working this fire?"

Buck answered over his shoulder, "Yeah, her team is on the front edge. Tough terrain."

"We'll pray for her safety," Hardy replied.

He turned and walked off, leaving Buck standing in the dark. Buck was concerned. He knew Hardy didn't make idle threats, and he also knew if Hardy had already gathered some information on the NETF, then he would have to move fast before Hardy and his friends decided to take things into their own hands.

He'd told the director he could handle Hardy, and he knew he could. Handling Mark Richards was going to be another story indeed. Mark Richards was a billionaire hedge fund owner and a heavyweight real estate developer, and he had a reputation for running over anyone who got in his way.

Richards had a lot of money and an incredible amount of power, and he had little regard for the government or people in general. All he cared about was getting whatever he wanted, no matter what. Buck smiled. "This is gonna be interesting," he said to himself. He turned from the fire and headed for his car. Before he pulled out of the parking lot, he asked the spirits of the forest to keep an eye on Cassie.

He pulled out onto Route 8 and headed back towards Meeker. It was time to start investigating, and Buck was more than ready.

CHAPTER EIGHT

They were sitting in the forest at the southern end of the campground parking lot and watched as Buck and Hardy talked. They had no idea who Buck was, but they were well aware of who Hardy Braxton was. They wished they had brought the parabolic microphone with them. The boss would be interested in knowing what those two had been talking about.

They thought about following Hardy Braxton, but they had been told to stay put and keep an eye on the fire efforts. The boss was not pleased someone else had set the lodge ablaze, and the fire set the forest ablaze. Even if it wasn't their fire, it was a significant mistake, and the boss was worried they would catch all the blame, and that would make for some terrible publicity. They were glad someone else started the fire.

They had checked the weather forecast earlier in the day, and the front was still hours away. They had no idea the front they had been watching picked up speed and dropped farther south than was initially predicted. The result would have been the same, and the forest would still be on fire, but they were glad it was not their fault. They would still need to follow orders, at least for a little while, until the boss got over being pissed.

The big guy pulled out his cell phone, held it inside his jacket so the light wouldn't shine like a beacon in the dark forest and dialed the boss.

"I hope you have a damn good reason for bothering me this late at night," said the boss.

The big guy went on to explain about the meeting between Hardy Braxton and the new guy. He also filled the boss in on the efforts of the hotshots and reported the fire was partially contained.

There was silence on the other end of the phone, and the big guy knew better than to interrupt. He waited while the boss thought about the report. The boss responded.

"Can you get close enough without getting caught and get me the license number from the newcomer's car? I have a way to track him down."

The big guy responded they could and would call back in a few minutes. He hung up the phone, and his partner headed off around the edge of the parking lot, hoping to circle in behind the car and get the plate number. He stopped where the forest met the lot and pulled out a pair of night vision binoculars. Through the green haze in the eyepieces, he was able to read Buck's license plate almost as well as if he were standing behind the car. He wrote the number on a small piece of paper and headed back to his partner.

Once they were back together, the big guy called the boss again and recited the license plate number. The boss hung up without any further comment. Cinching up their jackets against the late-night chill, they settled down and watched the area around the command center.

They couldn't figure out the newcomer. After he talked with Hardy Braxton and he turned and left, the newcomer stood there staring into the forest at the fire beyond. They decided the two men must have known each other, but whatever their relationship was, it didn't appear to be friendly. There was no familiar handshake or a slap on the back. They had a conversation in which neither man looked at the other, and then Braxton turned and left. He stopped after a few steps and said something to the newcomer, who responded but never turned around to face him.

The behavior of these two men confused them. They were students of human nature and over the years had developed a sixth sense about people. They had to. It was what kept them alive, and it made them good at their jobs, but they couldn't put their fingers on the relationship they'd just watched. Now, more than ever, they wished they had the parabolic mic with them.

They watched the newcomer for another twenty minutes before he turned and headed towards his car. Through the night vision binoculars, they could see he was an older guy and looked to be in pretty good shape even though the green haze. As he turned, his jacket flipped open, and the big guy could see the badge and gun clipped to his belt.

"Shit, he's a cop!" exclaimed the big guy.

"Are you sure?" asked his partner.

"Yeah. I saw his badge and gun. We need to let the boss know."

The big guy took out his cell phone and redialed the boss's number. When the boss answered, he explained what they had discovered about the newcomer. The boss thought about it for a minute and told them to follow him and see where he went. The boss told them not to engage him in any way until they could determine who he worked for.

Disconnecting the call, they both stood up and headed back through the forest to the small turnout where they had hidden their truck. They were sitting just off the road with their lights off when the Jeep Grand Cherokee passed by them on Route 8.

They followed the car for several miles until

it pulled into the parking lot of a small mom-and-pop motel in Meeker. The newcomer got out, walked into the office and walked out a few minutes later with the key he used to unlock unit number seven. They parked in the lot of the gas station across the street, shut off the lights and the engine and settled in for a long night of surveillance.

CHAPTER NINE

The restaurant that was attached to the small motel where Buck was staying was packed to the doors. Every seat was filled, and five waitresses, all wearing jeans and black T-shirts, moved seamlessly from table to table, taking orders and filling coffee cups. Buck noticed a few tourists who were also staying at the motel, but the crowd was mostly ranchers and farmers. Buck always looked for places like this when he was traveling, and this one was no exception. Good food, plenty of it, and fast service with lots of coffee. Just what working men and women wanted to start their day.

Buck was finishing off his fried eggs, sausages and hash browns when he looked up from his plate and spotted Ashley Baxter coming through the door. She stopped for a few seconds, looked around and spotted him sitting in the booth by the window. She waved and headed in his direction. She carried her ever-present backpack, and she looked like a girl on a mission.

Bax was attractive, with hazel eyes and long blond hair pulled back in a ponytail. She wore jeans, black Nikes and a light plaid shirt under her Carhartt vest. Buck watched as several of the ranchers and cowboys looked up to check out the new girl, and he also noticed a lot of them divert their eyes back to their plates when they spotted the gun and badge on her belt. Bax looked more like a college student than a cop, but Buck knew better. Bax was one hell of a cop in the eyes of Buck and a bunch of other people. She was smart, and she was fearless, but she also knew which one of those attributes to use and when. Buck had a tremendous amount of respect for Bax, and although it didn't happen often, Buck liked working with her.

Bax slid her backpack across the booth seat and slid in opposite Buck. Buck finished the bite of sausage that was still on his fork and nodded.

"Hey, Buck. Sheriff McCabe said I might find you here."

"It's nice to see you, Bax. Have you eaten?"

"Not yet. What's good?" she asked.

Buck waved over the waitress, and Bax ordered the same thing he was eating, but instead of a glass of Coke, she asked for coffee, which almost magically appeared in her cup. She looked at the glass of Coke and smiled. Buck's consumption of Coke was legendary around the CBI office.

Skipping the small talk, Bax pulled out a couple of files from her backpack and laid them on the table next to Buck's now-empty plate. Looking around and then keeping her voice low, she opened the first file, revealing several internet articles about the National Environmental Task Force. Buck was about to pick up the first article when he saw the waitress coming and closed the cover of the manila folder. The waitress set a huge plate of food in front of Bax and then stepped away.

Buck opened the first folder and briefly read the first couple of printouts while Bax devoured her breakfast. She had used a yellow highlighter to note pieces of information she felt might be important, and she had also attached lime green sticky notes to a few of the pages with comments or suggestions. Buck looked up from the papers and smiled. "She must have stayed up half the night going through this information," he thought to himself.

Bax finished her breakfast and pushed her plate to the edge of the table. She looked around the room and then leaned in towards Buck.

"The stuff in the first folder is internet background. A lot of press releases and newspaper articles about the NETF. There is some interesting information, which I highlighted for you. The sticky notes are some thoughts about how we might want to proceed."

She pulled the second file folder out from

under the pile. This folder was much thicker. Buck opened the cover, and Bax said, "I took the police reports the director sent you and did a deep dive. Most of the police reports and the investigations that followed are pretty weak, but I went back to the sources and was able to pull a lot more information up the director did not have access to."

Buck started to read the first police report, for a fracking site fire south of Craig. Bax continued, "I spoke to the fire chief up that way, and he told me he felt certain it was arson, but he couldn't get enough evidence to make a case, so this investigation pretty much died on the vine."

Buck went to interrupt, but Bax was on a roll. He held his questions and waited for a break in the briefing, which he knew from experience wasn't going to happen anytime soon.

"All told, there are fourteen unsolved fires over the last five years, including the big mountaintop restaurant fire in Vail that could be attributed to NETF, but there is almost no evidence pointing directly towards them. Whoever these folks are, they are damn good at what they do."

Bax stopped to take a breath and a sip of her coffee. Buck spent a few more minutes looking through the police reports, then he took off his reading glasses and looked at Bax.

"Nice job, Bax. This investigation just got big.

Can you pull away from whatever you were working on and spend a couple of days working this with me?"

"The director called me after I spoke with you yesterday and asked me to work with you on this full time. I think he's a little concerned about you, Buck, no offense."

Buck smiled. "No offense taken. He has every right to be concerned, and I appreciate that he sent you to help me out. Lucy's death hit me harder than I expected, but my head is on straight, and I'm ready to hit the ground running."

Buck thought for a minute. "Here's what I would like to do. I am heading back out to the lodge fire to meet the state fire investigator. Since you already laid the groundwork with the fire chief in Craig, why don't you head up that way and see what else you can find out? Have him take you to the site and see if you see anything he missed. Then work your way through the police reports and talk to whoever ran the investigation and get a feel for what happened. Once I finish up with the lodge scene, I am going to have the sheriff take me to the two other most recent fire sites here in Rio Blanco County. Give me a call tonight, and let's see if any of this takes us anyplace."

Bax pulled her backpack across the seat and

stood up. She reached into her pocket and set a twenty-dollar bill on the table next to her plate. Buck knew better than to stop her, so he left it there and placed his own twenty under his Coke glass.

"Thanks, Buck. I am looking forward to working with you again. It's good to have you back."

Bax took a last sip of coffee, flung her backpack over her shoulder and headed for the door.

CHAPTER TEN

Commander Jack "Fighting Red" Muldoon
sat at the center of the tribunal that had
been hastily called in the early morning
hours. The issue they were about to deal with
could conceivably cost the town everything they
had built up over the past couple of years, but
this was also a discipline issue, and Muldoon
wanted to get this over with as fast as possible.

Muldoon was an imposing figure of a man,
and few people ever crossed him. At over six feet
tall and built like a boxer, the redheaded former
Marine Corps captain and self-proclaimed leader
of this group of survivalists demanded full
allegiance from his followers. This was going to
be the first real test of his "power" since they
had established their little town a few years
back. Whatever decision was made here today
in the back of the old metal Quonset hut would
have wide-ranging implications for their future
success or failure as a group and as a business.

In the middle of the floor facing the tribunal
and duct-taped to a metal folding chair sat Elliot
Beech. Beech had been recruited by Muldoon

from the NSA, the National Security Agency, where he was a computer programmer and hacker extraordinaire who had made clear, on social media, his dissatisfaction with the policies of the United States of America when it came to cyber warfare. It was those same computer skills that had him sitting before the tribunal on this chilly morning, but Beech wasn't chilled; he was sweating profusely and was having trouble focusing after having been "interrogated" for the past eight hours by Muldoon's security team.

The other members of the town sat quietly in the audience and waited to see how far this would go. Everyone who'd decided to take up residence in the town understood the rules and regulations, but this was the first time anyone had committed a major breach of the rules, and how the tribunal would react was anyone's guess.

Muldoon looked at the other two members of the tribunal, and they each nodded in turn. Garret Tillman functioned as the chief financial officer for the town. At five foot ten and balding, the fifty-eight-year-old former accounting clerk had quit his job at a major accounting firm and moved his family to Colorado to join Muldoon's venture with the promise of becoming wealthy.

Margaret Windsong had dark black hair and a matronly way about her, but she didn't suffer fools lightly. She told everyone in town she was of Native American descent, but she couldn't seem to remember which tribe she was from since she told different stories to different people. The truth was, she was born and raised in a white evangelical family in Odessa, Texas, and had joined Muldoon after running away from home. She met Muldoon in a bar in Denver when he was first putting together his scheme. They were instantly attracted to each other.

Muldoon asked one of the security team to remove the tape from Beech's mouth, which he did with some vengeance. Beech started pleading.

"Red, you have to believe me, you have to believe me. I had no idea he was a Fed. I swear on my mother's life."

Muldoon picked up the paper off the table in front of him and stared daggers at Beech, who stopped talking. He read from the paper.

"Elliot Beech, you have been brought before this tribunal because you violated our most important rule. You involved an outsider in our business in an attempt to enrich your life and your bank account with little or no regard for the other members of the town. In doing so, you brought a DEA agent, an agent for the very government we have all sworn to oppose, into our midst, jeopardizing our entire operation and forcing us to deal with that agent in a manner we had hoped to avoid. We have no way of knowing how badly your actions will impact our business."

He stopped so the others assembled in the hut could digest the full effect of Beech's actions. He was going to use this as a teaching moment for the other members of the town, so none of them would think about crossing him.

Beech looked up through his two swollen black eyes and started to sob as urine ran down his leg. He had never been this scared in his entire life. He was a geek. He should be sitting in his mother's basement trying to hack into the Social Security Administration's website or some other innocuous government site and setting up ransomware, not sitting in a cold metal building in the middle of Colorado awaiting a sentence.

All he was guilty of was trying to set up a side deal between one of the town's Asian suppliers and a friend from his time at the NSA. How was he supposed to know his friend was working with a DEA agent who was working outside the box and offered him a great deal? Of course, the promise of a onetime payoff of two hundred grand and a plane ticket to Fiji or some other exotic place had helped to sweeten the deal.

Muldoon continued, "You have been found guilty by this tribunal of crimes against the town, and you will be banished from the town, but first, you will be locked up in our jail for ninety days of hard labor, and you will not be allowed any visitors. We want to make sure your actions didn't cause irreparable damage."

A gasp came from those assembled as Red handed down the sentence. Many were surprised at the harshness of the punishment. After all, Beech was one of them; there must be a better way. The town all assumed the DEA agent had been killed, even though they didn't know for sure, and no one questioned the action because it was needed to protect the town and their business. They all wanted to believe Beech would be spared and allowed to leave, but there would always be doubts.

Muldoon glared at the audience as the security team cut the tape holding Beech to the chair and dragged him towards the back door of the hut.

He addressed the rest of the town's residents. "Make no mistake. Beech's crime could have brought down our entire operation. I promised to make you all rich, but you also promised to follow the rules."

The tribunal stood up from the table and walked out the door, following the security team and Elliot Beech. The remaining members of the town walked back towards their homes. Everyone was aware that once the tribunal had resolved a matter before it, there would be no further discussion.

CHAPTER ELEVEN

Buck pulled his Jeep into the Vaughan Lake Campground parking lot and parked next to the fire command tent. He climbed out of his car, stretched, casually looked around the parking lot and walked into the tent. The sheriff and Pat Sutton, the incident commander, were looking over a topographic map of the area around the fishing lodge while one of Pat's assistants was reading from the latest weather forecast.

Buck stepped up to the table. "Good mornin'. How we lookin' for today?"

Pat and the sheriff looked up from the map, and Buck shook hands all around.

The sheriff spoke first. "Pat thinks the weather is going to cooperate, so we should be able to get to the lodge without a problem."

"We are expecting a little rain later today," said Pat, "but the forecast is for the winds to stay low through tomorrow. That should give you enough time to see what you need to see. Our containment is holding, so for right now, I can lead you in."

"Great," said Buck. "We can leave as soon as the state fire investigator gets here."

Buck and the sheriff headed out through the tent flap and walked to their respective cars. They each put on a yellow firefighter shirt and grabbed a white hard hat and a backpack full of the things they would need to perform as thorough an investigation as possible. Buck threw a rolled-up raincoat into his backpack, along with a couple of bottles of water and a few energy bars. He looked up as he heard a car pull into the parking lot.

Jack Spencer's white Chevy Tahoe parked next to Buck's Jeep. He slid out of the car, stood up, stretched and opened the back driver's side door. The big black Lab jumped off the back seat and headed straight for Buck and almost jumped into his arms. Buck grabbed hold of the dog in a big bear hug and shook him from side to side.

"Hiya, Gus. How are you, buddy?" The Lab, with his tail wagging nonstop, spun around several times as Buck let him go and then licked Buck on the side of his face. Buck laughed hard and stood up. He reached into a side pocket in the back of his car and pulled out a large dark brown chew stick and handed it to Gus, who lay down at his feet and started chewing away, tail still wagging.

Buck shook Jack's hand. "Jack, it's good to see you. Glad you had the time to join us."

"I'm glad to see you too, Buck. Hey, I was sorry to hear about your wife. Mary and I were heartbroken when we heard the news. Mary sends her best."

Jack Spencer had been the state fire investigator for the past fifteen years. He was five foot ten with a firefighter's build, and his almost white flattop haircut gave him the look of authority. Although his primary duties were with the state of Colorado, Jack—and Gus —worked fires all over the country, and his testimony had led to the incarceration of a lot of firebugs.

Buck was about to respond when the sheriff stepped around the car and looked at the dog at Buck's feet. Buck introduced the sheriff to Jack, and they shook hands. He then knelt next to Gus, who was still chewing away on his new chew stick.

"This is Gus. He's one of the best ADCs in the country, thanks to Jack and a great nose." Buck stood up.

The sheriff looked at Gus and said, "What's an ADC, if I might ask?" Buck was about to answer when Rick Carmichael stepped around Jack's car and beat him to it.

"Gus is a certified accelerant detection canine,

and like Mr. Taylor said, one of the best in the country. Hi, by the way, I'm Rick, I work with Jack." Rick shook hands all around.

Rick Carmichael was a twenty-something with a bald head and piercing blue eyes. Thin and a shade under six feet, he was Jack's forensic technician, and his job was to analyze any evidence they might find to see if this was a human-made fire or an act of God.

Jack opened the back hatch on his SUV and pulled out a yellow military-style vest, and as soon as Gus saw it, he dropped his chew stick and stood almost at attention while Jack placed it on his back and tightened the straps. The transformation from loveable pet to working dog was something to watch. Once in the vest, Gus knew it was time to go to work.

Jack grabbed his backpack, slipped it over his shoulder and closed the hatch of his car, and everyone headed for the tent.

CHAPTER TWELVE

Pat Sutton shook Jack's hand and rubbed Gus's head. He had everyone gather around the map table and gave a quick update on the course of the fire and the terrain they were about to walk into. He gave everyone a stern warning.

"This fire is erratic as hell. Right now, conditions are good, but that can change in a heartbeat. I will be with you the entire time you are at the lodge, and hopefully you can get what you need and we can get back, however, if I tell you we have to go, there will be no discussion and no hesitation, understood?"

He picked up a red Sharpie from the table and drew a circle around an area partway between the lodge and the parking lot. "This area here has already burned. We call it the black. If we have to evacuate in a hurry, we will head for this area first, so if you hear me yell for you to head for the black, this is where we are going as fast as we can."

Everyone nodded in agreement, so Pat grabbed

his radio, his handheld GPS and his hard hat off the map table and led the way out of the tent and down the trail.

Within a mile of the parking lot, the first signs of the devastation showed their ugly head. The trees were burned almost to the ground, and there was nothing left of anything that might have grown. Buck noticed several charred animal carcasses along the trail, evidence of a fire that moved faster than the poor creatures could react to. He could still feel the heat rising from the ash, and the air was thick with smoke, making breathing somewhat difficult.

By the time they reached the site of the lodge, they were tired, dirty and sweating profusely. It was no one's idea of fun, and the surrounding destruction made them all sad. This once pristine forest looked like an atom bomb had gone off. It was all so pointless.

What was left of the once majestic lodge was now a pile of smoldering logs, the smoke and heat still visible, swirling up from the huge pile. Buck told everyone to take a breather, drink some water to clear the ash out of their throats, while he walked off to survey the scene first. He took off his hard hat, wiped his forehead and took a drink from the water bottle he carried in. "This is going to be one tough crime scene to work," he thought to himself.

Jack and Gus stepped up next to him, and he rubbed Gus's head. "We are going to start working the site from here. If we find anything, I will give a holler and mark it with a flag. Once we cover the entire site, we will have a better idea of where to look for evidence."

Jack and Gus started carefully walking over the debris pile, with Gus walking gingerly on the logs. Now and then, he would stop and sit down, and Jack would walk over and stick a little red flag into the pile.

The sheriff walked up and stood next to Buck, a look of pure exhaustion on his ash-covered face. From off in the distance, a new sound entered the forest. Overhead, a huge Boeing 747 thundered over the ridge; it couldn't have been more than a couple of hundred feet over the trees. Buck and the sheriff watched with amazement as the huge plane flew just over the treetops and then a massive red trail started to flow from the belly of the beast.

"Since the wind died down this morning, we were able to bring in heavy air support," said Pat Sutton. He had walked up while they were watching the plane, and as they stood there, he raised his radio to his mouth.

"Jimmy, that looked like a good drop. When he comes back for his next pass, have him shift about a quarter mile south. Have the choppers start their water drops off that big cliff to the east and work along the ridgeline. Let's see if we can stop this mother from running over the ridgeline."

"Ten-four, boss."

Buck was about to say something when he heard Jack call his name, and he looked up to see him waving his hand for them to come over to where he and Gus were standing. Rather than walk through the crime scene, Buck, Pat and the sheriff walked around the perimeter of the lodge foundation, and, stepping carefully, they approached Jack.

"We have a problem," said Jack as he pointed towards the pile of burnt logs in front of him.

Buck looked where Jack was pointing, and at first, he couldn't see anything, so he focused harder, and he could just make out the charred hand sticking out from under the logs.

"Shit," said the sheriff. "This is now a death investigation as well. Fuck, Buck."

"Yeah," replied Buck. "Okay, let's see if we can move some of this debris out of the way so we can see what we have."

While Jack and Gus continued their search, Buck, the sheriff, Rick and Pat, who had wandered over to see what they were looking at, started removing the logs that were covering the body. It took almost an hour to clear away enough debris so they could see all of the body, or what was left of it.

CHAPTER THIRTEEN

Buck pulled a pair of nitrile gloves out of his backpack and knelt next to the body. The charring made it impossible to determine if this was a male or female, and it was so fragile he didn't want to try to move it. He was more concerned with the body falling apart than he was with trying to preserve evidence. The fire and the firefighting operations had all but destroyed any forensic evidence. He was about to stand when the sheriff asked him to look at a spot next to what he assumed was an ear.

Buck looked at the spot where the sheriff was pointing and at first wasn't sure what he was looking at. He reached into his backpack and pulled a long-handled cotton swab out of a tube. Leaning closer to the body, he cleaned a little of the char away and then probed with the swab. The swab disappeared into what seemed to be a hole. He left the swab in place, grabbed his cell phone and opened the camera app. He took several pictures from different angles and put his phone back onto his belt.

"Is that a bullet hole?" asked the sheriff.

"I believe it is," said Buck. "We could use a pathologist and a forensic team up here, but I don't think we are going to have the time. Have you looked to the east recently?"

The sheriff nodded. He saw the same thing Buck saw. Clouds were building, and the smoke from the fire seemed to be heading towards them more than it had been earlier. He could sense a change in the wind direction. They were running out of time and would have to work the crime scene themselves.

Buck reached into his backpack again and pulled out a neatly folded black body bag. It was not something your average investigator would typically carry with them, but once before, he'd had a murder scene get destroyed because of a sudden cloudburst, and he vowed after that to keep a body bag in his backpack, just in case. This bag had been in there for almost ten years, and he had not needed it since that day. Today he was grateful he had it.

With the help of Pat Sutton, they placed the body bag behind the body, opened it up and rolled the body onto the black plastic. Luckily for everyone involved, the body held together when they rolled it. There was nothing worse than a body falling apart as you moved it around. Buck zipped it up, and he and the sheriff carried it away from the crime scene to the side of the foundation.

Passing out new nitrile gloves, he and the sheriff returned to the scene and began a methodical search of the area. Buck couldn't be sure what part of the lodge he was standing in, so he took a bunch of pictures with his camera, trying to get as many landmarks as possible. He figured his son Jason might be able to help figure that part out, once they cleared the scene.

By late afternoon, they had surveyed and photographed everything and anything that looked like it might help with the investigation. Jack located what appeared to be the melted remains of several metal cans, outside the lodge footprint. He guessed they were gas cans, the most likely source of the fire. The arsonist had left them at the scene because he knew the fire would destroy any evidence, but Jack had Rick bag a few pieces for analysis.

The smoke from the fire was starting to block out the sun, and it was getting harder and harder to breathe. Buck was putting the evidence bags in his backpack when he heard Pat Sutton yell it was time to wrap up and head out.

While Buck and the sheriff were working the body, Jack and Gus made good time covering what was left of the lodge. By late afternoon they had covered everything that was safe to walk on or around, and looking back over the path of little red flags he'd placed at all the locations Gus had alerted, Jack felt he had a good understanding of what had transpired. He directed Rick to take samples from several charred spots on the ground and also from the burnt logs. Once the chemical analysis was completed on the samples by the State Crime Lab in Pueblo, Jack would know for certain what the accelerant was, but years of experience told him he already knew the answer.

Rick was cataloging the evidence bags before placing them in his backpack when Jack called him over to what appeared to be the remains of a rock fireplace. Most of the rock chimney had collapsed under the weight of the roof falling in, but you could still make out the bricks that were part of the firebox. Since these were heat-treated bricks, the fire hadn't destroyed them like it had the logs.

A few feet in front of what remained of the firebox, Rick could make out what appeared to be the remains of some springs and a partially melted metal frame, from a couch or love seat. Next to the frame, Jack was kneeling and using a small foxtail brush to sweep away the debris. When he finished clearing the area, he pulled out his cell phone and took several pictures of the large dark charred spot the debris removal had revealed.

Rick knelt next to him, pulled out a small plastic evidence bag and, using a small scraper, scraped up some bits and pieces from the charred mark on the floor. As Jack was about to stand up, he noticed what appeared to be a small pile of unburnt fabric on the outer edge of the area he'd swept. Scooting across the floor and followed by Rick, Jack reached the small pile and used a pair of forceps and lifted the fabric. The pile was most likely the remains of a couch or chair, which both surprised and pleased Jack, but what fell out of the fabric as he lifted it made his heart skip a beat.

Lying on the floor where the pile was, he saw a small, shriveled-up piece of plastic with a circuit board clearly visible. Jack had hit the mother lode, and he looked at Rick and saw the smile cross his sweat- and ash-covered face. Jack had found a piece of the igniter that hadn't burned up in the fire.

They were placing the circuit board in the evidence bag when they heard Pat Sutton yell, so they gathered up their gear, and with Gus at their heels, headed for the trail they came in on.

CHAPTER FOURTEEN

The four-mile trek back through the devastation was made even harder by the fact that after a full day of working in a hot, smoky environment, they also had to carry back the body bag. Buck and the sheriff made it look easy, but it was anything but, and not being able to breathe was making it worse.

Pat Sutton told them the winds had shifted, and they were now experiencing gusts of up to twenty-five miles per hour, which under normal circumstances is not bad, but when you are trying to beat down a forest fire, even a little wind is not your friend. The bad thing was the wind was blowing embers into new stands of trees that were already dry due to the drought conditions Colorado had been experiencing for the past couple of years. He now had new fires starting up in three locations around them, and he called for reinforcements and increased water and retardant drops.

The planes and helicopters spent all afternoon making valiant efforts to beat down the new fires, but the fire had already jumped one fire line, and part of Pat's containment area had disappeared. Two additional hotshot teams were on their way and would join the effort by nightfall. By the next morning, Pat would have almost four hundred firefighters working this fire, which was out of control and getting larger.

Earlier today, he had been planning to pull two of the original hotshot teams so they could get a well-deserved rest. Now, instead, those teams were working their way up the side of a ridge even a mountain goat would find difficult, so they could try to clear a new fire line. The days had been long, and the work was hard, but none of the teams balked when Pat issued the new orders.

As Buck and his team got closer to the incident command center, the air got a little clearer, and it was easier to breathe. A few hundred yards from the parking lot, they had to cross over a small stream. Gus was the first one to make a move, and as he stepped into the stream, he plopped down and let the water rush over him. Buck could have sworn the tired dog smiled. After a few minutes, he stood up, shook off and rejoined the team on the other side.

Each member of the team followed Gus's lead and, if nothing else, leaned down and washed the day's soot out of their hair and off their faces. The water was cold and refreshing, and it made them feel a little more human.

They walked up the embankment that led to the parking lot, and Pat headed for the command center. The parking lot was filling up with fire engines and emergency vehicles from all over the area, and Pat needed to get all these units positioned in the best places to fight this new threat.

Buck led everyone over to his Jeep, opened the hatch and placed his backpack down. He passed around a couple of bottles of water to each person and then pulled a collapsible water bowl out of the back of his car, filled it with water and set it down for Gus. Jack had already removed Gus's vest, and the dog knew he was now off duty. After drinking his fill, he found a shady spot under Jack's SUV and crashed. His job was done.

The sheriff had called the county coroner as they were nearing the parking lot, and he was waiting for an ambulance to show up to transport the body to the forensic pathologist in Grand Junction. Colorado was one of a handful of states that used the coroner system instead of the medical examiner system. In Colorado, the county coroner was an elected official and didn't need to have any formal training for the job. The coroner didn't even need to be a doctor or medical professional. In the event of a suspicious death or crime where an autopsy was required, the county coroner contracted with a licensed forensic pathologist, a specially trained doctor, to perform the autopsy.

Rio Blanco County, as well as several other Western Slope counties, contracted with the forensic pathologist in Grand Junction. This shared jurisdiction was common in counties that couldn't afford or didn't need a full-time pathologist.

Buck pulled the evidence bags out of his backpack and laid them on the floor in the back of his Jeep. Jack did the same thing with his evidence bags. While the others watched, Buck and Jack shared their thoughts. Jack went first.

"From what I can tell, the accelerant used —and there definitely was an accelerant used —was probably plain gas, nothing fancy or complicated. The burned-up gas cans were a dead giveaway, but we will run everything just to be certain. Most arsonists know it is much more difficult to analyze ordinary gasoline from a fire since it pretty much burns up almost completely. We will run the samples through the mass spectrometer, but it will most likely come back as gasoline. However, we hit the jackpot."

He pulled out the bag holding the igniter piece and handed it to the sheriff, who looked it over and passed it on to Buck. Buck smiled. This was a great piece of evidence—more than he had hoped for.

Jack continued, "We laid out a series of flags at every location Gus got a nose full of accelerant, and when we found this piece of the igniter and looked back over our trail, it was obvious what the arsonist had done. The evidence suggests the arsonist had doused a couch or chair with gasoline and set it in the middle of the floor near the fireplace. The fireplace chimney would help draw air from across the room as the fire grew. He then poured gasoline on all the furniture and ran a line of it from the couch to the rest of the furniture.

"We will probably find that this igniter piece is from a remote cell-activated igniter. That way, the arsonist could be long gone before he hit the button on the app—and yes, believe it or not, some igniters have cell phone apps. Once he pressed the button, the first thing to ignite would be the fabric inside the couch cushions, and then from there, the fire would follow the gasoline trail. If we hadn't found the igniter, this type of fire would be almost impossible to solve without a witness. This guy was good, but we now have a piece of evidence we can trace. Rick will send these off to the State Crime Lab tonight if we can get to the FedEx office before it closes."

CHAPTER FIFTEEN

B uck handed the igniter piece back to Rick, who put it back into Jack's backpack. The sheriff was looking at the pictures Jack had downloaded from his phone to his laptop and asked a question.

"Why didn't the fabric burn up if that was where the igniter was placed?"

"Well," Jack responded. "Could be any number of reasons, but to keep it simple for right now, let's say that fire does some funny things. Take a wildfire like this one. I have seen a wildfire rage through a neighborhood and destroy everything in its path, and then when the smoke clears, one house sits untouched by the fire. We have no real idea why. Lots of theories and opinions, but sometimes, shit happens. I know you were hoping for a better explanation, but right now, I don't have one."

The sheriff nodded and continued looking at the pictures on the laptop. Buck picked up his evidence bags, which numbered far fewer than Jack had, and said, "We don't have much to go on with the body. If I had to guess, it appears to be a male of indeterminate age or ethnicity. The only thing we found was a hole in the back of the head next to the ear. I can't be sure, but I think it's a bullet hole. So, for now, we are going to treat this as a murder. How he got killed and how he ended up in our fire still needs to be determined, as does the theory that the fire was set to cover up a homicide. We don't know yet."

Buck was about to say something else when they saw the ambulance pull into the parking lot and head their way. The sheriff walked over, spoke with the two attendants, signed the transportation order and led them over to the body bag, which they delicately picked up and placed on the gurney.

As the ambulance pulled out of the lot, Buck looked at his ragtag group of investigators and decided that anything else could wait till morning. It had been a long day, and everyone was beat. Buck suggested they head back to Meeker to clean up. He told them he would be at the Cozy Up at 8 p.m., and he was buying dinner for anyone interested.

They got in their cars and, after taking a moment, started up and pulled out of the lot. Buck stood next to his car and thought for the longest time about what they had discovered today. He had a feeling the body was going to be pretty much worthless, but the igniter piece, now that was a good find, and he knew Jack wouldn't give up until he identified the igniter. Once that happened, they could start to close in on the killer and the arsonist, possibly one and the same, although Buck had enough experience to know nothing was ever that simple.

Buck closed up his car and headed back towards the command tent. Inside, it looked like organized chaos as Pat briefed the fresh firefighters on the fire and gave out their assignments. His troops now briefed and heading for their vehicles, Pat waved Buck over to the map table. Buck told Pat about the evidence they'd found.

"We got lucky today with that igniter. If anyone can track that thing down, it's Jack Spencer. Who would have ever thought we'd uncover a murder?"

Buck nodded. "Yeah. Took me by surprise. However, it could move the investigation in a whole other direction. We'll know more once the autopsy is finished."

Buck stopped for a minute and looked at the map on the table. "How bad is it?" he asked.

Pat ran his eyes across the map and then looked at Buck. "It's never good when a fire flares back up. Luckily, we have a lot of resources on hand and more on the way. By the end of the day tomorrow, we'll have five hundred firefighters on the line, and the weather report is calling for rain. Every little bit helps, but we will tame this beast."

Buck could see the determination in Pat's eyes, and he knew the people in the area were fortunate to have this man running the show. Buck thanked him for his help and headed to his car. He needed a shower and some clean clothes.

CHAPTER SIXTEEN

Bax felt like she had been driving on this rutted dirt road, if you could even call it that, for hours. It was hot and dusty, and she couldn't wait to get to her destination. As she rolled over the next ridge, she stopped to let the dust clear ahead of her. There, below her, was her destination. She also noticed she was only a mile or so west of the city of Craig, Colorado. It was a shame the road she had to take couldn't have been straight. She would have been there by now.

She pulled forward and passed through the fence that surrounded the site. The sign on the gate read braxton global energy site 12. She was aware of who Hardy Braxton was and also his relationship to Buck. She knew she needed to do her best work, like always.

Bax parked her state-issued Jeep Grand Cherokee next to the fire-engine-red pickup truck with the Craig Fire Department emblem emblazoned on the door. The fire chief stood next to it and smiled.

"Hi, Chief Pierce. Ashley Baxter, CBI." They

shook hands.

"Please call me Clay," he said. "Everyone round here does."

"Nice to meet you, Clay. Please call me Bax, and thanks so much for meeting me here."

In front of them was the burned-out remains of what had once been an enormous drilling rig, along with what was left of what Bax assumed was the site office trailer, although it was hardly recognizable as anything.

"Clay, can you fill me in on what happened here?"

"Sure thing. Three weeks ago, we received a call from the county dispatcher asking us to assist with a well fire. Even though this is outside the city limits, we tend to help each other out around here. The closest county unit was several miles away working on a grass fire, so we headed on over."

The chief went on to explain that by the time they arrived, which was just before daybreak, the entire complex was ablaze. It took his entire force of four trucks, as well as two city tanker trucks, to get the blaze under control. He explained that firefighting foam takes a lot of water, yet even with the foam, the fire was a bear to put out, and it almost seemed like the fire only went out when it ran out of anything to feed on.

Once it was out, they had to wait almost two days before the twisted metal cooled down enough for them to get close to it, to try to figure out what happened.

The Craig Fire Department didn't have an arson investigator, so they called the state patrol for assistance. After two days of searching the rig, the findings were inconclusive. The night before, there were thunderstorms in the area, and the lightning was fierce, so without any evidence to the contrary, they concluded it was probably a lightning strike that set the place ablaze. Once the oil on the rig caught fire, it was a matter of time before everything in the yard went up.

Bax noticed the chief looked like he wanted to say something else, but he wasn't sure what to say.

"Clay, I sense you don't necessarily believe the report."

Clay Pierce was not a big man, but he looked like a little kid who had been caught with his fingers in the cookie jar as he shuffled his left foot back and forth in the dirt and scratched his thinning gray hair.

He looked at Bax. "Look, I don't want to give you the wrong impression. The state patrol was diligent in investigating this, but I don't think nature at its worst caused this. We did indeed have storms in the area, but the lightning that night stayed farther to the north. I can see this site from my back porch, and we didn't get woken up by any storm that night. We heard a small boom, which I believe is when the trailer went up."

"No worries, Clay," said Bax. "Anything you tell me will stay between us for now. Why don't we go take a look and see what some fresh eyes might uncover?"

Bax grabbed her backpack, and they headed over to what was left of the trailer. Anyone looking at it would never know this had once been an office trailer. The only things that marked this as a trailer at all were two twisted and partially melted axles. This must have been one incredibly hot fire to cause this much damage.

Bax put on a Tyvek jumpsuit and a pair of nitrile gloves and handed the chief a pair as well. After slipping on the gloves, they started a methodical search of the wreckage, beginning at the twisted axles.

She had learned a lot over the years working with Buck, and she was methodical when looking at a crime scene. Several times she pulled out a little yellow evidence flag and stuck it in the ground near something she wanted to come back and look at later. She never rushed this part of the investigation. She was well aware that many cases were solved because of the science, and Bax, like Buck, was a stickler for details.

The pair worked around the entire trailer site, and she took scrapings from several pieces of metal that she bagged and cataloged for the crime lab. She also took several samples of the soil below the trailer. It was while she was digging around in the dirt under the remains of the trailer that she found a small piece of plastic that seemed to have been part of a circuit board. She passed it to the chief while she slid out from under the metal.

Clay was looking it over when she stood up and dusted herself off. She was grateful she had remembered to pack a pair of Tyvek coveralls in her backpack before she left home this morning.

Clay raised his glasses to his forehead and held the piece as close to his eye as he could, trying to make out what was imprinted on it. Bax pulled out a bottle of water, and the chief washed the piece off, and then, lowering his glasses, he looked at it again.

He handed it back to Bax. "Do you think this might be important? Could just be from a phone or radio from inside the trailer."

She took the piece back and looked at it closely. "True, but right now, it's evidence until it's not."

She slipped the piece into a plastic evidence

bag, sealed the flap and signed it and put it in a manila envelope with the rest of her samples. They headed for the drilling rig.

CHAPTER SEVENTEEN

He had been watching them through the high-powered scope on his rifle since they had first arrived at the site. He had no idea who the blond chick with the ponytail was, but he was familiar with the local fire chief. Their paths had crossed several times over the years, and he had always come out ahead. Someday his luck might run out, but he never considered it luck. He always believed it was skill that kept him both alive and free.

He had been watching when the chief pulled into the site this morning, and he wondered what was going on until he saw the black Jeep Cherokee crest the hill and stop for a second. He figured whoever was driving wanted to let some of the dust clear before heading down towards the site. That road was one bumpy son of a bitch.

He concluded that the blond chick was some kind of investigator or something. The way she crawled around the wreckage, without fear, and handled the samples she had taken made it obvious she had done this before. He was intrigued by her. She looked to be about the same age his sister would have been if she were still alive. This woman carried herself with authority.

He adjusted his position on the ridge and continued to watch through the scope. He was even more intrigued when she handed something to the chief from under the trailer. He tried to focus on what they were looking at, but he couldn't make it out.

He knew the other investigators hadn't found any real evidence, but the way the chief and the blond chick were examining the piece of whatever they found made him wonder if he had made a mistake. The fire was hot enough; it shouldn't have left any evidence, but they seemed to have found something important.

He watched the blond chick put the evidence into a plastic bag, sign it and put the bag in a manila envelope. Now he was concerned. She'd found something he missed, and he was not happy about it. He continued to follow them as they walked towards the drilling rig. Without ever taking his eye off the scope, he smoothly pulled back the bolt on the rifle and, with three fingers, deftly inserted a high-powered ballistic round into the chamber and slid the bolt back into place. He hoped he wouldn't have to use the round, but he wanted it in place just in case.

CHAPTER EIGHTEEN

Bax and the chief started the process all over again once they reached the drilling rig. The damage was incredible. She had been part of several arson investigations since joining CBI, including one industrial warehouse full of chemicals, but she had never seen the kind of destruction she was looking at now. Every piece of metal that wasn't melted into a puddle was twisted and deformed. She thought back to pictures she had seen from World War II after the atomic bomb was dropped on Hiroshima. That was what this site looked like.

She followed the same procedure, placing yellow flags near some items, photographing everything as she went, and taking scrapings of anything that looked out of place or unnatural. The work was dirty, and by the time she was finished, she was covered in ash from head to foot and sweating profusely in her Tyvek jumpsuit.

As she was climbing around on what used to be the drilling rig base, some of the destroyed piping that wasn't melted together shifted and she found herself under a precarious pile. The chief rushed over to give her a hand getting out, but she waved him off. A glint of metal caught her attention, just out of reach in the pile.

Bax pushed against a couple of pieces of pipe, which seemed to have stabilized, and with the chief watching, she squeezed between the pipes and pushed herself into the cramped space. The chief was amazed at her agility.

She turned over on her back and let her head dip down under what she believed might have been the control panel, with its now-silent and melted gauges and buttons. She momentarily lost focus in the jumble of pipe and sheets of melted metal, but she stopped, took a couple of deep breaths and located the glint of metal she was hunting. Reaching out her gloved hand, she pulled out a small metal piece that had somehow become wedged between the base of the control panel and the pieces of the derrick that collapsed onto it.

With the help of the chief, she was able to pull herself back out of this human-made hell she'd crawled into and emerge back into the sunlight. She was never so glad to be back on real ground, even if it was just dust.

The chief was looking at what turned out to be a piece of a metal canister about four inches long; it had most likely been cylindrical, although there wasn't enough left to be sure of the actual shape. He handed it to Bax after she finished drinking a full bottle of water in order to get the ash out of her throat.

"I think I know what this is," said the chief. He continued as she looked at all the sides of the piece.

"A few years back, we had to clear an ice dam in the Yampa River to keep the whole valley from flooding, and dynamite wasn't doing the trick. The Army Corps of Engineers sent a guy down to help us, and he used a thermite charge, which burns so hot it pretty much vaporized the ice dam. This looks like the same kind of cylinder he placed on the ice."

Bax now looked even closer at the piece of metal. There were what appeared to be a couple of numbers imprinted into the outside of the piece, but it was so charred she couldn't read them. She held it up to the sun and turned it this way and that to try to get a better look.

The bullet slammed into the pile of melted pipe inches from her head, and it blew a huge piece of metal out of the pile. Bax instinctively dove sideways and slammed into the chief, knocking him to the ground. She never heard the rifle shot, so it either came from a long way off, or it came from a silenced rifle. She didn't much care. She heard the bullet fly past the side of her head, and that was all she needed.

The second bullet hit the pile of metal right behind where she and the chief found cover, and it showered them with rust and metal pieces. Bax unzipped her coveralls and pulled her Sig out of her holster. She didn't know who was shooting at them or where the shots came from, but she needed to be ready.

The chief pulled his radio from his belt, but his hands were shaking so badly he was having trouble working the radio. Bax placed her hand on top of his and softly said, "It's okay, Clay. I got this."

She took his radio and keyed the mic. "Dispatch, this is CBI Agent Ashley Baxter at Braxton drill site twelve. Shots fired. Officer needs assistance."

"Agent Baxter, this is Dispatch, is anyone injured?"

"No, ma'am," replied Bax. "Shots seem to have come from south of our position."

"Roger, Agent Baxter. Are you in pursuit?"

"Negative. I am with a civilian and can't leave him alone and unprotected."

"Roger. Deputies are en route. Stay protected. I will notify the sheriff."

"Thanks. Baxter out."

She handed the radio back to the chief, who was starting to calm down. He was amazed at how calm Bax appeared despite almost having her head blown off. She needed to get to her car and get her binoculars so she could try to pinpoint the shooter's position. She told the chief to stay down, and she slowly raised her head. It had been a while since the last shot, so she made a mad dash to the car and dove in through the open rear hatch, trying to keep as much protection as she could between herself and the shooter.

She found her binoculars and slid out of the rear compartment. Keeping as much of the vehicle in front of her as possible, she looked towards the hills in the distance. After a few sweeps of the hills, she spotted a dust trail fading off to the southwest.

CHAPTER NINETEEN

He watched the blond chick through the scope as she crawled into the guts of the destroyed derrick. He was amazed watching her and almost forgot why he was there. She looked like some kind of fearless monkey. He didn't know if he would have the guts to crawl into the spaces she was in, so he kept watching.

When she crawled back out, she was covered in ash, but she held a shiny piece of metal in her hand, which she and the chief were looking at. Even from almost a mile away, he knew exactly what it was. The damn canister should have burned up in the fire. What the hell happened?

He wasn't sure if the decision to shoot at them was a survival instinct or if he was just plain pissed off. But he took careful aim. He didn't want to kill them, because he knew that would make things worse, but he needed to do something, so he decided to put the fear of God into them.

He aimed for a spot of metal above her

head, slowed his breathing, momentarily held his breath and pulled the trigger. The silencer he had custom made for his rifle did an excellent job covering the sound of the shot, to the point he almost didn't hear it himself. He would have to bring the welder some more business as a way of thanking him for the excellent quality.

He watched the blond chick dive into the chief, and they took cover behind the pile of pipes. Without removing his eye from the scope, he pulled back the bolt, caught the bullet case in his palm and, once again deftly, slid a new round into the chamber and slid the bolt forward. The second shot slammed into the jumble of melted pipe above where he figured their heads would be. It, like the first bullet, disintegrated on impact.

He was about to load the third round when the radio next to him crackled.

"Dispatch, this is CBI Agent Ashley Baxter at Braxton drill site twelve. Shots fired. Officer needs assistance."

"Agent Baxter, this is Dispatch, is anyone injured?"

"No, ma'am," replied Bax. "Shots seemed to have come from south of our position."

"Roger, Agent Baxter. Are you in pursuit?"

"Negative. I am with a civilian and can't leave

him alone and unprotected."

"Roger. Deputies are en route. Stay protected. I will notify the sheriff."

"Thanks. Baxter out."

"Shit," he thought. "She's a state cop."

He took his eye off the scope, placed the third bullet into his pants pocket, picked up his brass and, with his rifle in hand, slid down the hill until he was no longer visible from the drill site; he raced for his car. He needed to put some distance between himself and the site. This was not the best countryside to find places to hide, but he knew a place where he could go, and it wasn't far.

CHAPTER TWENTY

It was twenty long minutes before the first Moffat County deputy arrived. The whole time she was waiting, one side of her brain kept telling her to get in the car and take off after the dust cloud that was fading to the south, while the other side of her brain kept telling her that she needed to stay where she was and keep the chief safe. After all, she was armed, and he wasn't.

The protection side won out, and she was sitting on the ground next to the chief when the first deputy pulled into the site with lights flashing. He spun his car sideways to the drill rig, so he was facing away from the shooter, jumped out of the car and took up a position behind the patrol car.

"You guys okay?" he yelled from behind his car.

"Yeah," Bax yelled back. "I think the shooter is gone. Saw a dust cloud heading away from us past those hills." She stood up and pointed over her shoulder.

The deputy stood up and holstered his pistol. He stepped out from behind the car and walked over to Bax. The chief was in the process of standing up.

"Hi, Chief. You okay?" asked the deputy.

"I'm fine, Jerry. Thanks for asking."

The chief dusted himself off and stepped up to where the deputy and Bax were standing.

The deputy looked at the ash-covered mess that was Bax and reached out his hand. "Deputy Jerry Garcia, ma'am."

She shook hands with the deputy, introduced herself and looked at his name tag with a questioning grin. The deputy smiled. "Yeah, I know. My parents were sort of hippies in their day." He laughed, and it broke the tension.

Bax was starting to explain what happened when two more sheriff's vehicles pulled into the lot, followed by a Craig police car. Sheriff Gil Trujillo stepped out of his car, walked up to Bax and the chief and shook hands.

Bax explained what had transpired and showed them the spot where she'd first spotted the dust cloud.

"Jerry, why don't you and Kate head up that way and see if you can find the shooter's nest."

Deputies Garcia and Thorn hopped into Jerry's patrol car, pulled out of the site and headed up the road towards the nearest set of hills, leaving a trail of dust behind them.

"Agent Baxter, can you fill me in on what happened? By the way, I appreciate that you checked in with my office when you got into the county. Most state folks don't bother."

Bax smiled and nodded. She gave the sheriff and Craig Police Sergeant Bob Calvin a quick trip through her investigation so far. She showed them the piece of plastic with the remains of what looked like a circuit board on it, and the metal piece the chief was convinced came from a thermite explosive device.

When she finished her debrief, the sheriff looked at the chief. "Clay, looks like you might be right. You said all along you thought this was arson, and it looks like this stuff is taking us in that direction."

"Agent Baxter, looks like all the dust and ash paid off. Nice work. We will follow up on the shooter. Why don't you check into a hotel and swing by the office in the morning and write this all up? I'm going to join my deputies and see if we can find a trail. By the way, thanks for not leaving Clay by himself. I will make sure your director knows how you handled yourself. Well done. Clay, you okay to drive, or do you need Bob to take you home?"

The chief nodded. He was okay.

While the sheriff was talking to Bax, several more city and county patrol cars showed up, and the sheriff and Bob assigned them to check out the roads that ran south from the site and headed towards the river.

Bax thanked the chief for all his help and escorted him to his pickup truck. They shook hands, and she promised to keep him apprised of the investigation. She watched him pull out, and she picked her backpack up off the ground and put it in the back of the Jeep along with her binoculars. She sat on the bumper and tried to get her hands to stop shaking. It felt like someone had let all the air out of her, and she felt deflated. She wiped a couple of tears out of her eyes and sat for a minute and breathed deeply. She realized she had never been more scared in her life than she had been today.

Calmed down, she got in her car and headed back to Craig. She needed to get the evidence bags overnighted to the State Crime Lab and a good night's sleep. She would start fresh tomorrow. She also made a silent vow to find the son of a bitch who shot at her.

CHAPTER TWENTY-ONE

Buck had pulled into the parking lot at the Cozy Up when his phone rang. He pulled out his cell phone, recognized the number and answered.

"Hey, Gil, long time. Is Bax behaving herself up there?"

"Hiya, Buck. Listen, first off, Bax is okay, but she's the reason for my call."

Buck listened as the Moffat County sheriff described the events of the day. The concern on Buck's face became more and more evident as the call progressed. Even though he wanted to interrupt several times, he had learned a long time ago that the best interrogators listen more than they talk, so he waited for Sheriff Trujillo to take a breath.

"Gil, did you find any tracks or evidence of the shooter?"

"We found an area of disturbed brush up on one of the ridges with a good view of the drill site, but nothing to indicate it was human-caused. Could have been a pronghorn bed for all we know. The spot was over a mile away. That would take one hell of a shooter from that distance. There were lots of tire marks not that far away, but it has been so dry up here for the past couple of weeks, they could be weeks old. You know as well as I do almost everyone up here drives a truck of one kind or another. We are going to head out tomorrow, first thing, and see if there was anyone in the area who might have seen a truck or car fly by."

Buck asked him how the fire chief was doing, and Sheriff Trujillo told him he had checked on him a little bit ago, and he seemed to be doing okay.

"Gil, you need me to come up there?"

"Nah. We're good for now. Bax is back in her hotel room, and I asked her to stop by and write up a statement tomorrow. What she needs now, most of all, is some sleep. We'll start again fresh in the morning. I'll let you know if I need any help."

Sheriff Trujillo also told him about the items Bax had found at the rig. The idea of the igniter piqued Buck's interest, since they'd found something that sounded pretty similar at the lodge. The possible use of thermite was something totally out of the blue. Most ecoterrorists did not have access to things like thermite. Thermite was extremely dangerous if mishandled, and the ecoterrorists Buck had encountered almost always tried to use easily obtainable materials that were not easy to trace, like gasoline.

"You think this might be related to your case?" Sheriff Trujillo asked.

"I'm having doubts about that. We don't know much about this group that potentially set this fire, but one thing we do know is that in all the fires they are accused of, they never used a weapon. I'm wondering if this is something else. Besides, why would an arsonist hang around a burned-out drill site for more than three weeks? Seems like odd behavior to me."

"You got that right, Buck, but you and I both know criminals do some weird shit. What do you want to do? We are at your disposal."

"I want to send up a full forensic team to take a look around. I've got this bug running around in my brain that keeps trying to tell me something is going on up there. Let me make a few calls and get back to you. Thanks, Gil. Talk soon."

Buck disconnected the call and hit speed dial one. Kevin Jackson, the director of CBI, answered on the second ring.

"Hey, Buck. How's it feel to be back in the field? I heard that fire took a turn and jumped containment. You all right?"

"Yes, sir, feels good to be back, and yeah, the fire made things interesting today."

Buck filled the director in on the fire investigation so far and discussed the body they'd found in the rubble of the lodge. After answering a few of the director's questions, he told him about the call from Sheriff Trujillo and Bax's close call. There was silence on the other end of the phone, and he could hear the director breathing. He knew not to interrupt.

"Fuck, Buck. What the hell is going on in Moffat County? Arsonists are known to come back to the scene of their fires, but not three weeks later, and armed with a sniper rifle. Doesn't make sense, even for ecoterrorists. What are you thinking?"

Buck told the director he was having trouble wrapping his head around the ecoterrorism angle when it came to the drill rig fire. He told him about the possible thermite link and the possible igniter piece Bax found.

"Thermite, huh?" said the director. "When was the last time you heard about a tree hugger using something as sophisticated as thermite?"

"My point exactly, sir," replied Buck. "That's what's not making sense. I think a few of the well fires Hardy Braxton is blaming on the NETF are something else entirely."

"Okay, Buck. What do you need from me?"

"I'd like to send a full forensic team up to Craig to go over that site with a fine-tooth comb. I would also like to take Hardy Braxton to the site to see if he sees something we may not see."

"Okay, Buck. I'll call Max and let her know you will be calling her and to get the team from Grand Junction rolling. Keep Bax up there working that scene unless you need her with you. Let me know what else you need as you go. I'm going to call the governor and fill him in."

The director hung up, and Buck headed into the bar. He hadn't eaten all day, and he was starving.

CHAPTER TWENTY-TWO

J ack and Caleb were already seated at a table for four when Buck joined them. They decided to take Buck up on his offer of a free steak dinner. Both men had a frosty mug of ice-cold beer in front of them. The bar was packed, which Buck was glad to see, and the noise level had gone up a few decibels since his last visit. The two waitresses working the floor made sure no one's beer glass ever went dry.

A young waitress with dark brown hair and an arm full of tattoos hurried towards Buck, but Sam cut her off with a wave and walked up to the table. She set a cold can of Coke on the table alongside an ice-filled glass and hugged Buck.

"Steaks will be up in a few minutes, boys. What else can I get you?" she asked.

"Sam," replied the sheriff, "looks like we have everything we need for now. Thanks."

Sam headed back to the bar but stopped to pat Gus on the head, which elicited a small tail wag from a sleepy-looking dog. Sam had lost her dog, Moose, a year or so back, but for some reason, she never got rid of his pillow at the end of the bar. Now it was used by special guests.

The guys took a few minutes to discuss the lodge fire and the sudden wind shift that caused the fire to explode all over again. The news had reported earlier that the fire doubled in size again and was now headed in a westerly direction and might require the evacuation of the lodges on the west side of County Route 8 and the town of Buford.

"We've already evacuated all the campers and fishermen from Trappers Lake, and Pat is pulling some of his teams from the east side of the fire and heading them towards Route 8. I am heading back out there as soon as I finish my free steak," said the sheriff.

"Hey, speaking of Buford. What's the deal up there?" asked Buck. "Looks like the town is being revitalized. Noticed a bunch of houses and trailers behind the old lodge."

"Well, not sure if revitalized is the right word," replied the sheriff. "Bunch of survivalists bought up a large parcel of land and kind of moved in and took over the town. Started building houses. Not that there was much of a town to begin with. They pretty much rule their own roost, and I try to stay out of it. I don't have the manpower to mess with them, and the county commissioners said to leave them be. I think everybody up there is armed, and they are not friendly to outsiders."

"They all wealthy?" asked Jack. "I imagine land isn't cheap up there. Any idea how they support themselves?"

Buck leaned forward, interested to hear the answer. He had been thinking the same thing.

"Don't rightly know what they do. I do know the local package delivery service in town had to add on two more drivers for all the packages coming and going. I'm guessing some kind of internet business, but until they break the law, I'm staying out of it."

Buck sat back in his chair as Sam delivered three huge porterhouse steaks and all the sides to the table. The waitress with the tattoos brought over two more mugs of beer and another can of Coke for Buck. The conversation lagged as the three men dug into their meals.

Between bites, Buck watched the people entering and leaving. He had a good eye when it came to people, and he played a little game with himself to see if he could figure out who was who and what they did for a living. It was a lot more fun when he used to do it while on a family vacation, but it still amused him.

Several times, when he looked up from his plate, he noticed the short guy down at the end of the bar. He couldn't be sure, because there was nothing overt, but he couldn't shake the feeling that the little guy was watching them. If he was, he was good at being subtle about it. Buck passed it off as curiosity and continued to enjoy his steak.

Finished with the meal and sitting back in his chair, Buck filled Jack and the sheriff in on what had transpired in Moffat County earlier that day. He told them about the close encounter Bax had with a bullet and about the possible thermite connection.

The mention of thermite perked up Jack's ears, and he laid his fork down and leaned into the table.

"Thermite is more than just a product. It is also a chemical reaction, and it can be some nasty shit. We used it in Iraq to seal up the guns on the tanks we captured. Burns hotter than almost anything out there. About twenty-five hundred degrees Celsius. Turns everything it touches into a molten pile of crap. No wonder it made such a mess of the drilling rig. Rust is one of the components needed to cause the reaction. I bet with all those rusty pipes, it made a hell of a puddle."

The sheriff was the first to ask. "I guess you can't just buy this stuff, right? Sounds like something the military or the government would keep tabs on."

"No, Sheriff, you would be wrong. There are

websites online that will show you how to make the product and how to use it. Anyone can do it. The good thing, if there is such a thing, is that it is tough to ignite, but boy, once it ignites, stand back, and just for shits and giggles, there is no way to put it out. It has to burn itself out. Like I said. Pretty nasty stuff."

He looked at Buck. "I will go out on a limb here, Buck, and tell you that if thermite was used on the drilling rig, then you are dealing with something a lot bigger than a couple of ecoterrorists burning down a fishing lodge. No eco group I am aware of would ever use thermite. Way too hard to control."

The conversation proceeded along that same line for a while longer, with both Buck and the sheriff getting a long lesson from Jack on fire starting and thermite reactions. Buck found it all very informative and scary. "What the hell did Bax uncover?" he wondered to himself.

The sheriff was the first to stand up and stretch. He shook hands all around and waved good night to Sam. Buck and Jack talked for a few more minutes, and then Jack looked at his watch, called Gus and headed for the door. He had a long drive ahead of him, and he said his goodbyes, telling Buck he would have preliminary results of their samples in a day or so.

Buck said good night to Sam, who was running

like crazy from one end of the bar to the other, and headed out into the cool night air. He could smell the moisture in the air once he stepped outside. Hopefully, it would be enough to help the firefighters.

CHAPTER TWENTY-THREE

Buck walked out of his hotel and headed for his car. Once there, he put his backpack in the back and pulled out his phone. He dialed Hardy Braxton's number. Even though it was just past six a.m., he knew Hardy would be up. Hardy may have gotten a little soft over the years, but he was still a rancher at heart, and ranchers started their days pretty early.

Buck heard Hardy's phone ringing, and after a couple of rings, a sleepy Hardy answered.

"You better have a damn good reason for calling me this fucking early," he said.

Buck almost laughed out loud. Well, maybe Hardy had gotten softer than he thought. Oops!

"Good morning to you too. You got some time today? I need you to run up to your number twelve site in Moffat County and meet me there. I am leaving for there now, so may be a couple of hours. Okay?"

"Why do I want to drive all the way up there, and why the rush?"

"Look," said Buck. "You started all this shit, so either you meet me there or find one of your drilling engineers and have him meet me there. You may have a bigger problem than some ecoterrorists."

Buck could hear Hardy talking to someone in the background, probably Rachel, and then he said, "Okay. If it's that damn important, I'll be there, but this better be good." Hardy hung up without even a goodbye. Buck laughed.

His next call was to Max Clinton. He dialed her number and waited for the phone to connect. Dr. Maxine Clinton was a matronly woman in her early sixties, about five foot five with short gray hair. She probably thought she carried around an extra fifteen pounds she didn't need, but she was still a handsome woman. Married for forty years, Max had four children, eleven grandchildren, and six great-grandchildren. She lived in a 150-year-old farmhouse in Pueblo, where she liked to tend her garden and sit on her porch and drink iced tea. She was also a bourbon girl and could drink most people under the table. She was loud and outspoken, but she knew her job.

Max had received her PhD in biology from the University of Colorado and worked as a biology professor for twenty years before joining CBI. Currently, she was head of the State Crime Lab, a job she thoroughly enjoyed. She was a harsh taskmaster, but she had a belief system that didn't allow for defeat. Her goal was to give the crime investigator, no matter which department or municipality they worked for, all the information they would need to solve any crime. She held that as a sacred obligation to the victims. She was incredibly dedicated, and her team at the lab practically worshipped her.

Buck would have been included in that group. Many times, during a tough investigation, it was Max and her team who lit the spark that led to a breakthrough. Max was one of Buck's favorite people, and she felt the same way about him.

Max answered her phone on the fourth ring. "Hey, Buck. How's my favorite cop? You doing okay?"

"Hi, Max. Yeah, I'm doing okay. Some days are better than others, but it's good to be back in the field."

"Well, you hang in there. God and your friends will help you get through the loss."

Buck never minded when Max invoked God into the conversation. She was very religious, and she believed without question the teachings of her church. Buck had realized a long time ago it wasn't God and faith he had a problem with; it was organized religion. In his many years in law enforcement, he had seen too many times the aftereffects of someone's religious beliefs. It amazed him that so many people of faith could cause so much hatred and crime. But then, nonbelievers created just as much havoc.

Buck always believed there was probably a higher power out there, but he didn't believe that whatever that power was, it cared about one individual over another. His football coach always offered up a prayer before each game, asking for help in defeating the other team. He always suspected the other team's coach was doing the same thing. How did God decide which side should win?

He knew a lot of people who said a lot of prayers for Lucy over the five years she was sick, but in the end, she still died. But Buck didn't carry any hatred for them. He was mad at God, but that left him conflicted. In order to get angry at God, he had to believe in God, and he wasn't sure if he did or not.

Buck believed there were spirits or a force all around us, and he always thanked the spirits for allowing him to enjoy the hike, or for allowing him to catch fish, or see the sunrise and the sunset. It wasn't a religion. It was something deeper. Something Buck didn't understand. He just accepted it, but no matter what, he always appreciated it when Max told him that God was watching over him. After all, what could it hurt?

Max explained to Buck that she'd already heard from the director, and she had the forensic team from Grand Junction on the way to Moffat County. She was curious about what Buck hoped to find, since the state patrol had already completed an investigation at the site.

"I'm not sure, Max. Someone took a couple of shots at Bax while she was on-site, and there's something about that that doesn't make sense."

"Is Bax all right?" asked Max, grandmotherly concern taking over her voice.

Buck told her Bax was fine, and she had some evidence heading to the crime lab, which should be there today. Max said she would keep an eye out for the package and get her people on it right away. She told Buck to let her know if there was anything else he needed, and then she ended the call the way she always did.

"You're a good man, Buck Taylor. God will watch over you. Stay safe."

Buck hung up his phone, hopped in his car and headed to Moffat County to meet Hardy Braxton.

CHAPTER TWENTY-FOUR

There was a full contingent of government vehicles at Braxton Global Energy site number 12 as Buck pulled his car through the security gate and parked next to Sheriff Trujillo's cruiser. The sheriff had several of his deputies standing around the front hood of his car, looking over a topographic map of the area. He excused himself from the group when he saw Buck pull in, and he stepped away and waited as Buck slid out of his Jeep. Bax spotted him as well and headed for the open door.

Buck shook hands with the sheriff and then looked at Bax. "Bax, you okay?"

Bax was already fired up and ready to charge ahead. Buck did not doubt that if she hadn't had to wait for him, she would have already been off towards the hills looking for signs of the guy who took a shot at her.

"Yes, sir, Buck. I told the director this morning I was good to go."

Buck smiled. "Okay, Bax. For now, the director and I want you to work this scene with the sheriff, his team and the forensic team. If I need you back in Meeker, I will let you know."

Bax interrupted. "Buck, why the forensic team? The state patrol already did their investigation."

Buck explained about the conversation he'd had with the sheriff the night before, and about the bug in his brain that was tugging at a string and wouldn't let go. He told her something wasn't right about this site, and he wanted a full-blown forensic search. The sheriff nodded in agreement.

"Buck and I talked, and we can't figure out why an arsonist would still be hanging around a site three weeks later and why he would take a couple of shots at you. Arsonists are not known to use weapons. They set fires and then sit back and watch them burn. This is weird."

"Sheriff's right, Bax. Something doesn't add up, so I called up the forensic troops to see what they can find. Who knows, we might not find a thing, but you already found two significant pieces of evidence that were missed, so let's see what happens."

Bax nodded in agreement. "The director said you were going to bring Hardy Braxton to the site. You think he can help?"

"Won't know until he gets here," replied Buck.

They heard a car pull through the gate, and Buck looked around to see Hardy Braxton's huge SUV pull to a stop behind his Jeep. Hardy stepped out of the driver's side, hitched up his jeans and put a tan Stetson on his head. Two other men, similarly dressed, climbed out of the passenger-side front and rear seats. Buck had never met these other two individuals, but he could sense that the guy getting out of the back seat was probably Hardy's attorney. He was shorter than Hardy and a lot thinner, with a thin mustache, and he had a computer bag slung over one shoulder.

The other fellow was tall and rangy with a gray ponytail and long sideburns. His craggy face was well lined and tan. Not a beach kind of tan, but the kind of well-worn tan that turns your skin to leather and comes from having spent most of your life working outside.

Hardy walked up to Buck. "Now, you want to tell me what the hell you meant when you said I might have more trouble than a bunch of ecoterrorists?"

"Same ole Hardy," Buck thought to himself. "Never one to mince words when being direct and in your face works just as well."

"We are not sure what we are looking at. That's why we want your opinion of the site."

Hardy waved over his traveling companions.

"Then let's get started. It's already hotter'n shit out here. This is my lawyer, Irv Tuttleman, and this tall fella is my chief drilling engineer, Carl Burkholder. Now, what do you want from us?"

Buck introduced them to Bax and the sheriff and asked them, for starters, to just walk around the site and see what they could see. He didn't expect much with this first pass, but every investigation starts at the beginning.

The sheriff excused himself and, along with Bax, headed back to the waiting deputies. Once again, pointing at the map, he gave each deputy a section of the topo map to check out. They were looking for any strangers in the area or speeding cars yesterday afternoon or anything that might be odd. He folded up the map, and everyone headed for the cars. He glanced over at Buck as he slid into his vehicle and thanked the Lord he didn't have to stay and deal with Hardy Braxton. They pulled through the security gate and headed in various directions.

Meanwhile, Buck stood back and watched Hardy and his associates wander around the burned-out well site. It was obvious Hardy was not taking this all that seriously, nor was the attorney. His drilling engineer, Carl, seemed to be in the spirit of things, and several times he got down on his knees to look under something. Once, he even called over one of the forensic techs to crawl under a pile of molten metal and retrieve something from underneath.

Hardy walked back over to where Buck was standing, pulled out a white handkerchief and wiped his brow under the Stetson.

"You think there is something here, or is this some kind of revenge thing by that no-count governor?"

"Look, Hardy, you know me better than to believe I would ever be involved in something political. Something is not right here, and I told you I would get to the bottom of it. This is how the process works. Did you bring the daily drilling reports from this site?"

Buck had sent Hardy a text on the drive over and asked him to bring any daily reports, inventories and any other paperwork they might have on this site. Hardy waved over the lawyer, who pulled a notebook out of the bag he had slung over his shoulder and handed it to Hardy.

Hardy handed the notebook to Buck but held on for a second. "This information is proprietary; that's why the lawyer is here. You can read it here with us, or you will have to subpoena it later. This doesn't leave my sight."

Buck nodded and started thumbing through the pages. Most of the information didn't mean anything to him, but he finally found what he thought he was looking for. He opened the tab marked Invoices.

CHAPTER TWENTY-FIVE

Sheriff Trujillo and Bax decided to make one more stop before calling it a day. It had been a long, hot couple of hours, and they had nothing to show for their time driving the back roads along the river except a long list of contact information. The sheriff had been getting reports all morning from his other deputies, and none of them were having much luck either. The search teams had been calling in to Dispatch all morning with IDs and license plates that needed to be run, but so far, nothing serious had shown up on the people they had interviewed. It seemed whoever the shooter was, he had vanished into thin air.

The day was getting hotter, if that was even possible, and the air was thick with dust as they pulled into the next small camp area along the river. It was a quiet spot and looked like an oasis. Here in the middle of all this dry, hardscrabble terrain was a little bit of heaven—a small copse of trees in an otherwise barren landscape.

There were three tents scattered about in the little oasis, and they could see several people lounging about in folding chairs they had set in the river. Two people were fly-fishing. It was an idyllic scene.

The sheriff and Bax parked the patrol car next to a beat-up-looking old Jeep Cherokee and slid out of the car. A young man was sitting in a folding camp chair under one of the trees sipping on a beer, which he set down under his seat as the sheriff approached. A young woman crawled out of the small dome tent and walked up to meet them.

"Mornin', folks. Looks like you found a nice spot to camp." The sheriff looked out over the campsites.

"Morning Sheriff," said the young man in the chair. "We doin' something wrong? The sign said public camp area."

"No, you folks are fine, just checking the area. You folks been here long?"

Bax walked off to talk to the two people who had stopped fishing while the sheriff spoke to the young couple. They were both pulling out their fishing licenses as she walked up.

"Catch anything?" she asked. Her badge and gun were visible, hooked to her belt.

"Couple of small ones, Ranger." They held out their licenses.

"Thanks, fellas, but I'm not the ranger." She

did look at their licenses and wrote their names down on the pad on her clipboard. "I'm working with the sheriff's department, and we are looking for a car thief who might have come this way yesterday afternoon. You guys didn't happen to see anything out of the ordinary yesterday, like a car or truck speeding by here?"

"No, ma'am. We set up camp this morning. We were working in Grand Junction yesterday. Didn't get here till about two hours ago and were lucky to find an open campsite."

Bax thanked them for their time and handed back their licenses. As they put their licenses away, she told them to enjoy the fishing. They turned and headed back into the river. Bax wrote down their license plate number on her pad.

Bax rejoined the sheriff, who was wrapping up with the young couple. They had been camping there for a couple of days, but yesterday afternoon they had been shopping in Craig for supplies and stopped for dinner. The young man was able to find two receipts in his car, from the restaurant and the grocery store. Both were time-stamped. Bax took down their contact info and their license plate number and thanked them for their time.

They walked over to the other tent on the site, but no one appeared to be around. The young woman told the sheriff that the owner of the tent was an older man who had been at the campsite when they arrived three days before, and he kept to himself. She said he seemed a bit unfriendly.

The sheriff thanked them for their time, and as he and Bax walked back to his vehicle, an old yellow Ford station wagon turned into the campsite and parked next to their vehicle. The door made a loud screech as the older fella driving pushed it open and stepped out. He nodded to the sheriff and then walked around to the back door, opened it and pulled a nice-sized rainbow trout out of an old beat-up cooler.

"Afternoon, sir," said the sheriff. "That's a mighty fine-looking fish you got there."

"Yes, sir, it is. Took damn near twenty minutes to land it. Best luck I've had this week."

He had longish gray hair and a gray beard, and he smelled of tobacco smoke. Bax worked her way upwind to avoid the smell. The sheriff didn't seem at all bothered by it.

"We were wondering if you might have seen a car or truck driving by yesterday? Might have been in a big hurry."

The man thought for a minute and then told them he had seen a newer model pickup truck fly down the road sometime late in the afternoon. He couldn't be sure of the time since he didn't wear a watch, but he knew it was later in the day. He told him he didn't think much of it at the time.

The sheriff asked for the man's driver's license and made a note of his information on a civilian contact form his deputies carried. It was always nice to know who was in the county. While the sheriff made his notes, the man told him he would be around for a couple more days before moving on. His final destination was California.

Bax asked the sheriff to step over to the man's car. She was standing at the back door, and she had a concerned look on her face. The sheriff handed him back his driver's license and followed the man back to his car, and they both looked at where Bax was pointing.

Barely visible under a pile of clothes was a large plastic rifle case, the kind used to protect valuable hunting rifles. The sheriff asked the man if he would mind pulling out the case, which he did willingly. He turned the case, so they could all see inside, unlocked the padlock from the one latch and opened the case, revealing an old but well cared for rifle and scope.

The sheriff asked if he could pick up the rifle, and the man told him it was fine. He told them it hadn't been fired in some time, because he hadn't been able to afford ammunition for it. While the sheriff examined the rifle and sniffed the chamber, the man told them it had been the only inheritance he received when his father died a long time ago. He told them his father, a retired marine, had been a stickler for keeping his guns clean and in perfect working order. Even though the rifle was fifty years old, he felt obligated to do the same. So, even though he hardly ever shot it, he made sure to take it out of its case and clean it every week. He hoped his father would be proud.

The sheriff handed him back the rifle, which he delicately placed back in the case and closed the lid and locked it. He slid the case back under all the clothes. The sheriff thanked him for his time and told him to enjoy the fish for dinner. He and Bax headed for his car, hopped in and headed back towards the drill site.

CHAPTER TWENTY-SIX

Buck wasn't sure of the names for a lot of the materials listed in the invoice section of the report, but he was getting the idea that opening a new drilling site was a pretty costly operation. He started feeling bad for Hardy. He had a considerable investment in materials and manpower, and now it was a melted pile of slag.

The forensic team had spent the better part of four hours crawling all over the pile of metal, and their white Tyvek suits were no longer white. Buck noted they stopped several times and took samples of metal or ash or some other unknown substance. At one point, one of the techs had even taken a sample of a stain in the parking area. He liked working with these guys. They were incredibly thorough. Of course, Max Clinton wouldn't have it any other way.

He was reading through the daily reports in the notebook when he heard Carl Burkholder call over to Hardy. Hardy, on his phone, as he had been since he arrived, held up one finger and continued to talk.

Carl, who had a similar blue-covered notebook to the one Buck was reading, was standing next to what Buck had been told was the drilling rig control panel and was flipping pages in the notebook. He watched Hardy disconnect the call and walk over to Carl. Hardy seldom smiled, and today he looked downright pissed off. Buck thought to himself, "How times have changed." Hardy was always the guy in school who got busted for pulling some lame, dumb stunt. As long as it got a laugh from the other students, Hardy was in on it. Now he was a hard-bitten international businessman, but somehow, Buck didn't think he looked happy.

Buck watched from a distance as Carl pointed to the pile of materials in the field and then pointed to some note in the notebook. Hardy would look at the notebook where Carl was pointing and then say something. A few times, Buck thought Hardy was going to have a heart attack. He would gesture and point and then get red in the face, and Carl or the lawyer would say something to try to calm him down. This episode went on for about twenty minutes until Buck decided it was time to get in the middle of whatever this was.

"You guys okay?" Buck asked as he approached the group. Carl closed the notebook and looked at Hardy and the lawyer. "Looks like you found something that's not right. You want to fill me in?"

Hardy threw up his hands and stared at Carl. "Give him your theory."

The lawyer looked like he wasn't sure what to do. "Mr. Braxton, we should discuss this fully before making any kind of statement."

He started to say something else, but Hardy cut him off with a wave of his hand.

"We came here with the intent to help Buck figure this out, which is what I asked him to do." He looked at Buck. "You don't know this man like I do. He is like a bulldog. He is going to find this out anyway, and I would rather he heard it from us than from the newspapers."

Buck stood by silently and waited. He'd spent a lifetime developing patience into its highest art form, and his silence had never failed him. Hardy looked at Carl. "Tell him."

Carl looked at Buck. "Well, sir, something doesn't add up. According to the drilling plan and the daily reports, they were supposed to drill a four-inch shaft down to a depth of forty-nine hundred feet, turn due west, and horizontal bore for another thirty-nine hundred feet. This should have put them into the best part of the fracture zone, so when they started pumping in the fracking fluid, the shale would fracture and give off the desired amount of oil. What's odd is that what I see here doesn't match what is in the reports."

"How so?" asked Buck.

Carl hesitated, and Hardy lowered his voice a couple of octaves and said, "Finish it."

Carl started again. "These reports follow this plan to the letter. Almost too exactly. They didn't miss a date or a depth, and they didn't have one issue arise with either equipment or conditions. This is the most perfect drill site I have ever seen. Problem is, it's all a lie. No site is ever this perfect. I don't care who is running it. The second problem is the inventory and the invoices. Nothing matches what's lying here in the yard."

Carl opened the notebook to the inventory page, and Buck looked at the page he turned to, as Hardy walked away.

"The inventory matches the daily reports. Again, almost perfectly. Except here, where they list four-inch pipe casing. There is none. All the pieces that are left are eight-inch casing. They also list enough pipe to hit their marks. The problem is the invoice is for twice as much pipe, and there are only a couple of hundred feet of pipe left in the yard. Now, there isn't a drilling company anywhere in the world that will buy more materials than they need or pay more for larger pipe than the engineer calls for."

"Okay. Bottom line it for me," said Buck.

At this point, Hardy walked back up to the group, looking slightly calmer than when he walked away.

"The bottom line is either someone can't read a fucking engineering report, or someone is drilling a larger, deeper shaft for a specific purpose. I think it's the latter," said Hardy.

Buck thought about what Hardy said. "What other purpose?"

"Mr. Braxton, you need to be careful what you are about to . . ." But Hardy waved the lawyer quiet.

"My name is on this fucking site! Not yours, mine! And it's my responsibility to make this right." He looked at Buck. "I think someone may be using the well to dispose of toxic waste. I could be dead wrong, but I don't think so. Carl?"

"I agree with Hardy. I've seen this before in several third-world countries, but not here. Waste is a lot more profitable right now than oil, and it takes decades for anything to happen to draw attention to the problem."

"Hardy, how could this happen under your nose, and you not know about it?" asked Buck.

"We used a new drilling company on this one." Hardy stopped and got this "oh shit" look on his face. He looked at Buck and Carl.

"The same company drilled four other wells

in this field. We used these guys because Mark Richards insisted we give them a try. Fuck."

Buck was about to say something when the sheriff and Bax pulled into the site. He excused himself from the group and walked towards the sheriff's vehicle. They were all about to step into a hot mess, and Buck was not happy about it.

CHAPTER TWENTY-SEVEN

The Rio Blanco County deputy slid to a stop on the gravel road that led to the makeshift town. The road was blocked by two Hummers and four men, all armed with AR-15-style assault rifles. The deputy placed his mic back in the holder and stepped out of the car.

"This here is private property, and you are not welcome," shouted one of the men manning the gate. They all held their rifles at the ready position, pointing towards the ground.

The deputy stopped next to his front tire. "The sheriff has issued a mandatory evacuation order for this town. The fire is out of control and heading this way. You need to gather your things and move out. You will have twenty minutes."

"We are a sovereign nation," shouted the man at the gate. "You have no authority to issue any kind of orders to us. Now turn your car around and get out of here before we are forced to defend ourselves."

The deputy was unsure of what to do next, so he took a step forward, and the two men on the outside edges of the group raised their rifles chest-high, pointing towards the deputy. The deputy stopped in his tracks and rested his hand on the backstrap of his pistol.

"Don't you understand that there is a forest fire headed your way and . . ."

"No. What you don't understand is that you made a threatening gesture towards us after we warned you that your laws are not recognized here. Take one more step towards us, and we will open fire."

Now with four guns pointed directly at him, the deputy chose the better part of valor and stepped back towards his car door, never once taking his eyes off the four men. He pulled open his door, slid into the seat and backed down the gravel road until he was far enough away and then made a K turn and headed for the main road.

Once on the main road, he pulled over to the side and sat for a minute. His hands were shaking. He was also getting madder by the minute. He represented the county, and who the fuck did they think they were talking to him that way? He was tempted to go back up to the gate and have it out with them. His smarter brain decided that it was a bad idea, so he headed towards the Vaughn Lake Campground to find the sheriff.

County Route 8 was starting to look like a parade with all the cars and trucks making a run for Meeker. The campers had already been evacuated from Trapper's Lake, and now it was the ranches and resorts to the west of Route 8 that were on the move. The deputy passed a number of trucks pulling horse trailers, even though he knew a lot of the ranch and resort owners had chosen to ride out the firestorm. They could get all the people out, but there was too much livestock to move in the short amount of time they had to move. Many of them had their own employees, using their own light and heavy equipment, creating firebreaks and clear zones around buildings. They were running whatever sprinklers they had, and they had people hosing down the roofs of the buildings.

The deputy didn't understand why many of them chose to stay, but he figured he might think differently if it was his ranch or resort he was trying to save. He didn't have time to second-guess any of them. He pulled into the Vaughan Lake Campground to report to the sheriff.

In the meantime, back down the road in the new town of Buford, Muldoon stood on his front porch and looked east. The wall of smoke was getting closer, and he could see lots of cars and emergency vehicles out on Route 8. He called the front gate on his radio.

"Front gate, this is Muldoon. What did the

deputy want?"

"This is the front gate. He wanted us to pack up and leave. Seems the sheriff ordered an evacuation. We told him to turn around and leave."

"Good. We can deal with our own problems. We don't need them. Keep two men at the gate and send two more back to me. Out."

When the two gate guys arrived in one of the Hummers, Muldoon ordered them to get all the women and children who weren't working and move them into the underground shelter inside the big barn. He then told them to gather up all the men and all the available hoses and start watering down the areas around the houses and the houses themselves.

Even with the smoke a couple of miles away, he still believed this was all a setup and that once they evacuated, the government would come in and raid his property. There was no way he was going to let that happen. They had worked too hard to build their little town, and no one was going to take it away from them. He was positive the DEA agent had told someone, even though he didn't admit anything during the entire time they tortured him; they still needed to be ready.

Muldoon called back into the house and told Margaret Windsong to gather up the computers and put them in the safe. The safe was rated to

3,500 degrees, and he was told by the salesman it could pretty much survive an atomic bomb blast. He headed off towards their makeshift jail. He needed to have a few words with Elliot Beech. He had to find out what the government knew, and so far, Elliot hadn't talked. He would make sure that changed and changed right away.

He hopped onto his ATV and headed towards the back end of the property, where they had located their jail in an old pump house that had been abandoned years ago. It was far enough away from the central part of the town that no one was able to hear what went on inside.

Muldoon pulled up outside and hopped off his ATV as the door swung open, and one of his security guards, wearing a long black apron as if he were a butcher, stepped out and lit up a cigarette.

"Has he talked?" asked Muldoon.

The guard blew a smoke ring and then blew a stream of smoke through the middle of it. "Nah. He still swears he didn't know the guy was a Fed and he never told him anything about our operation."

"You believe him?"

The guard looked at Muldoon. "I was pretty hard on him. If he was going to crack, he would have by now. What do you want to do with him?"

Muldoon told him to wait outside, and he stepped in through the old metal door and pulled it shut. Beech sat on a metal chair, naked and strapped down with wire ties and duct tape. His face was a bloody mess, and he had burns and cuts all over his body. Muldoon spotted the cables running from the battery. One was hooked to the chair, and one was lying next to it. He also noticed the charred hair around his man parts. He smiled his approval.

He stood there and looked at Beech. "How pathetic," he thought.

"Elliot, looks like you're having a bad day. I can make this all stop if you tell me the truth about how much you told the government agent. It will all be over in a minute if you tell me." His voice was so soft Beech had to cock his ear to one side to hear him.

"Nothing" was his raspy response.

Muldoon had seen too many men tortured during his long military career. He knew they weren't going to get the truth out of Beech. At least not the truth he wanted to hear. They had been at this for two days, and he didn't think anyone could resist that long. There was no sense wasting any more time. Jack pulled his pistol from the holster on his belt, screwed on the silencer and shot Beech through his right ear. He put the pistol away, opened the door and stepped out into the fresh air.

"Clean that up," he said, and he hopped onto his ATV and headed back towards the center of town.

CHAPTER TWENTY-EIGHT

B uck filled in Bax and the sheriff about the conversation he'd been having with Hardy Braxton and his team as they pulled up. Bax looked confused, but the sheriff looked like he wanted to walk over and strangle Hardy.

The more Buck explained, the madder the sheriff got until Buck said, "Look, Gil. From what I can gather, Hardy was unaware of any of this. He was pretty much hands-off on this site, as well as the other sites in the county, and he appears to be as pissed off as you are. So, get hold of yourself, and let's go finish this conversation so we can figure out a course of action."

Buck and his team walked back to where Hardy, the lawyer and the engineer were standing, still deep in conversation. Buck looked at the engineer. "Tell me about pumping toxic waste into these wells. We need to know what we are dealing with."

"Without chemical analysis, we could be talking about anything. I once saw an entire village in Africa decimated because some warlord decided to make a ton of money pumping crap into the ground. He ended up contaminating the entire water source for the village, and people started dying terrible deaths. I don't know if that is what we have here, and I hope to god it's not, but we should plan for the worst."

"Do you think the other wells in the county were drilled for the same purpose?" asked Bax.

Hardy hung up his phone and stepped up to the group. "I may be able to answer that, young lady. I just got off the phone with our office, and we have no oil or gas production information for any of the sites in Moffat County."

The sheriff looked at Hardy with a fiery stare that could have caused the same amount of damage as the fire. "Are you telling us you might have poisoned my county?"

Buck stepped between them before Hardy could answer. He held his hand, palm out, towards the sheriff, and looked him in the eye. "Calm down, Gil. We will get to the bottom of this, so let's bottle up the anger for a minute. We are going to need everyone at the top of their game. We could have a serious problem here, so let's work this out." The sheriff stomped away from the group.

The lawyer started to say something, but

Hardy cut him off with a stare, and he backed away silently. Buck looked at Carl. "Could we also be talking about radioactive waste here?"

"I've never heard it done anywhere else in the world, but I guess anything is possible. I haven't heard of anyone trying to get rid of radioactive waste, but I am sure if you check with Homeland Security, they will be able to tell you. From what I understand, the government takes a real interest in stuff like that."

Buck was thankful the sheriff had walked away before he asked the question. His anger level was about as high as Buck had ever seen it, and the last thing he needed right now was for the sheriff to blow up.

Buck took Bax aside, and they had a serious discussion about where this was going to go. Mark Richards was possibly involved in a serious environmental situation, but right now, it was Hardy who was pretty much hung out to dry. Bax nodded a couple of times, and then Buck called over the sheriff, and he and Bax walked back over to Hardy.

"Okay, folks, here is what we are going to do. Hardy, I want you and your team to head over to the sheriff's office and write up a statement about everything we have discussed here today."

The lawyer started to object, but this time Buck cut him off with a wave.

"This is not a statement about guilt or innocence. I want to get the facts as we know them down on paper. This could potentially be used later at a trial, but right now, we need everyone involved to understand that besides the facts about the materials and the drilling records, we have a working theory that will need to be further explored. If I were you, Hardy, I would give Bax copies of the reports we all looked at today, but all I can do is suggest it. Your lawyer will tell you we will be requesting a subpoena for the records anyway, but for right now, that is your call."

He went on to explain that he would like to have Carl remain available to work with Bax since he was the subject matter expert on the whole drilling and extraction process. Bax nodded in agreement.

"Bax, please call Bill Unger at the EPA. We are going to need an emergency response team out here immediately to investigate this and the other four wells and try to determine if they have been used for illegal dumping. Bill will make that happen."

Buck caught the eye of Tim Jacoby, the lead forensic tech on the site, and waved him over. Tim pulled off his mask and Tyvek hood and unzipped his suit. He was sweating like a pig. Buck explained the situation to him and could see the concern that appeared in Tim's eyes.

"Tim, please have your team wrap up what they are doing, double bag all your samples, and then let's get everyone off the site. We do not know if there is any contamination on this site. I think the fire would have destroyed most of it, but let's err on the side of caution and set up a decontamination station and implement basic decontamination protocols."

Tim nodded, zipped up his coveralls, replaced his mask and hood and headed back for his team. The sheriff pulled out his cell phone and called the fire chief and told him to send out his hazardous materials unit to help with the decontamination and to do it quietly. The last thing he wanted right now was to stir up the people of his county. There would be plenty of time for that later if they did discover that poison had been dumped in the wells.

Buck took Bax aside. "I need to head back to Meeker unless you need me here. You know what you need to do. Open an investigation file, and let's take this one step at a time. Keep me posted, and be careful. We don't know where our shooter is. Questions?"

Bax shook her head. "I'm good to go, Buck. I'll have the file set up by the end of the day, and I'll call Bill Unger right now. I'll let you know if I need anything else. Thanks for your help with Hardy Braxton."

Buck smiled, told her to call if she needed him and headed for his car. He pulled out his phone as he stepped up to the car and dialed the director. This case had just taken another strange turn, and they were just getting started.

CHAPTER TWENTY-NINE

Buck sat through part of the interview with Hardy and his team at the request of the director, and he was impressed with Hardy's attorney. He requested that before any conversation took place, they meet with the county attorney, and he negotiated a fair arrangement to protect Hardy as much as possible.

In exchange for "informational testimony" regarding the drilling and fracking process, no one was to be Mirandized, and Hardy would not be held criminally responsible for anything that was said during the interview unless new facts came to light that might change that outcome. Buck was aware that criminal prosecution was the least of Hardy's worries. If word got out that his company, even without his knowledge, deliberately caused potential harm to the residents of Moffat County, the civil lawsuits alone would cost him millions of dollars. Buck felt bad for Hardy, who looked utterly spent, but there was nothing he could do to help him at this time.

After watching an hour of the interview, Buck was confident that Bax and the sheriff had things well in hand, and he decided to head back to Meeker. He needed to shift focus from this investigation to the probable murder and arson investigation he was preparing to roll into. He pulled out of the parking lot and swung through one of the fast-food restaurants that had sprung up all over Craig since his last visit.

He grabbed a burger, fries, and a Coke and headed for Route 13. He watched in his rearview mirror as the white pickup truck that had been following him since the first time he left the fire command center pulled onto the highway a few cars behind him. He wondered why they followed as close as they did since there was no place else to go between Craig and Meeker. It made him laugh at the ineptitude of the two guys in the truck, unless his knowing they were there was part of some plan he was unaware of. He decided not to worry about the two guys and the pickup for now. He would deal with them later.

Buck arrived at his hotel room a little after dark, parked his car, grabbed his backpack and headed for the lobby. For kicks, he looked across the street, and sure enough, there in the restaurant parking lot was the white pickup truck. He was almost tempted to walk over and see what they wanted, but he decided that was a bad idea. He unlocked his room and stepped inside.

Buck set his laptop up on the small desk table, logged on to the internet, and logged in to the CBI website. CBI had gone digital a few years back, and Buck was getting used to setting up his investigation folder in cyberspace. He used to set up his investigation book in a blue notebook, which meant a lot of paper, and if someone took the notebook from him to add information, he would have to track that person down to find the book. With Buck seldom working in the office in Grand Junction, this sometimes made the transfer of information difficult. This new system was so much easier.

Once he filled in a couple of blanks on the title page, the file was created and given a case number, and he could then email access to that file, under the case number, to anyone involved in the investigation and they, in turn, could upload documents right into the file. No searching for the blue notebook, and no need to look for documents or reports. Everything in one neat, tidy package.

Buck clicked on the file he'd created the night before and clicked on the investigation timeline page. This was a snapshot of each step of the investigation. Each time he opened the file, the first order of business was to note the date and time the file was accessed. Buck was meticulous about his notes, and this was how he ran each investigation. He never lost a case in court because something was missing from his file.

He noticed that an entry was made a few hours before from the forensic pathologist in Grand Junction, so he closed the timeline and opened the report folder.

Dr. Sima Kalishe had posted the preliminary autopsy report and left a note for him to call her if he had any questions. Buck clicked on the report and spent the next hour reading and then rereading it and making notes on his yellow pad. Even with all kinds of technology available, Buck still, sometimes, reverted to paper and pencils. When he was finished reading the report for the third time, he picked up his pad and looked at his notes. There wasn't much there.

The report was straightforward and concise. The victim was a male of unspecified ethnic background. The victim's height, as best as could be determined due to the condition of the body, was estimated at between five feet eight inches and five feet eleven inches tall. Weight was estimated to be between 140 and 160 pounds. Hair and eye color could not be determined. There were no distinguishing marks on the body as far as could be found. He did have one pierced ear, but no earring was found.

Cause of death was one bullet to the side of the head above and posterior to the left ear. It was a small-caliber weapon, and the bullet had been sent to the State Crime Lab. The pathologist noted what appeared to be subcutaneous bruising around the face and chest, but nothing was visible on the surface due to the excessive charring of the skin.

The pathologist took X-rays of the victim's teeth, and those were included in the file along with some gruesome pictures of the body. There was nothing unusual regarding the victim's organs; however, in severe fire victims, the organs tended to cook and boil as the body was burned. That was the case here.

She did note there was no charring inside the victim's lungs or nasal passages, indicating he was not alive when the fire started. The preliminary cause of death was the gunshot to the brain, pending the outcome of toxicology tests. Samples of skin, organs and teeth were sent to the crime lab for DNA analysis.

Buck sat back and rubbed his eyes. He looked at his notes. There wasn't a lot to go on, but it was a start. Hopefully, the DNA results would shed some light on the victim's identity. Buck closed the report and uploaded it to the national missing person database. It wasn't much, but maybe someone else in law enforcement was looking for someone who matched some of the information.

With no other reports to review at the moment, Buck decided to shut down his laptop and get some sleep.

CHAPTER THIRTY

B uck was awakened by the ringing of his phone and had trouble locating it on the table next to the bed. He finally found it, noted the time and answered.

"Taylor."

"Buck, Jack Spencer, did I wake you?"

"Hey, Jack. No, I'm good. What's got you up so early?"

"I just got a call from the lab," said Jack, "and I was wrong. The accelerant wasn't gasoline at all. It was something else entirely."

Buck listened as Jack explained the lab results. The remains of the cans they'd discovered outside the structure area definitely contained gasoline. That was confirmed by the mass spectrometer results. The problem was the residue samples they took from inside the lodge. The mass spec results showed a cocktail of strange ingredients, which Jack had never seen used in this combination before. He started giving Buck the names of the chemical compounds they found when Buck cut him off.

"Jack, can we discuss this in English? I flunked high school chemistry."

"Sorry, Buck. What all this gibberish says is someone made up a custom cocktail to start this fire. This is pretty sophisticated stuff, and you can't just go out and buy this stuff at the local hardware store."

Jack explained that the combination of chemicals made a napalm-like substance and would have an almost puttylike consistency. The final product, besides being sticky, would smolder for a while before bursting into flames when exposed to a lot of oxygen and would burn extremely hot.

"Now, the other product we found . . ."

Buck wasn't fully awake, but he was becoming more focused as the conversation went on, and he stopped Jack again. "What other product?"

"That's what I was getting to, Buck. We found the chemical signature for a second accelerant. This product was a liquid, and it had the same chemical properties as white lightning—you know, moonshine."

Buck was now wide awake and looking for his notepad, which he found on the desk next to his laptop.

"Did you say white lightning and moonshine?"

Jack explained further. "It appears whoever

lit the fire first covered all the furnishings and the flooring with a product similar to white lightning. This product was almost pure alcohol and would have burned fast and hot. Fast enough and hot enough to catch the rest of the building materials on fire. Once the logs caught, the whole building would have gone up in a matter of seconds."

Jack's assessment was that the puttylike product was stuffed inside the couch or chair, and when the igniter was activated, it started a slow fire that would have sucked all the oxygen out of the room and then sat there and smoldered.

What happened next was still speculation, but either someone opened a door or a window or a piece of glass failed in the vacuum and blew into the space. Either way, the sudden inrush of oxygen would have caused an almost instantaneous back draft, and boom, the whole place would have exploded.

"The open valves we found in the kitchen on the propane tanks, and the chemicals on the floor and the furnishings, would have created a massive explosion. The closed valve on the sprinkler system didn't help, but my guess is the fire would have blown right past the fire sprinklers, and they would have been completely ineffective."

Buck, now sitting at his desk, was making notes as Jack spoke. He could tell from Jack's voice that this was exciting for Jack.

"Okay, so let me see if I have this straight. Someone spread a lot of moonshine around the inside of the lodge. Then they set up this smoldering fire, which worked almost like a timer, to give whoever set the fire a chance to get away, and when oxygen entered the space, everything blew at the same time. Is that about right?"

Jack told him it was close enough, but even so, it was all still speculation as to the sequence of events. Jack went on to tell him he had never seen the chemical signature for the puttylike product and he'd sent it on to the Denver office of the ATF. The Bureau of Alcohol, Tobacco, Firearms and Explosives has an extensive database of every chemical ever used in a bombing, or any other attack, and he was hoping they might have run across this chemical composition before. If they had, it could be a signature product of the arsonist, which might help them find this person.

Buck let Jack take a minute to catch his breath before he started asking the questions he'd written down on his notepad. Buck wasn't sure how this information might help them at this point, but if Jack was excited about the information, he would respond accordingly.

"Jack, what about the gas in the can remains we found? Sounds like almost overkill to me."

"Yeah, me too. I can't figure that one out. Anyone who would put together a product this sophisticated would not also bring along several cans of gasoline. It would serve no purpose. It would take a lot less white lightning to get a fire going than it would gasoline, and it would burn hotter and faster."

Buck thought for a minute. The nagging bug was back in his brain. He never knew when it would show up, but he had also learned a long time ago to never discount the bug. He sat and rubbed his temples, and then it came to him.

"Jack, suppose for a minute the arsonist didn't bring the gas with him. We already talked about the fact these ecoterrorists almost always use gas because it is easy to obtain and hard to trace. We know the ecoterrorists sent a letter to the local paper claiming responsibility, but the sophisticated chemical used kind of shoots that idea to hell. What happens if . . . ?"

"Buck, you're thinking we have two arsonists working the same location at the same time without either one aware of the other? That's almost too bizarre."

"Yeah, but it would also explain," Buck interrupted, "the forest fire. The NETF has never made a mistake like that before. They either got careless, or someone else set the fire to cover up the murder and didn't care about the weather or about what happened later. The ecoterrorists could have arrived with the gas and found the fire already happening. They might have dropped the gas cans and just bolted. It would explain a lot, except for why two separate groups wanted to destroy the lodge."

"Fuck, Buck. If you're right, we have a real mess on our hands."

CHAPTER THIRTY-ONE

J ack uploaded the mass spectrometer report to the investigation file, and Buck took a few minutes to read it and reread it. The chemical names were outside of Buck's knowledge base, but the rest of the information was exactly as Jack explained. Buck needed to get back out to the lodge. "What was it about that lodge that would cause two different groups of people to want to destroy it?" he thought to himself.

Buck jumped in the shower, got dressed, grabbed his backpack and opened the door. The smoke in the air hit him like he was sitting at a campfire when the wind shifted. There was a distinct haze, and he could see the soot that had accumulated on the cars in the lot overnight. He knew this was not a good sign.

He walked next door to the restaurant, sat down at the only open booth and picked up the menu. He could overhear the conversations around him, and it seemed like almost everyone was talking about the fire. He also got the distinct impression a lot of people were blaming the fire on the lodge built by Mark Richards, which was true, since the fire was a direct result of the lodge being there.

He put down the menu as the waitress approached and ordered the ranch special: two eggs over hard, sirloin steak and hash browns, with a Coke to wash it all down. He was about to pull out his phone to check messages when a shadow crossed the table, and a woman sat down on the booth seat opposite him.

"Agent Taylor, my name is Stephanie Street." She slid her business card across the table, but Buck didn't reach for it. "I represent the Western Colorado Conservation Alliance, and my clients want to be certain you understand they had nothing to do with the lodge fire. If you continue your investigation by looking into conservation groups in the region, I will be forced to file for a restraining order to prevent you from harassing my clients. Have I made myself clear?"

Buck sat for a second and looked at Ms. Street. She was a lot younger than he was, but then again, he felt like most people he encountered were, and she was attractive with a round face, deep blue eyes and jet-black shoulder-length hair. The combination was almost mesmerizing. He reached over and picked up her business card and looked at it.

"I'm sorry, Ms. Street, is it? Have we met

before?"

The waitress stepped up to the table and set down a huge plate of food in front of Buck. She asked him if he needed anything else, and then she looked at Ms. Street, who shook her head no. The waitress walked away, and Buck unrolled the silverware from the white paper napkin and then looked at Ms. Street.

"Ms. Street. I have no idea who your clients are. This investigation is in its earliest stage, and at this time, I don't have a clue who I will need to interview. Now, I appreciate the fact you have brought your clients to my attention, and I will make sure to make a note in my file that I might need to talk to them at some point, but right now I have no interest in harassing your clients, just eating my breakfast."

Ms. Street looked almost perplexed. She'd dealt with law enforcement types before, and she knew the direct approach usually worked best, but she wasn't sure what had just happened. She had received information her clients were being investigated about the lodge fire and subsequent forest fire, but here was the lead investigator, and he acted like he had no idea who her clients were. She didn't know what to do next, which was a position she rarely ever found herself in.

"Are you trying to tell me you haven't attempted to locate my clients and have no interest in speaking with them at this time?" she asked.

Buck cut a piece of his eggs, slid it onto the fork and held it poised below his mouth. "That would be correct, Ms. Street, but now that I am aware of your clients, I will definitely run a background check on their organization. If I find the need to interview your clients, I will give you a call." He waved her business card in the air. "If there is nothing else, I'd like to finish my breakfast, as I have a busy day."

Ms. Street started to slide out of the booth, and Buck said, "I would be interested in finding out why your clients think they are under investigation for the fire since, so far, I haven't interviewed anyone."

Stephanie Street didn't lose the perplexed look from her face as she stood up. "Know this, Agent Taylor, I will protect my clients at all costs. Good day, sir."

Buck watched her walk away and smiled. "Did my first lead just walk up and present itself to me?" he wondered. He dug into his breakfast, paid the check, left the waitress a nice tip and headed out the door into the smoky haze.

CHAPTER THIRTY-TWO

Sheriff Trujillo arrived at his office early the next morning and found Bax sitting at the table in the conference room that was attached to his office, hard at work. They had wrapped up the interviews with Hardy Braxton and Carl Burkholder late the night before and hadn't had a chance to discuss their impressions of the interviews. She was clicking away furiously on her computer and didn't look like she had slept at all. She didn't notice the sheriff's arrival until he put a fresh cup of strong black coffee down in front of her.

"Did you get any sleep, or have you been here all night?" he asked, noticing the growing pile of papers strewn all over the table.

"That son of a bitch lied to us!" she said excitedly.

"Who, Hardy Braxton?"

"No, James Robert Galvin."

The sheriff stopped and thought for a minute, but he had a confused look on his face, so Bax stopped clicking her laptop keys, took a sip of her coffee and filled him in.

"The guy from the river with the fish and the rifle."

"Okay, I remember him, but what is this about him lying to us?"

Bax dug through the piles of paper on the table until she found one of the items she was looking for. She handed the first pile of documents to the sheriff. While he looked through the papers, she explained what she had discovered during the night.

The clerk in the office had run all the names and license plates the sheriff and his deputies collected while checking along the river for anything unusual. Most of the names came back clean, but a couple had some past minor infractions. Nothing serious. However, James Robert Galvin was a different story.

Galvin's name didn't show up in the motor vehicle database in Colorado or any of the surrounding states, which was odd since he gave Bax a Colorado license. What she did find was an arrest warrant, now closed, for a James Robert Galvin of Lake County, Colorado. The charge was two counts of murder.

Bax had left a message on the voice mail at the Lake County Sheriff's Office and was waiting to find out the particulars of the case. It was odd that the arrest warrant was never acted on and even odder that it was closed out without explanation.

She rummaged around on the desk and found a couple more printouts, which she handed to the sheriff. She hadn't been able to find a criminal record in Colorado, but at some point during the night, she started running a deep dive internet search on Galvin and came up with some interesting information. She found a news article about a wrongful death lawsuit filed by James Robert Galvin's attorney on his behalf.

"Mr. Galvin's wife and young daughter both died from a rare form of cancer, and he tried to sue the chemical company that sold him some kind of fertilizer he'd used on his land."

Using her superior computer skills, she was able to find a little more information on the lawsuit, mostly from some local press releases. The Galvins owned a small ranch in Lake County, Colorado, and Galvin purchased a new fertilizer combination to use on his vegetables from an unnamed chemical company. There was something wrong with the fertilizer, some cows died, and Galvin blamed the fertilizer for his family's cancer.

She hadn't been able to find out any more about the lawsuit, except it had been dismissed because the attorney didn't have any standing, according to the judge. This would have been odd all by itself since the lawyer represented the party that had been wronged, but she couldn't find anything else, because the records were sealed.

She'd started working through channels to get the records unsealed. There had to be a reason he wasn't in the motor vehicle database, and there had to be a damn good reason to seal the records for a lawsuit that was dismissed. Her interest was piqued, and she wanted answers. She was also pissed she had been lied to.

The sheriff looked at the papers in his hands and then looked at Bax. "Okay, Bax. The question now is, how does this connect with the oil well fires?"

"That's what I was working on when you came in."

"Good, then grab your stuff, and let's go see if we can find Galvin. I think we need to have another chat with him and see what he has to say. In the meantime, I'm going to have one of the clerks start running a more in-depth background check on him."

CHAPTER THIRTY-THREE

Buck spent the better part of the drive from Meeker to the fire incident command center talking to Dr. Kalishe. The charred body was in such bad shape any distinguishing features would have been destroyed. He asked her about the subcutaneous bruising she described in her report, and she told him that when she opened up the body, she was able to see the bruising on the underside of what was left of the skin.

She told him it was pretty much just luck that led to that find. It was not something she would typically look for in a body with this much damage.

"So, at this point, Doc, there is pretty much no way to identify the victim?"

"Unless the DNA is still viable, and we get a hit through the national DNA registry, I'd say the chances are pretty slim. We could hope for a dental match, but if you read farther down the report, several of his teeth are missing. I can't determine if they were knocked out or if they blew out due to the fire."

Buck thanked the doctor and pulled into the Vaughan Lake Campground. The fire was running south, so they hadn't had to relocate the fire command center, but the smoke was another matter. He noticed it got a lot denser the farther he drove up Route 8. At one point, as he passed Buford, he looked over towards the town and noticed they still had their security guys manning the gate to the town, but this time they were all wearing surgical masks and had their heads covered. Glancing the other way, he could see the fire looked a lot closer to the town than it had been the day before.

He was contemplating what would possess a bunch of survivalists to stay in an unprotected area when they were looking down the throat of a fire-breathing monster. He decided he had better things to do than to start getting philosophical about what made people do dumb things. His entire career had been based on people doing stupid things, and that wasn't going to change anytime soon.

He stepped out of his car, grabbed his backpack and headed for the fire command tent. Pat Sutton was where he had been for the past couple of visits, hunched over his topographic maps while several other people clicked away on their computers with lightning speed. As he walked through the tent, he noticed several of the computers were open to what looked like different satellite views of the fire. None of them looked good.

Pat looked up from his map and keyed the mic on the desktop radio. "Mike three, come in."

"Go ahead, Skip," came the reply.

"Mike, can you move your team about a quarter mile to the south? The latest pictures show the fire creeping up on a steep draw, and if it gets in that draw, it could make a run for about a mile. We need to stop it there."

"You got it, Skip. Mike three out."

Pat laid down the mic and looked at Buck. The weariness in his eyes was telling.

Buck asked him how things were going, which he realized after he asked was a dumb thing to ask, but Pat, good-naturedly, took the time to show him where things stood, and it didn't look good. A small finger of fire had jumped Route 8 south of the command center, but luckily, they spotted it right away, and with the help of the rancher who owned the property, his crew of cowboys and a helicopter, they were able to beat it back.

The biggest issue right now was that the fire was blowing towards a good-sized stand of spruce trees that had been killed off by the spruce budworm. Once the fire got in there, it could burn up a lot of acreage in a short amount of time. Pat was concentrating a vast amount of resources on that edge of the fire. He did mention the wind had calmed down enough overnight that he could begin airdrops again, and he had two huge 747 tankers en route. If the wind held off, he was hoping to get back to about 30 percent containment.

"Pat, what do you think the chances are I can get back out to the lodge site?"

Pat thought for a minute, checked with one of his weather forecasters and said, "Right now, pretty good. The fire did all the damage it can do at that end of the burn scar, and the winds are predicted to keep blowing from the northeast, so the fire and a lot of the smoke will blow away from the site. You want someone to go with you?"

"No. I don't want to cause you any trouble; you got your hands full. I would appreciate one of your radios though, just in case."

Pat pulled one of the spare radios out of the charger, set it to the correct channel and handed it to Buck, who clipped it to his belt.

"Just like the other day, Buck, if I call and tell you to move, you get your ass out of there, okay?"

Buck nodded and thanked him for the radio. He headed back to his car and took his hard hat and his bright orange traffic safety vest out of the back and put them on. He made sure he had his flashlight, a camera, a couple of bottles of water and some energy bars. He grabbed his backpack and headed across the parking lot to the trail.

He wasn't sure what he was looking for, or what he hoped to find once he got to the lodge site, but things weren't adding up. He understood why the conservation people were upset and why they would want to burn down the building, but why would another group decide to do the same thing at precisely the same time? There had to be a damn good reason.

CHAPTER THIRTY-FOUR

Sheriff Trujillo and Bax left the sheriff's office by the rear door. Their first stop was at Bax's Jeep so she could get her ballistic vest out of the back, which she put on and snapped shut. She also grabbed her backup weapon and strapped the thigh holster onto her leg. She was now ready to go. While she was getting herself ready, the sheriff was doing the same thing at his car.

He and Bax climbed into his marked unit and headed for the highway. He also unclipped his radio and called Dispatch to have Deputies Garcia and Thorn meet him a quarter mile east of the campsite. They had no idea of Galvin's state of mind or his abilities, but they wanted to take every precaution, especially if he was the one who'd shot at Bax.

Twenty minutes later, they were parked on the side of the road on the downslope side of a ridge. Garcia had already climbed to the top of the rise with his binoculars and was scanning the area. He came sliding back down the hill and caught his breath.

"Nothing visible, Sheriff. There is one tent under the trees, and all I see are two fishermen in the river."

The sheriff decided to err on the side of caution and directed both deputies to follow him down to the camp. Garcia would follow him into the camp while Thorn took up a position at the entrance. He gave the word, and they all jumped back in their vehicles and headed to the camp.

The two fishermen, who were sitting in chairs along the edge of the river, looked startled when the three sheriff's department vehicles pulled into the campsite and stopped in a cloud of dust. They looked more concerned when they noticed everyone had on a ballistic vest and their weapons were drawn. They thought it prudent to stay right where they were, so they set down their beers and sandwiches and waited for the cops to come to them.

Checking all three campsites to make sure they hadn't missed anything and feeling confident Galvin wasn't hiding in the trees, the sheriff released Garcia and Thorn back to their patrol routes, and he and Bax approached the fishermen.

"Afternoon, gents," said Bax as she holstered her weapon. "Did you guys see what happened to the older fellow we spoke to yesterday?"

"Yeah," said the one fisherman. "He cooked up

that big trout last night, gave us and the young couple next door a bunch of it and then, right after dark, packed up and pulled out."

Fisherman number two continued. "He didn't say much, just all of a sudden he was dropping his tent and packing up his old station wagon. Didn't seem in a big hurry when he left, so we didn't think much about it."

Fisherman number one said, "He do something wrong?"

"We just had a few more questions for him," replied the sheriff as he holstered his pistol. They looked at the sheriff like they didn't quite believe him.

"When did the young couple leave?" asked Bax.

"They left about an hour or so ago. Said they had to be back at work in the morning. We were getting ready to call it quits ourselves and head back to Grand Junction. Tom here needs to be at work tonight. I get one more day off."

Bax thanked them and handed them each one of her business cards. She asked them to keep an eye out as they were leaving, and if they spotted the old station wagon to please give her a call.

As they walked back to the sheriff's car, he keyed the mic on his shoulder and told Dispatch to issue a statewide all-points bulletin for the car and the driver. He asked the dispatcher to also include Utah and Wyoming. They climbed in the sheriff's car, and Bax punched the dashboard with her fist.

"Shit. He could be anywhere by now if he left last night!" She was not happy.

"Well, look," said the sheriff. "We can't do anything out here, so why don't we head back to the office. I'd like to look at the tapes from the interviews with Hardy Braxton and his team. Maybe we can find something we missed while we wait for the EPA to arrive."

After arriving back at the office, they walked back to the conference room, grabbed a couple of bottles of water and some snacks and made themselves comfortable. Bax fired up her laptop and pulled up the interview tapes from last night.

After two hours, the tapes ended, and they both stood up to stretch. The sheriff walked over to the coffee maker in the corner and poured himself and Bax each a cup of black coffee. Bax sipped hers as she looked over her notes.

"Well," she said. "It looks like we have plenty of information on the process, and we can put together a drilling timeline, and a comparison of the invoices and what's on the site. The question is, what do we do with it, and can we use any of it to convict someone of a crime?"

"I doubt we have anything right now that is actionable, and believe me, I wish there was, because if this is all true, I want to make someone suffer. The problem now is all we have is the opinion of the people who are responsible for the wells. Mark Richards's name doesn't appear on any of the documents we've seen so far. Everything right now points to Hardy Braxton as the bad guy."

"I know, so here is what I'd like to do. I think we should do a deep dive into Hardy Braxton and his many companies and see if we can make anything fit with the illegal dumping scheme. At the very least, we have to find anything that can be connected to Richards, but as Buck would tell me repeatedly, the investigation will go where the evidence takes us."

They worked out a plan of attack and were in the process of deciding which task was to be completed by whom when one of the deputies knocked on the conference room door. He told the sheriff the EPA crisis team had just arrived at the well site.

Bax downloaded the interview tapes and all the papers from the internet searches into her case file, shut down her laptop and headed for the door. She wanted to talk with the EPA investigators before they got too far along.

CHAPTER THIRTY-FIVE

The fire had devastated the forest around the lodge. What was once a beautiful pristine wilderness was now a charred mess of burned sticks, but even with all the burned landscape, Buck could see the first sprouts of Indian paintbrush pushing their way through the dusty soil, and he stopped for a minute and marveled at the resilience of nature. This was one of those moments he wished he could share with Lucy, and he got a little misty-eyed.

His hike to the lodge was uneventful, and the smoke wasn't bad. He could still hear the helicopters as they flew to Trapper's Lake to fill their huge buckets with water for the fight that was still going on south and west of the lodge. He knew this fight wasn't even close to being over. He passed several firefighters hiking back towards the command center, and they looked exhausted. He wondered how Cassie and her team were doing.

Buck reached the lodge and sat down on a burnt log, took off his hard hat and wiped his brow with the back of his hand. He was no expert, but it seemed to him the humidity was up. Maybe that would mean rain, since the storms that had been predicted for the last two days never materialized. He shrugged off his backpack and sat for a moment, looking over what was left of the lodge. He knew from experience that sometimes the best thing to do during an investigation was to sit and look around. Get a real good feel for the area.

After a few minutes of looking around, Buck pulled a pair of heavy-duty leather work gloves out of his backpack along with a handful of blue nitrile exam gloves. He stood and started walking around the lodge. He wasn't looking for anything specific, just possible areas to look at further. He had no idea what he was looking for, so this was the best approach.

It took close to two hours to walk around the lodge. Occasionally, he would stop and look harder at something that caught his eye. Several times he stepped into the lodge itself to look at something only to find it was a reflection or something else insignificant.

With his first pass complete, Buck stepped onto the floor of the lodge and began moving about the burned-out logs. He had to push a couple of logs out of the way to see under them. As he moved, he had a destination in mind: the couch or chair where they'd found the victim.

He was trying to get into the killer's head as he moved through the building carrying a dead body, and figure out what he did along the way.

Several times he stopped and examined something he found on the floor. He would take a picture of it with his cell phone and then put it in a plastic evidence bag, sealing it and noting the date, time and rough location. He also made a mental note to call his son Jason and see if he could email him a floor plan for the lodge.

As he got closer to the area where the body was discovered, he slowed his pace and moved with determination. He was looking for anything that might give him a clue as to what was so important about this building that everyone, it seemed, wanted to burn it down.

The body had been lying under a bunch of massive logs that Buck assumed must have come from the roof. It was also near where the small plastic igniter part was found under a scrap of unburnt material. Buck wondered if the body had been hidden someplace and came crashing down with the roof, or if it had been sitting or lying on a couch or chair and the roof had collapsed on top of it. He decided to work from the assumption that someone had placed the body on the furniture, and the fire caused the roof to collapse on top of it.

He started pushing and pulling the big logs

he could move out of the way so he could get a better view of where the body had been. He found a few more pieces of fabric that had not completely burned, along with some partially melted foam rubber—most likely, the cushion filling from the furniture. He took a couple of pictures and then placed the pieces in an evidence bag. There was enough of the material left; they might be able to determine which piece of furniture it came from. That could help with the placement of the body in the space.

Buck spent the next couple of hours crawling around on his hands and knees. The fire had done an amazing job of destroying all the evidence that might be found. During his long career, Buck had never believed a crime scene was worthless for evidence gathering, but he now thought he had encountered his first one. Other than the few pieces of fabric and foam he had found, the fire had destroyed everything else. Buck stepped back over to the log where he left his backpack, put his meager samples inside and sat down on the log.

He'd never felt so frustrated at a crime scene. The little bug running around in his brain was not satisfied and continued to stomp around, but he was no closer to getting any answers. He'd been confident all along something would lead him to understand why this building had to burn, but after several hours of backbreaking work, there was still no clear answer. The little bug was going to have to wait.

He started to wonder if he was losing his touch. He had been at this job a long time; or maybe he came back too early after Lucy's death. Perhaps he wasn't ready. Buck hated these thoughts. He had never been the kind of person, even during those tough years of dealing with Lucy's illness, who would fall into self-pity or despair. No matter what happened, he always managed to persevere, but now he was sitting literally like a bump on a log and filling his head with self-doubt.

Buck took a long drink from his water bottle and poured the rest of the water over his head to clear away the dust. When he shook the water out of his hair, he realized how stupid this was. He'd worked tougher cases before, and this one was no different. Besides, if Lucy saw him sitting here thinking like this, she would have kicked him right in the ass. That thought made him smile, and he decided the little bug was right. Something didn't make sense, but he wasn't going to find the answer here. He picked up his backpack, put on his hard hat and headed back to the command center. This site, as far as being a crime scene, was dead. He would need to look elsewhere for the answers.

CHAPTER THIRTY-SIX

Hardy Braxton's face was bright red as he listened to the person on the other end of the call. Rachel, who was standing nearby, thought he was going to have a heart attack. She'd seen Hardy get mad before, but this was something new and scary. She didn't have all the details yet, but she'd never heard him talk to Mark Richards like that before.

"Look, Mark," shouted Hardy. "Who the fuck do you think you're playing with here? I asked you a straightforward question. Are you using our wells to pump toxic waste into the ground?"

"Now, Hardy, I have a lot of businesses under my name, I can't remember all of them, for Christ's sake."

"That's bullshit, Richards. Right now, my neck is stretched out about five miles, and I need an answer. Yes or no?"

"Hardy, it's not that simple."

"The fuck it isn't. We are in some deep shit if you pulled this stunt."

"Now, hold on, Hardy. As I recall, you haven't complained once about all the nice fat checks you get from our ventures, and besides, as you said earlier, your neck is out five miles, not mine. As I recall in our business ventures, my name doesn't appear anywhere, but oh my god, yours does."

Hardy sat back and blew out a breath. He couldn't believe what he was hearing. The smug son of a bitch was going to throw him under the bus and let him take all the blame and the lawsuits. He needed to be careful where this conversation went from here. He knew he had a temper, and Richards had just about pushed him over the line. There were two things Hardy didn't like. Not being in charge, and being pushed around by pompous assholes. He had reached his limit.

Hardy looked at Rachel, who was signaling for him to calm down. He had built this business up from a small cattle company into one of the biggest livestock and energy companies in the world, and he wasn't going to let the likes of Mark Richards tear it down.

Mark was still rambling on with that smooth Southern accent, the one Hardy knew was as fake as the guy using it, when he shouted into the phone and cut him off.

"You listen to me, motherfucker. I know I

haven't done anything illegal, but I am damn sure you can't say the same thing. So, maybe I should call the attorney general in Washington and have a nice conversation with him."

Mark's voice changed, and the smooth Southern twang was gone, replaced by all New York. "Hardy, are you taping this conversation? Because know this. I am Mark Richards, and there is nothing you can do to hurt me. I will bury you in lawyers and paperwork. As far as I am concerned, you used our business relationship, and the oil wells we drilled together, to run a side scam involving toxic waste, and I am appalled. I might call the FBI and swear out an arrest warrant for you and your whole family. And know this also, Hardy: your cop brother-in-law doesn't scare me one fucking bit. So, you chew on that, my friend, because by the end of the week, I might end up owning your ranch and all your livestock, which might be a lot of fun."

Hardy heard the phone disconnect on the other end and sat there for a minute, holding his cell phone. "Maybe I should have taped the conversation," he said to no one in particular. Rachel, who was now sitting in one of the big leather chairs in front of his desk, looked at him. She could see the fire in his eyes, and she got very concerned. Mark Richards may be worth a lot more than Hardy Braxton, but he had never dealt with Hardy when Hardy was mad. And right now, Hardy was furious.

Hardy opened his cell phone contact page and speed-dialed Irv Tuttleman, his lawyer. Irv and Hardy went back a long way, and Irv had been a big part of all the successes they had enjoyed on the way to this moment. Irv didn't look the part of a tough-as-nails attorney, but looks were deceiving, and Hardy found over the years that Irv had one of the best legal minds around.

Irv answered the phone on the second ring, and Hardy explained the phone conversation he'd just had with Mark Richards. Irv didn't interrupt once as Hardy repeated the conversation as best he recollected. Exhausted, Hardy stopped talking. He sat back in the desk chair and put his feet up on the beautiful burled wood desk.

For a moment, there was silence on the other end of the line, and Hardy was afraid he might have lost Irv, but then Irv spoke. He explained that the way they had Hardy's multiple businesses structured, each business was isolated from the others, so Mark Richards could try as hard as he liked, but there was no way he could own Hardy's companies. He did tell Hardy that any lawsuits coming from the oil well issue could tie them up in court for a long time and might cost Hardy a lot of money.

He told Hardy that threatening to go to the attorney general was a bad move because Mark Richards would now be on the defensive, and he was probably already directing his lawyers to destroy any evidence of his involvement in the oil wells. Irv promised he would do everything to protect Hardy, but they were going to have to go on the offensive and get ahead of this. Once this became a criminal matter, it would be a lot harder to fight.

Hardy listened to everything Irv said and started to calm down, much to Rachel's relief. He knew Irv had his back. As he listened, he began to think about how to go after Mark Richards. He was pissed Mark would hang him out to dry, and at this moment, he wanted nothing more than to destroy him, even though he knew it would be impossible. But he could still dream, couldn't he?

Irv was talking about having his staff gather all the documents related to the oil wells they had partnered with Mark Richards on, and then they could sit down and see where they stood. Then he said something Hardy never expected to hear from Irv.

"Hardy, you need to sit down with Buck and fill him in on everything you told me. You always told me Buck was the most honest guy you ever knew, so it's time to tell him everything we know."

Rachel, who had been listening to the conversation, nodded at Hardy. In a whisper, she said, "Call him. I trust Buck a hell of a lot more than the attorney general. Buck can't be bought."

Hardy knew she was right, and he told Irv to start working on the documents, emails and phone calls. He knew what he needed to do.

CHAPTER THIRTY-SEVEN

It had been a long time since anyone had talked to Mark Richards the way Hardy Braxton just did, and Mark was not happy. No, he was pretty pissed, and everyone sitting in his office knew it as he threw his cell phone across the room; it shattered when it hit the Frederick Remington statue sitting on the credenza.

He jumped up out of the chair behind his Montana-sized teak desk and stormed around the office. No one breathed.

"Who the fuck does he think he is? No one talks to me like I'm a piece of shit on the bottom of his shoe! I will crush that son of a bitch! I will crush his entire family! He is nothing but a pompous little asshole! I'm Mark Richards, and I'm like the fourth richest man in the fucking world. No one treats me like I'm filth!"

He looked at his attorney sitting in the chair opposite the desk. "As of right now, our relationship with that fucker is done, finished. I want you to cancel every contract we have with him, and then I want to crush him!

"When I get done with him, he is going to be worthless, and then I'm going to make him suffer! I will own his ranch and his livestock, and then when I have it all, I will kill everything he values and burn his new house to the ground, while he sits and watches! He has no idea who he just fucked with!"

This tirade lasted for another twenty minutes, and everyone in the room knew not to interrupt until he was finished. They had all seen this behavior before. Behind his back, his staff called it his petulant little boy behavior. He calmed down, walked over to the bar, poured himself a big glass full of bourbon and chugged the contents of the glass. He sat down in his chair and looked around the room.

"Everyone get the fuck out of here except for Steve!" he screamed.

It was like someone fired a starter pistol: everyone made a mad dash for the door like they couldn't get out of there fast enough. Mark watched them all leave and then looked at his attorney, Steve Fletcher.

Steve looked at him. "You feel better now?" he asked with a smile.

Mark let out a huge, straight-from-the-belly laugh and got up and poured himself another glass of bourbon. He poured a glass for Steve as well, handed it to him and then sat down on the edge of the desk. Of everyone in his company, he knew Steve was the one who would talk to him straight, and Steve knew it too, which was why he never worried about his job.

Mark asked the attorney how bad this was going to get, and Steve didn't hold back. "I told you when we decided to go down this road that we were going to make an ungodly amount of money. I also told you that if the shit hit the fan, we could lose just as huge. We may be facing that time right now."

"Civil or criminal?" Mark asked.

"Both," replied the attorney. "If this goes public, we are going to get sued by anyone who lives near one of your wells and has ever had a runny nose, and the criminal case is going to depend on how good they do their jobs. What do you know about Hardy's brother-in-law? Anything we can use?"

Mark explained that Buck Taylor was pretty much a Boy Scout, but the way Hardy described him, he was going to be a force to be reckoned with. The female agent he had no information on, but if she was working for Buck, she would also have to be a straight shooter.

Mark walked around the desk and sat down in his chair. He kicked his legs up onto the desk and rubbed his temples. The bourbon was starting to dull his senses, but it was also making the headache go away. He looked pleadingly at Steve.

"Look, Mark. I think you need to take the wife and head for your island for a couple of weeks." Mark owned a private island in the Caribbean where he had another huge estate, and it was far away from the prying eyes of the government and the court system of the United States.

"I will get the private investigators to look into the cops, but I am not hopeful. We also need to find the guy you hired to look into Muldoon. With that big fire raging out there, we need to close that investigation up and let it die. You won't be having any of your powerful friends visiting that resort anytime soon, if ever, so we don't need to worry about that one. In the meantime, I will have our people scrub all the files and get rid of anything relating to the waste disposal business. I am also going to talk to our folks at that big East Coast newspaper you own and have them start a smear campaign on Hardy Braxton. Now, go tell your wife you are going on a vacation, and get packing. I will alert the airport to have the jet fueled and ready whenever you are."

He looked across the desk at Mark, who was now sleeping with his head back and his legs up on the desk. He had no idea how long Mark would be asleep, but he figured he would let Mark's wife know to get ready to leave, and she would take care of everything. That was the way it always was with Mark Richards. Mark would make these rash, boneheaded decisions, and then everyone else would have to pick up the pieces. To be fair, they were all paid a great deal of money to take on that responsibility, but it was also a fact that Mark owed a lot of his success to the people around him.

CHAPTER THIRTY-EIGHT

Bax wasn't sure what to expect as she crested the ridge leading to the well site. Maybe she expected to see a bunch of people wandering around in space suits carrying fancy instruments in their hands. Boy, was she wrong. What she saw as she looked down on the well site was a group of what looked like college students out for a Sunday picnic. She was almost disappointed. There wasn't a space suit among them.

She pulled into the parking lot and parked next to a white panel van with government plates. There were no signs anywhere indicating the van came from the EPA. The sheriff would be pleased.

As she slid out of her car, a tall, thin man with a straw cowboy hat walked up and introduced himself. Bill Unger was older than she expected, but he had an awesome tan and looked to be very fit in his jeans and T-shirt.

"Hi, Agent Baxter. Bill Unger, EPA," he said with an easygoing smile.

"Nice to meet you, Bill. Please call me Bax."

With pleasantries exchanged, Bax asked about the lack of protective gear. Bill explained that since she'd asked him to keep this low-key until they were sure what they were dealing with, he decided jeans and T-shirts were more appropriate than space suits.

"So, what's the plan, Bill?" she asked.

Bill explained they were getting their gear unloaded, and once they were done, the first order of business would be to cut away some of the melted pipes to expose the wellhead. He mentioned that after a preliminary look over the site, they'd determined there was probably nothing toxic in this well, since they hadn't finished drilling it. Once they were confident this well was clean, they would visit the other four wells in the field.

Bax heard a loud noise as one of the techs, wearing protective gloves and a face mask, fired up a large reciprocating saw with a sturdy diamond-edged blade and started cutting away the pipes around the well. Bill explained they had first checked the opening on the pipe for natural gas. Not finding any, they decided to move forward with getting rid of the pipe.

Bax watched as the tech made quick work of the pipe, and after about two hours, he and his colleagues managed to clear away most of the excess debris, continually monitoring the well for any kind of gas. They cleared away enough of the pipe to give them access to the top of the well. It was a dirty job, and it was a good thing they weren't wearing white space suits because they would be filthy by now.

With the top of the well casing exposed, another tech slid a tiny detector tip down alongside the pipe still in the well. The detector tip bottomed out somewhere around twelve thousand feet. It was hooked up to several very high-tech monitors, including a gas chromatograph and a portable mass spectrometer, and the techs kept a constant watch on the monitors, looking for any change in the readings.

Just as Bill had expected, there was nothing in this well yet, which was evidenced by the drill pipe still in the well. Bill had his team pull all the equipment and load up the van.

Bax was disappointed. It seemed like every step they took led to another dead end.

He invited Bax to join them for dinner in town, and she accepted. She wanted to know more about the work they did. So, leading the way, she drove them to a decent steak restaurant in Craig.

The conversation was light at first, and Bill and his team laughed about the places they had been and the crises they had seen during their careers. Surprising to Bax was that these young technicians had all worked for the EPA for well over ten years each. She'd assumed Bill was the boss and the techs were college kids working on their degrees. Boy, was she ever wrong.

Only one team member had just a master's degree. The rest of the team all had PhDs, most in chemical engineering. She came to realize as the night wore on, and the stories got more detailed, that this was a top-notch team—the kind of people you wanted on your side in a crisis. Of course, she should have realized that from the start. If Buck suggested someone to help with a problem, you could bet your last dollar that that person or persons would be the best around. She had never known Buck to work with anyone but the best.

Eventually, the group petered out, and they all headed to their hotel rooms. Tomorrow would be a much harder and, from the way they were talking, a much more dangerous day.

Sitting alone in her hotel room, Bax uploaded her notes into the investigation file. She looked through everything she'd loaded and saw a lot of information. Unfortunately, there was very little of any real evidentiary value. She closed her file and picked up her cell phone. Buck answered on the second ring. He sounded as frustrated as she felt.

"Hey, Buck. Hope your day went better than mine?"

She filled him in on the hunt for James Robert Galvin and the disappointing results at the first well site. He suggested a few avenues for her to pursue, and then they talked about the lodge fire. The eight-hundred-pound gorilla in the room was Hardy Braxton. It seemed like they were dancing around Hardy's involvement in everything that had happened so far. Right now, Hardy and Mark Richards were the common denominators in both events. They discussed the videotape interviews she'd recorded the day before and they discussed the fact there was nothing startling in the tapes.

Buck suggested she focus her attention on Hardy, which didn't surprise her. Brother-in-law or not, Buck was about the law and the evidence. He told her to keep the faith and to call if she needed anything. Buck hung up, and Bax turned out the lights and just lay on the bed. Hopefully, tomorrow would bring a break in the case.

CHAPTER THIRTY-NINE

After talking to Bax and having already filled out everything he could in his investigation file, Buck decided to walk over to the Cozy Up. He didn't drink, but he felt like he needed a diversion, so he put away his laptop and left his room. He had always been a student of people, and he liked sitting in bars and restaurants, watching the people. It used to drive Lucy nuts because wherever they were, he would try to analyze each person who walked through the door.

It would have been a beautiful night except for the smoke in the air. You could also feel the humidity in the air, and he was hoping maybe it was knocking some of the crap out of the air. He stepped out of the front door of the hotel, and before doing anything else, he checked to make sure his two shadows were still in the parking lot across the street. He had no idea who they were or what they wanted, but it was almost comforting, in a weird way, to see them sitting there keeping an eye on him.

The Cozy Up was unusually quiet, and he

figured most of the locals had already gone home for the evening. After all, this was an agricultural community, and, in his experience, folks involved in that kind of livelihood usually went to bed early.

Buck grabbed the same seat at the end of the bar he'd sat in the first time he walked in, what seemed like weeks ago but was only three days. Sam lit up when she saw him come in, and by the time he sat down, a cold Coke was sitting in front of him. She served a couple more customers down the bar and then asked him if he wanted anything to eat. Even though the kitchen was closed, she would make an exception. Buck politely declined.

Since it was slow, Sam stood on the other side of the bar and listened while Buck filled her in on the sorry state of his investigation. She was about to offer him words of encouragement when the front door opened and a dozen tired, smoky hotshots stepped into the bar.

The few people who were still at the bar, Buck included, stood and applauded, and you could see the firefighters perk up. Sam walked down the bar and started taking drink orders. They asked her if the kitchen was still open, and before she could answer, Buck stepped up to the group and told them it was, and dinner was on him.

Sam smiled at him and walked back into the

kitchen to stop her two cooks from leaving, and Buck introduced himself and started pouring beers. Sam walked up behind him as he was pouring a beer from the tap and placed her hand on his back. He looked at her, waiting for the explosion since he'd volunteered her place without any discussion, but what he found was a big smile.

He was about to say something when the swinging door to the kitchen opened, and the two waitresses, who had been getting ready to leave, walked back into the bar, tying on their aprons as they walked. Without hesitation, they started taking orders from the firefighters. Sam playfully pushed him out of the way of the beer taps with her hip and told him to talk to the chef. One of the cooks had already gone home, and the chef was going to need help.

Buck headed into the kitchen and grabbed an apron, and the chef handed him a dozen porterhouse steaks to put on the grill. While the chef cooked up the side dishes of baked potatoes and corn on the cob, Buck played grill master. It was amazing. For the first time since Lucy died, Buck seemed to be enjoying himself. Between steaks, he stepped through the swinging door into the bar and was amazed to see several more people had arrived, and the mostly empty bar looked like a party was going on.

The locals treated the firefighters like royalty,

and someone passed around a cowboy hat that was now brimming with money to pay for their meals and drinks. The atmosphere was exciting. One of the firefighters walked up to the small stage in the corner, picked up one of the guitars off the rack and started to play some old favorite country-western songs. It turned out the guy had an excellent voice, and soon, the whole place was singing and clapping along with the music.

Buck physically worked harder than he had in a long time, cooking steaks and cleaning dishes, and by the time last call came around, the party was in full swing. Sam was almost reluctant to call an end to the party, and then the mayor of Craig walked in with his wife and told her to stay open as long as the firefighters wanted to stay. The mayor and his wife introduced themselves to each of the firefighters and thanked them for their service, and the party continued.

Buck, finished in the kitchen, took off his apron and hung it over the back of his chair. The party looked like it was winding down, and he picked up the cold Coke Sam placed in front of him and turned his chair to watch the crowd. One of the firefighters walked up and reached out his hand. "The bartender told me your daughter is out on the fire line," said the firefighter.

"That's right," Buck replied. "Cassie Taylor. She's with the Helena Hotshots."

"Wow, that is one tough crew. Those guys have been on the front line of this fire since the beginning. You must be proud of her."

Then he called over the other firefighters, and introductions were made all around. More stories were told, and more songs were sung, and then the party, once again, started to slow down. Sam's crew cleaned up the kitchen with Buck's help, and after the firefighters thanked everyone in the place and promised to be back with their friends, everyone left the bar, and it was just Buck and Sam.

Buck started to apologize for volunteering Sam's place, but Sam walked around the bar, touched her finger to his lips to silence him and then kissed him like he hadn't been kissed in a long time. Buck returned the kiss, and Sam took him by the hand.

Buck left Sam's apartment over the bar just as the sun was starting to break through the smoky haze. It had been quite a night, and Buck felt good. He also felt bad, if that was possible. It had been five months since Lucy died, and tonight, even though Sam proved to be a fantastic lover, he felt like he'd cheated on Lucy. But she would have told him to stop being such a baby, that it was time for him to get out in the world and live his life.

He smiled at the idea that Lucy would have

approved, and he walked down the street to his hotel. He felt invigorated, and he realized that last night, all of it, was what he needed to get his mind back into the investigation. He felt like the next big break was on its way. He didn't know how true that was.

CHAPTER FORTY

B uck stepped out of the shower and was getting dressed when his phone rang. He picked it up, looked at the caller ID and smiled.

"Hey, Jess. It's been a while. How ya doing?" he said as he answered the call.

Jessica Gonzales was the DEA agent in charge of the Grand Junction field office. She'd worked with Buck on several investigations over the years, and they became fast friends. She was one of the first people to show up at Buck's house in Gunnison the day after Lucy died. She had been to their house several times, and she had developed a real fondness for Lucy.

Jess was one tough girl. Raised in Brooklyn, New York, she was the youngest DEA agent, male or female, ever to be offered a position as an agent in charge. Buck had no idea how old she was and was afraid to ask. She had a thirteen-year-old son from a previous relationship, and they lived with her mother. Jess was about five foot four, weighed about a buck twenty-five and was all muscle. She prided herself on her less than 10 percent body fat and worked out most days for two or three hours. She was also proficient in several martial arts styles.

She typically wore her gray hair short and spiked, and her favorite outfit was black jeans, laced-up boots and a black T-shirt that accentuated some impressive curves. It was rumored she had several tattoos, but no one Buck knew had ever seen them. Her record at the DEA was impeccable.

"I'm good, Buck. Heard you were back in the field. You doing okay?" she asked.

Buck and Jess spent a few minutes catching up, talking about some past cases they had worked together, and then she asked Buck how his current case was going. Buck filled her in on his lack of progress, and she was stunned to hear that Buck's brother-in-law might be the center of attention in both cases.

"You think you might have to arrest him? I'd like to be there to see that," she said with a laugh.

"Too early to tell, but who knows. So, what's up, Jess?" he asked during a lull in the conversation.

"I got an odd call last night from the AIC of our Memphis office. He has a missing agent, and he was calling because he saw a post about a burned-up body you have at the Grand Junction

Coroner's Office. He called to see if I knew you and if I would check it out."

Buck listened as Jess filled him in on the details of the disappearance. One of the DEA agents had told his girlfriend he was going on an undercover assignment and he would be gone for a couple of weeks. Even when he was undercover, he tried to contact her every other day to let her know he was safe. A couple of days ago, he fell off the grid and stopped calling her. Being a good agent, he gave her an emergency number to call if anything ever happened to him and she lost contact.

She was worried enough after a couple of days that she called the emergency number and got his supervisor on the phone. Well, the supervisor had no idea what she was talking about. He told her that her boyfriend was not working any kind of assignment he was aware of, and he had requested a couple of weeks' leave of absence to take care of a sick parent in Oklahoma. The problem was both his parents were deceased. The supervisor automatically assumed he was shacked up with some bimbo in a hotel someplace, but because the girlfriend was so upset, he assigned one of his agents to start tracking him.

The agent pulled his phone and credit card records and soon discovered the last place he used his phone was at the airport in Denver to call his girlfriend, and the last time he used his credit card was to rent an RV. Since then, he'd completely dropped off the radar. Now his supervisor began to worry as well. He knew it wasn't like him to drop out of sight like that, so the supervisor opened a full-blown missing person investigation.

According to Jess, the agent investigating spotted the post from the Grand Junction Coroner's Office on the national missing person database, and here they were.

"Jess. Do you have the missing agent's vitals?" Buck asked.

"Yeah. Five foot seven and about one hundred fifty pounds. Brown over brown. He's Asian. Name's Jimmy Kwon. Could this be our guy?"

Buck thought for a minute. The pathologist had estimated five foot six and about 140 pounds, but with the condition of the body, it was almost impossible to tell with any certainty.

"It's possible. The body was badly burned— well, charred would be a better description—but based on the pathologist, the stats are close. Do you have any idea what this guy might have been doing here?"

"None," she replied. "Like I said, his boss thought he was on leave."

"Okay. Can you get me his dental records and

send me the name of the company he rented the RV from, and I will check it out? Don't hold your breath, but I will see what I can do."

"Thanks, Buck. I'll send the dentals as soon as I can get them. Shit, I hope your burned body isn't our guy. Shit's gonna hit the fan. Washington doesn't like it when our guys go off the reservation."

They talked for a few more minutes, promised to get together for dinner and then Buck hung up.

CHAPTER FORTY-ONE

Bax was sitting in the conference room, running a computer search on everything Hardy Braxton. It had been a long morning already, and she felt like she was getting cross-eyed from looking at the computer screen, but she knew she was making some headway. Many of Hardy's businesses were privately held, so that information had to come from other sources than the internet; his business ventures with Mark Richards were partnerships, so she was able to get a lot of information from the Secretary of State's website. There was also a lot of information on the internet because pretty much anything Mark Richards got involved with made headlines.

She began to develop a picture of how Mark Richards did business. He would team up with some local company—especially energy companies, which he seemed to have an affinity for—let them do all the work and sit back and collect huge profits. None of the documents used by those companies, for permits or land purchases, contained any mention of Mark

Richards's involvement. He was pretty much isolated in case anything went wrong.

Hardy Braxton, on the other hand, had his name on everything. She was able to get her hands on some profit and loss statements for a couple of his partnerships and forwarded those over to the forensic accountant. Math was never her strong suit, so she figured a little expert help couldn't hurt.

She was reading through the documents she'd printed off when her phone rang. She looked at the unknown number and decided to answer it anyway.

"Ashley Baxter."

"Hi, Bax, Bill Unger. Do you have a minute to talk?"

Bax had been waiting for Bill to call, but she felt worried now that it was happening. She put down the papers she was reading and told him to go ahead.

"Okay. The bad news is we found toxic waste contamination in two of the four wells we checked today. We are certain we will find the chemicals are persistent bioaccumulative toxic substances, or PBTs. The worse news is that the levels so far seem to be much higher than anything we have seen in any of the Superfund sites."

Bax started a Google search for PBTs, and what she found did not make her very happy. Bill went on to explain that they were taking samples back to their lab, but he had no doubt the lab would confirm his findings. PBTs included chemicals and toxic minerals such as arsenic, lead, beryllium or zinc, but as a class of toxins, it also included persistent organic pollutants, or POPs, which included dioxins, hexachlorobenzene and a mess of other extremely hazardous chemicals. All in all, the stuff was bad news.

Bax was feverishly working the keys on her computer as Bill spoke, and she almost missed the most important part of the conversation. She stopped what she was doing and asked him to repeat himself.

"What I said was that while we were on one of the sites, a small tanker truck pulled into the lot. Since none of us were wearing anything that said EPA on it, he asked us if he could dump his load. He needed to get back to the transfer site, and it was a long drive."

"Holy shit. Can you hold him there until I get there?" she said.

Bill told her to take a breath. He'd already called the sheriff, and a deputy was being dispatched to the scene to bring the driver in. He told her their preliminary test of the tanker found the same chemicals as they found in the well.

Bax could not believe their luck. She'd had a feeling something was about to give, and then this fell into their laps. This was the break she was waiting for. Bill told her they were wrapping up, and they would be back at the sheriff's office in two hours. He clicked off, and Bax started printing off another ream of paper on toxins.

She pulled out her phone and called Buck. She could not contain her emotions as she told Buck what she'd found out about Hardy's various businesses and about Mark Richards and his relationship to Hardy, and then she told him about the toxins and the driver.

Buck was thrilled to hear about the driver. The fact they were dumping PBTs into the ground in Moffat County did not make him happy. He had run into chemicals like that early in his career when a dam holding back a mine tailings pond collapsed, and they found the remains of two bodies in the sludge at the bottom of the pond. Buck had solved the murders and sent several of Colorado's leading mine operators to jail. It was a big case for him and ended up in a huge Superfund designation for the area around the pond.

Buck told her to upload all the information she had so far into the investigation file, and he would read it later that night, then they would sit down and strategize about the next step. A lot would depend on what the driver had to say.

Buck told her about the call he'd received from Jess Gonzales regarding the missing DEA agent. He said he called the RV rental company Jess sent him the contact information for, and the RV was GPS tagged, so he was waiting for the clerk in the CBI office to fax the RV company a copy of the court order requesting the current location of the RV. He also told her Jess was sending him a copy of the agent's dental records. They talked for a few more minutes, then Buck clicked off, and Bax sat back in her chair and gave herself a minute to feel good.

Sheriff Trujillo stuck his head in the door as he headed for his office.

"Hey, did you hear the EPA guys nabbed a driver coming to one of the sites to drop a load?"

Bax told him she had, and he told her the deputy had just radioed in, and he should be at the office in about twenty minutes. He said she could use interrogation room one, and he would join her once they processed the driver.

CHAPTER FORTY-TWO

Buck hated waiting, especially on things that pertained to the cases he was working on, so he decided to fill his time doing a little research. He pulled his car into the parking lot at the sheriff's office, walked through the front doors, presented his ID to the desk officer and was buzzed into the back. He found an empty desk in the bullpen and fired up his laptop.

He was curious about the young woman who'd confronted him in the restaurant at breakfast the day before, so he decided to do a little research on her and her clients, the Western Colorado Conservation Alliance.

Stephanie Street appeared in several of the results of his Google searches. She specialized in environmental law, a field Buck was not familiar with. The more he read about her, the more he realized she sued companies for violating environmental law. These cases rarely went to court and usually resulted in some low dollar settlement. If her clients were accident victims, she might have been described as an ambulance chaser, which surprised Buck because her credentials were impressive.

She'd graduated at the top of her class at Yale Law School and clerked on the U.S. Court of Appeals in Washington for several years before moving west and taking a job as a litigator for a large downtown Denver law firm. Her record of wins was impressive as well, until three years ago, when she suddenly quit the law firm.

The next time she showed up was in a lawsuit brought by the Western Colorado Conservation Alliance against a mining company in Leadville, Colorado. The suit alleged that the mine was letting acid mine drainage (AMD), a toxic mix of subsurface water and mining residue, flow into a nearby creek, and it was destroying the habitat of the endangered humpback chub. The case went to trial and attracted national attention. Stephanie and her clients prevailed, and the mine was forced to spend a half million dollars to clean up the stream.

Buck figured she could have written her own ticket to anywhere after receiving that verdict, but she stayed put. It looked like, for the last couple of years, she'd filed a bunch of lawsuits on behalf of her clients, but none that attained the level of the mine case. Some even seemed a little frivolous.

Buck was now a lot more curious about this

woman, so he worked his way through several social networking sites and some attorney associations until he found what he was looking for. On a popular social networking site, he found a page dedicated to the Conservation Alliance, and there, in one of the pictures, were a proud Robert and Marilyn Street celebrating the mine victory with their daughter, Attorney Stephanie Street.

That explained a lot. He was still curious as to why she decided to stay and work only for the Alliance, but that would have to wait. His phone rang with an unknown number, and Buck answered.

"Taylor."

"Agent Taylor, this is Rosemary at Mountain RV in Denver. We spoke earlier. I have the location information on the RV you sent over the court order about."

"Thanks for calling me back, Rosemary. I do appreciate it. So, where is the RV right now?"

"The RV is located south of the town of Meeker on Highway Thirteen. I can't be more specific than that, but I did do a Google map search, and there are two RV parks just outside of town. The White River Campground and the Riverside RV Resort."

"Thanks, Rosemary. This is a huge help."

Buck hung up and called Sheriff McCabe and filled him in. The sheriff, who was out on patrol, suggested they meet at the Riverside RV Resort first since that one was the closest to town. Buck said he could be there in about fifteen minutes, and he hung up and headed out the door.

Fifteen minutes later, Buck pulled into the parking lot of the resort and parked next to the sheriff's SUV. Buck slid out of his car and looked around. The RV park sat alongside the White River and was heavily treed and beautifully kept. It was apparent the owners of the resort were very proud of what they had. Buck noticed about twenty-five RVs of every different make and size.

The sheriff walked out of the small office, followed by a small elderly woman, and walked up to Buck. He introduced him to Mrs. Talbot, the owner, and Buck told her he was very impressed with the resort from what he could see. Mrs. Talbot mentioned that she and her late husband built the resort almost forty years ago, and after her husband died, she wanted to give it to her kids, but neither one was interested, so she decided to keep doing what she had been doing for all those many years.

The sheriff interrupted. "Mrs. Talbot remembers the young Asian man. She said she put him in site twenty-seven because it was closest to the river and farthest from the office."

"He said he was looking for privacy," said Mrs. Talbot. "I hope he isn't a wanted felon. I wouldn't allow that kind of person in here."

Buck smiled at Mrs. Talbot. "No, ma'am. He's a police officer on vacation, and his family have been trying to reach him. We are here as a courtesy."

Mrs. Talbot looked cross-eyed at Buck and then looked at the sheriff, who nodded. Buck knew right away he wasn't putting anything over on this woman. She may have been elderly, but she was as sharp as a tack, and she read him like a book. The sheriff asked if she would wait inside the office, and they walked off towards the far end of the park, nodding at curious campers as they went.

They reached the end of the park and found spot number twenty-seven. Buck checked the license information on the RV against the information he had received from the RV company and nodded to the sheriff. The sheriff stood off to one side of the side door and, as inconspicuously as he could, pulled his pistol and held it down against the side of his right leg. Buck stepped up to the door and, having already drawn his pistol, knocked loudly and called out Jimmy Kwon's name.

Receiving no response from inside the RV, Buck checked to see if the door was locked while the sheriff worked his way around, looking in all the windows. They now had a problem. This was primarily a welfare check, and since no one was home, they should have walked away and notified his supervisor that they'd found the RV. They could also call a judge, get a search warrant and hope Jimmy Kwon wasn't inside lying on the floor bleeding. The sheriff made the decision for them and pulled out his phone and called a friendly county judge.

Judge Elena Morales answered on the second ring. The sheriff filled her in on their dilemma and asked her for her legal advice. Judge Morales thought for a minute and told the sheriff that since the life of a federal agent might be at stake, he should go ahead and enter the RV and do a thorough search. She would have her clerk write up the search warrant and fax it over to the sheriff's office.

The sheriff thanked her, and Buck pulled a small zippered leather pouch out of his pocket, opened it and pulled a pair of lockpicks out of the pouch.

"Damn, Buck. Do I want to know why you have those?" he asked with a grin.

Buck laughed. "In case I forget my house keys."

With the sheriff laughing behind him, Buck knelt next to the door and proceeded to unlock it. They both raised their pistols; he nodded to the sheriff, and then he swung open the door. Once inside, Buck went left and the sheriff went right. From everything they could see, the trailer was empty, and a quick walk through the RV confirmed that.

Buck was looking through the back bedroom when he heard the sheriff call him. He turned and walked back to the front and looked at the table the sheriff was looking at. The dining table was covered with photos of people, lots of people. Buck took a pen out of his pocket and slid the pictures aside, revealing several manila file folders.

Using the tip of the pen, he opened the first file. It contained a series of reports, written in a very professional manner and detailing what appeared to be an investigation into an illegal prescription drug ring. Buck was looking through the files when the sheriff pulled out a large folded map. He put on a pair of blue nitrile gloves and unfolded the map.

"Buck, this is a map of the area around Buford. There are symbols handwritten on here indicating houses and warehouses with what appears to be the names of the people who live in them."

Buck slid a picture out from under one of the files and pushed it towards the sheriff. "This is a picture of an EpiPen, but it's not from this country. Lucy kept an EpiPen handy while she was on chemo, in case she had a bad reaction. It didn't look like this one. The packaging is different."

They spent the next hour going through the files and looking at the pictures. The conclusion they came to was chilling.

"This guy was investigating the entire town of Buford. There is information in these files on dozens of people in the town who are involved in selling counterfeit EpiPens and other foreign medications."

"Yeah," agreed Buck. "But who was he investigating for? His boss thought he was on leave, and since this is Jess's turf, he wouldn't have been working undercover without her knowing about it."

"Fuck, Buck. What the hell was this guy into?"

Buck had no idea at this point, but he knew one thing. He would find out.

CHAPTER FORTY-THREE

Antonio Gonzales looked up as Bax and Sheriff Trujillo walked into the interrogation room, sat down and laid a file folder on the table. Bax had been watching him through the glass for the past fifteen minutes, and this was a nervous guy. The whole time he looked like he wanted to be anywhere but where he was.

She removed her pocket copy of the Miranda warning and read him his rights. She asked him if he understood what she had told him. He said he did, and she put the card back in her shirt pocket.

Bax opened the folder and sat for a minute, not saying a word, looking at him. She had watched Buck do this dozens of times, and she understood what was at play. People hate silence, and they feel the need to fill it, especially when they are in an uncomfortable position. She'd watched Buck get a full confession out of a murder suspect without asking one question. He just sat there for a couple of hours and didn't say a thing. By the time he was finished, the suspect looked like he was ready to climb the walls.

She slid the papers around in front of her and looked like she was intently reading what was in the file. The truth was there was very little in the file. Mostly it was old printed papers she'd found next to the printer and borrowed. A deputy was still running his prints through the system, but she had enough to get things started. Antonio watched nervously without saying a word.

"Antonio, we've got a problem," she said. "Not only have you been arrested for illegally dumping toxic chemicals, but . . ." She picked up one of the papers in the folder. "This report from ICE says you are here illegally."

She sat back and waited for a reaction as sweat appeared on Antonio's brow. He picked up the water bottle they gave him when they first brought him in, and he drank half of it in one big gulp.

"I have a green card," he said softly. "I have been here twenty years. I have a family." Tears rolled down his face.

Bax felt bad for him. After all, he wasn't the ringleader of this crime; he was an errand boy— someone who had the misfortune of being in the wrong place at the wrong time. The truth was, she had no information about his legal status, but she'd decided to give it a try and see where it went. She hit a nerve.

Bax looked at the sheriff. "Look, Antonio," she said. "We have not alerted ICE that we have you in custody. So, for right now, no one knows but the three people in this room. We don't care about your immigration status. We need to know who you are working for, and where you are getting the chemicals. If you help us, maybe we can help you."

Antonio sat for a minute and thought about what Bax said. If he told them everything they needed, would they keep him from getting deported? He had spent his whole life, up to this point, flying under the radar. He loved this country, and he loved his family. It would kill him to have to leave them, but back home, you never trusted the police.

Bax sat back and let her offer sink in. She was getting pretty good at this patience thing. In her early years, she would have gone after him with both barrels. She knew she could be tough if she needed to be. She'd played bad cop several times, but she enjoyed this kind of challenge more. The whole spirit of cooperation thing was pretty cool.

Antonio looked into her eyes. "You can keep me from getting deported, but will I have to go to jail?"

Bax pulled her list of chemicals out of the folder and read the names and the descriptions of the kinds of illnesses they could cause. She could see the fear in Antonio's eyes as he listened to her words.

"The chemicals I have been dumping can do those things you described?" he asked.

It was apparent from his reaction that he had no idea what he was hauling. He explained that no one had ever talked to him about using protective gear when picking up and dumping the chemicals. He asked Bax if the chemicals he was dumping could be hurting children. When she told him about the kind of illness and deformities children could get from drinking water tainted with those chemicals, he broke down, put his face in his hands and wept.

Bax and the sheriff stood up, she picked up the folder and they walked out of the room. They would give him a minute to let it all sink in.

Outside in the hall, keeping an eye on Antonio through the glass, she looked at the sheriff.

"He doesn't seem to have a clue what he was dealing with, and right now, he is in there thinking about his kids," she said. "Why don't you call the district attorney and see if we can get him a deal that doesn't involve jail time?"

"What about his immigration status?" asked the sheriff. "He has never even had a parking ticket, and he owns a house and pays taxes."

Bax thought for a minute. "Sheriff, this is your jurisdiction. I'm a guest here, but I know if Buck was here right now, he would tell me to do the right thing. When I told him I didn't care about his status, I meant it. I will go along with whatever decision you make."

Bax walked back into the room, and the sheriff headed for his office to call the district attorney. She sat down opposite Antonio, who looked like he was finished crying, and asked him if he was ready to talk to her. His nod was almost imperceptible. She asked him to say the words for the videotape, and he did. She slid a document across the table to him, along with a pen, and asked him to read it and sign it. She explained that he was giving up his right to have an attorney present and was willing to talk with them on the record. He picked up the pen and signed the paper.

The sheriff walked back in, and she slid the paper over to him. He looked at it and nodded.

For the next two hours, Antonio filled them in on the who, what and where of his job. Antonio and several other drivers worked as contract drivers for a larger company. Three times a week, they would drive to a large warehouse outside of Rangely, fill up their liquid waste trucks and take the load to a specific location. They never knew which location they would be going to until they arrived at the warehouse. In the last couple of months, he'd off-loaded the liquid at three different locations.

He said he spoke with a few of the other drivers, and they had been to places in Utah, Wyoming and Nevada, as well as Colorado. He said there could be as many as fifty other drivers; he wasn't sure. He wrote down directions to the warehouse and then sat back in his chair, totally spent. He told Bax he never liked delivering the liquid because it smelled terrible, but the money was good. He said he used to pump out pit toilets from campgrounds and porta-potties at construction sites, but this was a much better job.

Bax told Antonio she would be right back, and she stepped out of the room. The sheriff had stepped out earlier to meet with the attorney from the district attorney's office, and they were both standing outside the door.

The sheriff introduced Bax to Amber Hunter, and Bax asked, "Do we have enough to go after the warehouse?"

Amber looked like she knew the answer she was about to give was not going to satisfy Bax. "Right now, no. We have a connection between the well sites and the warehouse, but what we need is corroboration, which we don't have. Can you get another driver to confirm his story?"

Bax looked disappointed, but she'd known

what the answer was going to be before she asked the question.

"Let's find out," she said.

CHAPTER FORTY-FOUR

B uck and Sheriff McCabe spent most of the day going through all the information they'd found in Jimmy Kwon's RV, and as it turned out, he had amassed a lot of evidence against the people of Buford. They found documents relating to the purchase of the property and to the establishing of various companies online, and a massive amount of information on the drugs that were purchased. The most critical piece of information they found in the files was the names of the companies overseas that the town had been buying the illegal drugs from.

What Buck and the sheriff found amazing was that they were running this business right out in the open, and no one ever caught on, at least not until Jimmy Kwon came knocking. The big unanswered question was, who was Jimmy Kwon working for? They ran the numbers in his cell phone, and several came back to burner phones, which Buck sent over to his office in Grand Junction, and two other agents were now trying to track down those numbers.

The sheriff had asked a local accountant to look at the financial records they found, and he finished his initial review and stepped into the sheriff's office.

"Sheriff, we are definitely in the wrong business," he said. "If these records are correct, these guys were making two hundred grand a month selling these drugs."

Both Buck and the sheriff stopped reading and looked up.

"Seriously?" asked Buck.

"Quite seriously," replied the accountant. "Last month alone, they took in close to four hundred thousand. They have a hell of a scheme going. Take the EpiPens alone. They were buying these low-quality drugs from companies in India, Pakistan and China for about twenty cents each and reselling them for three hundred dollars here in the U.S. That's a huge markup, and that's only the pens. They have entries for at least six other drugs they are buying and selling."

Buck looked at the printout. "Look at the information under clients. These numbers are huge."

"From what I can tell, they are not only selling to the public through the internet, they are also acting as a wholesale distributor and selling to other companies here in the U.S. and abroad. That is where the bulk of their income comes from."

Buck sat back and looked stunned. "How the hell can this go on, and no one is aware of it? This has to be dangerous, selling cut-rate drugs to people who rely on this stuff to stay alive."

Buck was about to dive into another pile of papers when his phone rang. He recognized the number and answered. "Hey, Doc. Did the dental records help?"

Buck listened to Dr. Kalishe. When he hung up the phone, he did not look happy. "The forensic dentist is ninety percent certain the body belongs to Jimmy Kwon."

"Shit," said the sheriff. "That means we are going to be crawling with Feds."

Buck walked over to the conference room refrigerator and took out another can of Coke, his fourth so far today, and looked out the window. He noticed the smoke in the air was thicker than it was a couple of hours ago. "The wind must have shifted again," he thought to himself.

He walked back to the table. He hated situations like this and hated losing the investigation to the Feds. There were people out there who needed to know about Jimmy Kwon, but the sheriff was right. As soon as he called Jess, the Feds would be all over this. He also knew if they sat on this information and Jess found out they knew, his credibility would be shot. "I need to call Jess and fill her in. While I'm doing that, why don't you call the district attorney and see if he can come over here and look at what we have?"

The sheriff stood up and turned to Buck. "I'm going to send a deputy over to sit on the RV. Can we get the forensic team out of Grand Junction to go over the RV? It might be a crime scene."

"I will make that call as soon as I'm done. I need to call the director first." The sheriff headed to the dispatcher, and Buck pulled out his phone.

Director Jackson answered on the second ring. "Hey, Buck. What's up?"

Buck filled him in on the missing DEA agent and all the evidence he had collected about the town of Buford. He gave him a quick rundown on the arson case and the fact that, more and more, he didn't think the NETF was responsible for burning down the lodge, but he still hadn't been able to nail down what was bothering him about the whole thing. The director listened, remaining quiet for the longest time. Buck waited patiently.

"Fuck, Buck," the director said. "How do you always manage to get into these kinds of messes?"

Buck knew he was joking, but he also knew he was half serious too. Buck had made a career out of turning simple cases into complex cases, and this one was proving to be no different.

"Okay, Buck, so what's our next move?"

"Well, sir. First, I need to call Jess Gonzales at the DEA. She needs to know. Second, we are calling the DA to come by and look at what Jimmy Kwon collected. If we have enough for a search warrant, we might be able to move before the Feds get here."

Buck's phone beeped with an incoming call, but he ignored it. The director agreed with the plan. He didn't see an alternative other than to try to get ahead of the Feds. He was aware how quickly his people would react if it was one of theirs who had been killed. They would move heaven and earth to find the killer. He knew the DEA would be no different.

"Okay, Buck. Do you need me to send up some help?"

"No, sir. Not yet. But we do need the forensic team from Grand Junction to go over the RV. We have no idea where Kwon was killed, so right now, it is a crime scene."

"I'll call and get the CSIs rolling. Keep me posted on how you want to play this. I've got your back, whatever you decide." The director hung up, and Buck sat back in the chair and rubbed his temples. He picked up his phone, looked at the most recent call list and dialed his voice mail. He listened to the message, hung up and dialed the number from his recent call list.

"Agent Taylor, thanks for calling me back."

"No problem, Mr. Earp, is it? What can I do for you?"

"Well, I've got some information about Mark Richards that you are gonna want to see."

CHAPTER FORTY-FIVE

Bax walked back into the interrogation room and sat down opposite Antonio. She had a feeling this next ask was going to be very difficult for Antonio. She was going to ask him to give up one of the other drivers. This was the part of the job she hated. She held all the power over this man, and his entire life was in the palm of her hand. She'd already made up her mind that she wasn't going to force him. That wasn't her style. She wanted his cooperation, not his fear.

She looked into Antonio's frightened eyes and told him she needed his help. She needed someone else to corroborate the information he had given them. She didn't coerce him, and she never raised her voice. He was just a guy trying to do right by his family, and he deserved a little respect. She told him she needed to talk to another driver. Then she sat back and watched him.

Antonio sat and stared at the table. He never looked at her, and for ten minutes, she just sat. She was surprised at herself that she had the patience to sit and wait. That never happened before she met Buck.

Antonio looked up and asked her if he could use a phone. She knew it wasn't the smartest thing to do, since he could just as easily call his boss and rat her out, but she had a feeling about Antonio, and she decided to play along. She handed him her phone, and he picked it up and dialed a number from memory. Her first thought was, "Who does that anymore?" She couldn't even remember her parents' phone numbers without looking at the contact list on her phone.

Antonio started speaking in rapid-fire Spanish. The conversation often sounded heated, but he kept making his case to the person on the other end of the phone. What he had no way of knowing was that Bax spoke fluent Spanish, and she was listening to his side of the call. He hung up and slid her phone back to her.

Antonio had convinced his cousin, one of the other drivers, to come in and talk to Bax. He told him that unlike the police at home in Mexico, this senorita could be trusted. Bax thanked him, stood up and left the room.

Antonio's cousin, Armando, arrived at the sheriff's office twenty minutes later and was led back to the other interrogation room by a deputy. Bax and the sheriff followed them into the room and sat down. They introduced themselves and took down his name and contact information. The sheriff gave it to the deputy as he was walking out the door and asked him to run Armando's name through the various crime databases.

Since Bax had listened to Antonio's side of the conversation, she knew where to start with Armando, so she spent a few minutes talking about his family and his kids. She never brought up his immigration status because she didn't want to spook him. She showed him the list of chemicals they had been dumping and told him about the way those chemicals could impact the health of the people in the county, including his kids.

Armando read down the list of side effects and health issues caused by the chemicals and then looked at Bax.

"All this can happen because of the chemicals we have been carrying?" he asked.

Bax explained this to him in more detail. What she told him caused tears to form in his eyes.

"Is this what made my little Jennifer sick?" he asked. He went on to explain that his six-year-old daughter had been diagnosed with a rare form of brain cancer, and she was getting radiation treatments. The tears flowed freely as he asked, "Did I do this to her?"

Neither Bax nor the sheriff was sure how to

respond, so Bax reached across the table and put her hand on top of his. She held it there until he was able to calm himself down. She now understood why Antonio called Armando.

For the next hour, Armando told Bax the same story Antonio had. She asked some clarifying questions, but for the most part, she let Armando just talk. When Armando was finished, Bax thanked him, and she and the sheriff stepped out of the room.

Amber Hunter met them as they exited the interrogation room. "Nice job, Agent Baxter," she said.

She turned to the sheriff. "I think we have enough to hit the warehouse. I'll have one of my people write up the warrant if you will call the sheriff in Rio Blanco County and the Rangely police and coordinate the raid with them."

She turned and walked down the hall towards the front door. Bax was looking in the window at Antonio. "What do we do with them?" she asked. "I don't want to turn them over to ICE."

The sheriff smiled. "ICE doesn't know we have them."

Bax kind of cocked her head sideways and looked at him. "We must have forgotten to include ICE when we were running their background checks. I already chewed out the deputy who did the background checks." He smiled. "I will have one of the deputies work up their release papers." The sheriff turned and walked towards his office. He had a raid to coordinate.

Bax called Bill Unger to make sure his team hadn't left Craig yet, and when she reached him, she told him about the warehouse. Bill sounded like a kid on Christmas morning, he was so excited. He asked her if she wanted him to call in more federal people, but she told him they could handle it. He said his team would head to Rangely and stay out of sight until they were needed.

Her next call was to Buck.

CHAPTER FORTY-SIX

B uck, the sheriff and a team from the district attorney's office were sitting around the conference table, organizing the files Jimmy Kwon had collected. The whiteboard at the front of the room was covered with squiggly lines leading from one picture to the others. With the help of several deputies, they were able to identify most of the people in the pictures and were creating a hierarchy chart of the organization. Jimmy's notes were clear, but he hadn't marked any of the pictures with names or positions.

At the top of the chart was John F. Muldoon, aka Jack Muldoon. From everything Kwon had written, it appeared Muldoon was the guy in charge. Under his picture was a picture of a heavyset woman with long black hair. Kwon identified her as Margaret Windsong, but Buck doubted that was her name. Her skin was way too pale for her to be of Native American descent, but then again, you never know.

Elliot Beech, the third picture, to the left of Muldoon, was much younger than the other two. Kwon listed Beech in his notes as simply "Hacker." They had no idea what his job was, but his name appeared quite a lot in the notes. From what they could determine, they believed Beech was Kwon's contact. Below them were about two dozen other people, along with about a dozen children. The deputies finished putting names and faces together, and when they stood back, they were missing only a handful of connections.

Buck was about to say something when his phone rang. He looked at the number and answered.

"Hey, Bax," Buck said. "What's going on?"

She told him about the information they had gotten from the two drivers, and about the raid the sheriff was now coordinating. Buck listened as she filled him in on the rest of her investigation. He was impressed with everything she had accomplished. He told her to make sure to document everything in the investigation file and include all the information she had gotten on Hardy Braxton and Mark Richards.

He asked her about the suspected shooter.

"Nothing yet. We've got an APB out to all of Colorado, Utah and Wyoming, but so far, no sign of him."

Buck asked her about his background, if he

had ever worked with explosives or chemicals, and if she had pulled the death certificates for his wife and daughter. He listened to the silence on the other end of the line.

"Shit, Buck. We got so busy with the drivers I forgot to dig into his background. God, what an idiot. I feel so stupid."

"Hey, Bax. Don't worry about it. You've had a lot on your plate. His info is in the file; I'll have someone in the office run it down."

Buck heard the intercom on the sheriff's desk go off. "Sheriff, Sheriff Trujillo on line one." The sheriff stepped away from the table and walked into his office, kicked the door shut with his foot and picked up his desk phone.

Bax continued. "Buck, this thing has gotten big. Bill Unger and his team are already heading to Rangely, and Trujillo is calling McCabe to coordinate the raid. With any luck at all, we can get something at the warehouse to link Richards and the chemical dumping. I hope it's enough."

Bax took a break, and Buck said, "Even if we can't get Richards this time, you guys should feel good that you're about to stop a chemical dumping operation that could have ramifications for years to come and could affect the health of thousands of people. That's not a bad couple of days' work." Buck hung up his phone.

The sheriff waved Buck into his office. "I just got off the phone with Gil Trujillo. They are going to move on a warehouse outside Rangely to look for toxic chemicals. I'm going to round up a couple of deputies, and we'll meet them at Rangely PD in two hours. I assumed you would want in."

"Hell yeah. That was Bax on my phone. She filled me in. I need to call the office and get someone to do a deep dive into the possible shooter. Give me a couple of minutes. Can you have one of your clerks start running background on everyone we have on the whiteboard?"

The sheriff said he would take care of it, and they would head out in about twenty minutes. Buck took a minute to call the director and fill him in. The director listened as Buck relayed his conversation with Bax and then gave him the details of the upcoming raid.

"Good news all around, Buck. Now, give me your take on where Bax is headed."

"She's doing fine, sir. So far, she has followed all the procedures you would expect someone to follow on an investigation like this. She ran everything by the attorneys, and everyone is good to go. McCabe spoke with Trujillo, and they are working out the details of the raid, and I think she has done a pretty good job. Good as I would have done; besides, we usually talk before she makes a move."

"Okay, Buck. What do you need from me, anything?"

"We haven't been able to run background on the possible shooter, Galvin, yet, and I would like to have someone check on the deaths of his wife and daughter. Can you get someone to do that?"

"You got a hunch about something, Buck?"

"Not sure, sir. I'm just trying to figure out his motivation."

"Okay, Buck. We will get you what we can. Keep an eye on Bax and stay safe. Now that you're back, I would hate to lose either you or her."

Buck took one more look at the whiteboard as he packed up his backpack. He wished he had more time to spend running background on all these people, but he would have to rely on the sheriff's people to take care of that.

He slung his backpack over his right shoulder, grabbed a can of Coke out of the refrigerator and headed for the door. He was almost out of the building when a deputy called to him.

"Agent Taylor, Sheriff said to tell you that the CSIs just arrived at the RV park."

Buck waved his hand over his shoulder, yelled his thanks and headed to his car. He stashed his backpack in the back, jumped in and pulled out of the parking lot right behind the sheriff. Once on the highway, he flipped on his flashers and hit the gas.

CHAPTER FORTY-SEVEN

The little caravan of law enforcement vehicles ran south on Highway 13, turned onto Route 64 and headed west. They pulled into the parking lot of the Rangely Police Department and parked behind the building. Bill Unger and his team were already on-site with their nondescript white panel van and were briefing the Rangely chief of police and two of his officers on the dangers of PBTs. The chief was concerned these chemicals were being stored and transported through his community.

The people of Rangely were no strangers when it came to chemicals. The area was primarily agricultural, but there were a great many fracked gas wells surrounding the town. They had been part of the boom-and-bust cycle of well drilling for years, and they always had a healthy respect for the fracking industry, but this was something new: people deliberately poisoning the ground and potentially the groundwater. The chief of police was not pleased.

Sheriff McCabe climbed out of his SUV, walked over and shook hands with the chief. The sheriff and Chief Applegate had worked together many times, and they maintained a very close, friendly relationship. The sheriff introduced Buck, who had walked up and joined the little group. Buck thanked the chief for his cooperation and then stepped over to talk to Bill Unger.

"Bill, good to see you." Buck reached out, and they shook hands. "How bad might this be?" he asked.

"Based on what Bax learned from the two drivers, it looks like this has only been going on for a year or so. If that's the case, then it might not be too bad. We'll know more when we can look at the disposal company's records." He pulled a sheet of paper out of his pocket.

"I took the liberty of pulling a federal warrant to search for the records and chemicals. I wasn't sure if you guys thought to include that in your warrant. Besides, since mine is federal, it will supersede yours anyway."

"Good thinking, Bill." They were walking back to join the group talking with the sheriff when the team from Moffat County pulled into the lot. Bax pulled in and parked next to Buck's Jeep. She walked over to the group, and more introductions were made.

Speaking to the group, Bax said, "I want to thank you all for being here today. We are going to do this operation by the book all the way. Once the scene is secured, we will turn the building over to Bill and his team. We do not believe any of these individuals are armed, but we need to be careful anyway. Stay on your toes. Keep an eye out for anyone trying to destroy records or computer files. This could be the tip of the iceberg and could help us close out several cases. I will now turn it over to Sheriffs McCabe and Trujillo."

Chief Applegate pulled out a set of plans he had gotten from the building department and laid them on the hood of his patrol car. Everyone gathered around. He showed them the two entrances into the building and where the office was. Since they didn't have any idea if there were any PBTs being stored on-site right now, he couldn't say for sure where they might be, but he reminded everyone to be careful. The state patrol provided a hazardous materials unit with full decontamination capabilities just in case of an accident of any kind.

Sheriff Trujillo continued with the briefing and then broke everyone up into teams. They all headed for their vehicles to gear up. Buck walked back to his Jeep with Bax.

"You guys have done a good job," he told Bax. "Now, let's hope this raid will give us what we need to finish this part." He told her about the call he'd received as he left Meeker and the offer of documents about Mark Richards.

"Do you think this is legit?" she asked.

"No way of knowing. I told him I would meet with him tonight at the Cozy Up, and he was okay with that."

"Do you need me to back you up?"

"Thanks, Bax. Let's see where we end up after the raid."

They both opened their back hatches, pulled on their ballistic vests, checked their pistols and stood by, waiting for the signal. The signal from Sheriff McCabe came five minutes later, and they all hopped into their cars and pulled out of the parking lot, heading west on 64.

Two miles after crossing the White River, they pulled into the dirt parking lot of a nondescript metal building. There were four cars and pickup trucks in the lot. One team pulled behind the building, and everyone piled out of their vehicles. Sheriff McCabe gave the word, and the teams pulled open the doors and moved into the building.

"Police, search warrant!" shouted Sheriff McCabe as the teams spread out, and within seconds they had three workers lying face down on the ground, with their hands handcuffed behind their backs. Buck and Bax headed for the office in the back corner of the building. As they opened the office door, they saw one man sitting behind the desk, his fingers poised over the keyboard.

Buck raised his pistol and pointed it at the man's head. "Touch that keyboard, and it will be the last thing you ever do." The look in Buck's eyes said it all, and the man wisely pushed his chair back from his desk and raised his hands over his head.

Bax walked behind the desk, handcuffed one of the man's hands and then, with a nod from Buck, told the man to stand while keeping her hand on the cuffed arm. Once he was standing, she told him to put his other arm behind his back, and she finished cuffing him. She led him out the door and into the arms of Chief Applegate. She turned around and headed back into the office.

Buck was seated behind the desk. Luckily the guy who was sitting there hadn't closed out the program, so Buck had full access to the computer, which didn't do him much good since he was pretty much a dinosaur when it came to operating a computer. Sure, he could enter data into a predesigned program, and he knew how to do an internet search, but after that, it was all foreign to him.

Buck stepped from behind the desk and let Bax take over. He watched in amazement as her hands flew over the keyboard. While she worked her magic, he checked out the rest of the office, including the file cabinets in the corner. He could hear what turned out to be the owner of the company loudly discussing his rights with Chief Applegate.

Buck walked out of the office when Bill Unger called from the back door, "Buck, we think we found it."

Buck noticed the owner became very quiet. He walked out the back door, followed by Sheriff McCabe. Two members of Bill's team were in the process of donning white hazmat suits, while the other members checked the breathing tanks and attached the hoses to the suits. The two men opened the door of a small outbuilding and closed it behind them.

"One of the workers told us to look in the outbuilding, so we did. There is an underground storage tank under it with a very elaborate pumping system," said Bill.

While Bill's team investigated the underground tank and took samples to run through the mass spectrometer, Buck went back inside to see if Bax found anything on the computer. He stepped into the office as she was starting to explain what she found to both sheriffs.

She was able to find files hidden within other files, and when she opened them, she hit on a treasure trove of information. It would take a lot of time to decipher all of it, but she had a good idea where the chemicals were coming from and how much had been distributed so far. The answer could have been a lot worse. The one thing she hadn't found so far was a link to Mark Richards.

Buck had stopped listening about halfway through her presentation and was looking at all the pictures the owner of the company had framed and hung on his wall. He stopped, pulled down one picture and reread the caption. It was a newspaper clipping from the local paper, and it talked about the new growth plans for the company, now that they would have increased operating capital thanks to a new partner. What got Buck smiling was what he saw in the picture that accompanied the article. The picture showed the owner shaking hands with his new partner, Mark Richards.

CHAPTER FORTY-EIGHT

B uck set the picture down on the desk, and everyone stopped what they were doing and looked at it. Bax was the first to respond.

"Oh my god. We have been searching high and low to find some connection between Mark Richards and the company doing the dumping, and after all that work, it is going to be a newspaper clipping that nails him."

"I think we need to have a little talk with the owner of this company," said Sheriff Trujillo.

Buck and Sheriff Trujillo walked out while Bax and Sheriff McCabe continued working on the files in the drawers and on the computer. Two deputies were standing next to the owner of the company, Randy Stewart, and they stepped to the side as Buck and the sheriff walked up.

"Mr. Stewart, my name is Buck Taylor, with the Colorado Bureau of Investigation, and this is Sheriff Trujillo from Moffat County. We'd like to ask you a couple of questions, if that's okay?"

Stewart looked them both over and said, "I

want my lawyer."

"No problem, Mr. Stewart. I am going to read you your Miranda rights, and then the sheriff and I are going to tell you where things stand. You will be able to call your attorney when we are finished."

Buck pulled his Miranda card out of his pocket and read the warning word for word. He asked Stewart for a verbal acknowledgment that he understood his rights. Stewart was eager to say he did, and reiterated he wanted his attorney.

Buck pulled up a chair and sat with his knees touching Stewart's. "See, Mr. Stewart, the nice thing about your rights is it's perfectly fine for us to talk to you as long as we don't ask you any questions."

Buck started to explain about the toxic nature of the material they had been handling, making sure he was clear about the health risks. He talked about federal charges from the EPA as well as county charges for the dumping, and the possibility of lawsuits. The entire time he was speaking, Stewart got paler and paler, with little beads of sweat forming above his lip.

"I have no idea what you are talking about; we deal with household and light commercial waste. We would never be caught dead handling PBTs."

Bax walked in and tapped Buck on the

shoulder. She handed him a couple of pieces of paper she'd printed from Stewart's computer. Stewart could see from where he was sitting that she had circled several items with a red Sharpie. Buck looked over the papers.

"The household waste business must pay pretty well, Mr. Stewart. Your bank records, which we found on your computer in a file marked Safety Information, show a very successful business. You should be very proud. Odd though that they would have gotten misfiled. I guess things like that happen sometimes."

Buck smiled and watched Stewart's reaction. He seemed to be turning a lovely pale shade of green. What pushed him over the edge was when Bill Unger walked up with the letters epa emblazoned on his jacket. Stewart hadn't seen the EPA team, since he was in the office. At the sight of Bill walking up, he almost passed out, and one of the deputies had to reach over and hold him up in the chair.

Bill handed Buck a printout from the mass spectrometer. Buck was having a little too much fun watching Stewart squirm in the chair, so he asked Bill to explain what he found, even though Buck could read the printout without any issues.

Bill took back the printout and proceeded to explain that they'd found a roughly five-thousand-gallon tank under the floor of the outbuilding, and the tank contained the same chemicals they found at the two dump sites in Moffat County. He told Buck that the match was as good as a fingerprint match in people.

Bill also added that the federal violations alone would probably net a thirty-year jail sentence plus millions in fines, and that didn't include the lawsuits from anyone who got sick. Buck sat back and watched Stewart. He could see it in his eyes the moment survival mode kicked in.

"I had no idea we were dumping toxic waste," he said.

"Well, that's kind of strange since . . ." Buck picked up another sheet of paper from the pile Bax had given him. "You were the one who gave the drivers their assignments and destinations. Since there are no legal dump sites up there for these types of chemicals, I would have to wonder what you thought they were doing with the chemicals once they got there?"

For almost a full minute, no one said a word, and all eyes were on Stewart. It looked like Stewart was about to say something when Chief Applegate walked up to the group.

"The municipal court judge approved the search warrant for Mr. Stewart's house. Sheriff McCabe, two of his deputies and one of my guys are on their way over there right now to execute the warrant."

Buck smiled at Stewart and over his shoulder said, "Bill, you might want to have a couple of your people go to his house as well. He might have exposed his family to the chemicals. Maybe they should put on their hazmat suits just in case. Maybe check his neighbors too, for contamination. We will also need to check his employees' houses for contamination."

At this point, poor Mr. Stewart lost it. The image of people in hazmat suits talking to his neighbors and searching his house was too much to bear. After all, Rangely was a small community. Tears flowed down his face, and he broke out into a major sweat.

"I changed my mind! I don't want an attorney. I will tell you whatever you want, just don't embarrass my family."

"Okay, Mr. Stewart, how much involvement in your company does Mark Richards have?"

Stewart looked stunned. "How do you know Mark Richards is involved in this company? There are no documents with his name on them. This is my company, and I alone am responsible for this mess. No one else."

Buck had set the picture he had taken from the wall in Stewart's office next to the chair he was sitting in. He reached down and held the picture so Stewart could see it.

Stewart stared at the picture. "Fuck" was all he said.

"Tell us how Mark Richards is involved," said Bax, over Buck's shoulder.

"Okay, okay. Mark Richards gave us the money to expand. He owns eighty percent of the company, only it was set up so his name didn't appear anywhere. The tank under the outbuilding was at his direction. He even provided the specs for the transfer system. We could have gotten a system for much cheaper, but this is what he demanded we install. Eventually, we would have had a dozen five-thousand-gallon tanks, but he was having trouble getting them shipped in special from India or China or someplace like that. He told me he made arrangements to have a special kind of fracking fluid manufactured, and we would be the first to have it. It was going to revolutionize the fracking industry. Until you guys showed up today, I had no idea what the chemicals were. Now I feel awful. My employees have no idea they have been exposed to shit that bad."

Once Stewart got started, he talked nonstop until he sat back in his chair, exhausted. Buck now had a much better picture of how Mark Richards did business. He either bought entire companies or set up some kind of convoluted partnerships without his name ever being attached to the businesses. Then, if things went bad because of some shady deal he worked out, it was the owner of the company who got burned, and he walked away scot-free with a huge profit. Buck was starting to dislike Mark Richards more and more.

Buck stood up and thanked Stewart for his openness. Buck could see in Stewart's eyes the realization that he had been hung out to dry by Mark Richards. He told Bax where to look on his computer for other files that were "misplaced."

Buck stepped away, and the two deputies from Moffat County escorted Stewart to a waiting car for the trip up to Craig.

CHAPTER FORTY-NINE

Things had gotten so crazy Buck had forgotten to call Jess Gonzales. He felt bad. Jess was a good friend who'd asked him for a favor, and he felt like he blew her off. He wondered if his mind was still filled with too much of Lucy's death. He knew Lucy would never let him think that way when she was alive. The thought of her brought tears to his eyes, and he was glad he was driving by himself, so no one could see him. He wiped the tears from his eyes and shook his head to clear his mind.

He pushed the green phone icon on his steering wheel and said, "Call Jessica Gonzales."

Buck heard the phone ringing on the other end, and Jess picked up. "Hey, Buck. Is this a good or a bad call?"

"Hey, Jess. I'm afraid it's gonna be a bad call."

"Fuck, Buck. It's our guy, isn't it?"

"Pathologist says ninety percent. I'm sorry, Jess."

"Thanks, Buck. This is not going to go over

very well in Washington. Any idea how it happened? Could it have been an accident?"

Buck explained about the bullet hole behind his right ear and the missing teeth, some of which could have been caused by the fire, some of which may have been pulled out. She listened in silence until Buck was finished.

"Did you find his RV?" she asked.

Buck filled her in on what they found in the RV, and about the investigation he seemed to be running. He told her about the pictures, the files and the spreadsheets they were presently looking at.

"Who the hell was he working for?" she asked, not expecting an answer.

"Not sure at this point. What can you tell me about the illegal prescription drug market in this area?"

"That's just it. We haven't had any chatter about this kind of drug ring operating in this area. We busted a huge fentanyl lab in California a couple of months back, which surprised everyone because most of that shit comes in from Mexico, but we haven't done any investigating in this area. How could something this big operate right under our noses?"

"Look, Jess. Don't beat yourself up over this. The sheriff was in the dark as well. These guys think they are a sovereign nation, and they won't let anyone on their property. They have also been operating right out in the open, and no one was suspicious. I can tell you this, right now, the DA's team is going through the stuff we collected from Jimmy Kwon, and if they have enough for a warrant, I am going to find out what's going on. You can take that to the bank."

"Okay, Buck. Don't make a move without me. I need to call Washington and fill them in. Keep me posted, and thanks."

Jess hung up, and Buck called the director to fill him in on the call with Jess. One of the DEA's own was killed, even if he was working on his own, and they weren't going to sit still very long. Buck figured they had twenty-four, maybe thirty-six hours at the most before Meeker would be crawling with Feds, and the director agreed. He needed to move quickly to figure this out, and the director told him to call if he needed help.

Buck pulled his car into the driveway of the Riverside RV Resort and drove down to Jimmy Kwon's RV. The forensic techs were in the process of loading up their van as Buck slid out of his car.

Kelli Vaughan stepped away from the van, met Buck halfway and gave him a big hug. Kelli was about Buck's age and wore a silver-blond wig. She had been diagnosed with breast cancer about a year ago, successfully finished her first round of chemo and was now back at work on a limited basis. She'd reached out to Lucy and Buck several times during her surgery and treatment and was heartbroken when Lucy passed away.

"How you doing, Buck?"

"Not too bad, Kelli. It hits me sometimes that she's gone, but I've been able to work through it. What have you found?"

Kelli explained they'd found very little. She told him unequivocally that Jimmy Kwon had not been abducted or killed in the trailer; they found no indications of a struggle of any kind, and everything they did find led to only one person. As far as she and her team were concerned, the trailer was clean.

Buck thought about it for a moment. "If Jimmy Kwon wasn't taken from here, then it is likely the people he was investigating had no idea what kind of information he had collected, since it was all here when we arrived this morning. So, he was killed someplace else, most likely in Buford. Great job, Kelli. Thank your team for me."

Buck hugged her and told her to keep in touch, and that he was always available for her and her family. She handed him the keys to the RV and headed for her van. Buck slid back into his car, turned around and drove down the road to the office. Mrs. Talbot was sweeping off the front porch when she saw him pull up. She set down the broom and walked towards his car. He rolled down the window.

"Mornin', Agent Taylor. Did you folks find what you were looking for?"

"Unfortunately, we did," he replied. "I wanted to let you know I will call the rental company and have them make arrangements to pick up the RV. It may take a couple of days."

"So, I assume the young Asian man will not be returning for his package?" she asked.

Buck looked at her for a moment. "What package?"

"He left a package a couple of days ago before he disappeared and asked me to hold it until he came back for it. He said if he didn't come back to give it to the authorities. I kind of forgot about it until I was cleaning the office this morning and it was sitting under my desk. Do you want it?"

Buck shut off the car and slid out. "Yes, ma'am. I do."

Buck followed her into the office and waited on the customer side of the counter until she was able to bring him the package. Buck pulled a pair of nitrile gloves out of his pocket and put them on. He pulled out his knife, flipped it open and slit the tape on the end of the package. Putting away his knife, he opened the end flap and slid out a pile of papers about an inch thick. Buck leafed through the papers and noted they were mostly copies of what had been found inside the RV. He looked at the letter on top that was addressed to the agent in charge, Grand Junction Field Office.

The first part of the letter was introductory. It explained who he was and that he was running an off-the-books investigation into an illegal prescription drug ring involving the entire town of Buford, Colorado.

The letter went on to explain that he was being paid by Mark Richards to develop a case against Jack Muldoon and others in the town, which his lawyer, Steve Fletcher, would then present to the proper authorities so a legitimate investigation could be launched, and the town closed.

"What I discovered during my investigation is that Mark Richards was an early investor in getting the operation in Buford off the ground. Mr. Fletcher revealed to me during one of our meetings that Mark Richards did not want his involvement in this criminal enterprise getting out to his guests. I was not going to reveal that last little bit of information in my investigation notes.

"I know I have violated a lot of laws and DEA procedures by going off on my own, but the money was too good to pass up, and I used some of it to put a deposit down on a small ranch in Brazil. If you are reading this, then I guess I will not be making the trip since I am either in jail or dead. If it is the latter, please let my boss know I am sorry about violating my oath and let my mom and sister know I loved them. The deed to the ranch is in my bedroom closet in a fireproof box. The key is in my desk. When you find the box, you will also find digital audio tapes of my initial meeting with Mark Richards and subsequent meetings with Mr. Fletcher."

Buck put the letter down and gave a soft whistle. He sat down in the chair next to the counter and stared at the letter. Jimmy Kwon, besides being an excellent investigator, had left an insurance policy. He had Mark Richards on tape, setting up an investigation that would have sent Jack Muldoon to jail for a long time. Buck needed to hear those tapes. There was nothing illegal about all this unless it led to the death of Jimmy Kwon.

He put down the letter, pulled out his phone and speed-dialed Jess Gonzales.

Jess answered on the second ring, and before she could even say hello, Buck said, "Jess, I need you to call Jimmy Kwon's boss in Memphis."

CHAPTER FIFTY

Bax and Sheriff Trujillo were sitting opposite Randy Stewart in the interrogation room. They reread him his Miranda rights and had him sign a statement indicating he waived his right to have an attorney present. They sat quietly while he wrote out his statement on a yellow pad.

Finished, he looked up from the pad and slid it over to Bax. She read through all nine pages and then slid it over to the sheriff, who picked it up and read it. The sheriff nodded and stood up and left the room. Bax looked at Stewart.

"Randy, the DA will read your statement and then come in and talk to you. We have called your attorney, and he is on his way in. Just sit back and try to relax." He raised his cuffed hands and looked pleadingly at Bax.

Bax smiled. "Sorry, Randy. Those have to stay on until we book you. Once we are finished with the booking process, Bill Unger from the EPA will come in and sit down with you and your lawyer. I want you to understand that their investigation is separate from ours. We are concerned with the illegal dumping of hazardous chemicals within the county. They will discuss possible civil and criminal proceedings on a federal level. I would urge you to cooperate with them as you have with us."

Randy buried his head in his hands, and tears flowed as he thought about how this was going to affect his family. They allowed him to contact his wife, and the sheriff had suggested he might want to have them leave town for a while. So far, only limited information had spread around town, but as his neighbors learned more about the crimes he was accused of, things might turn ugly.

Bax sat back in her chair. "Randy, how come you didn't ever question dumping these chemicals? You knew the fracking fluid story was false; didn't you think to question what you were handling?"

Randy picked up his head. "The money was too good to pass up. We struggled for a couple of years as oil prices crashed again and everyone stopped drilling. When someone like Mark Richards calls you with an offer, you assume it is a good thing. After all, the guy is a billionaire. He told me one of his companies developed a method to render the chemicals safe so that he could use them for fracking. I guess I should have questioned the deal a little more."

"Randy, do you know anything about the fires at four of Braxton Global Energy's sites?"

"No, ma'am. The news reported they were caused by some environmental group. That's as much as I know, swear to god."

Bax thanked him for his honesty and stepped out of the room. The sheriff and Amber Hunter were sitting in the sheriff's office, and Bax stepped through the door.

"Well?" said Bax.

Amber looked at her. "We are going to charge him with the illegal dumping, which will allow us to process him and hold him in a cell. It will also give us time to put together a criminal conspiracy case against him and Mark Richards. We are still a little light on the evidence against Mark Richards, but I think we can at least get an indictment on the conspiracy charge. I also want to look at some health code violations. I want to throw the book at the son of a bitch."

"Do we have enough evidence to at least bring in Mark Richards and question him?" the sheriff asked.

Amber thought for a long minute. "If nothing else, he has been implicated in a crime by Mr. Stewart. We should ask him to come in voluntarily, so we can try to clear up the allegations. I will convene the grand jury in the morning and see what we come up with. I am also going to issue an arrest warrant for Hardy Braxton. It is still his wells being used, and we haven't cleared him of any wrongdoing. Do you have any issues arresting him, Agent Baxter?"

"No, ma'am. I do want to discuss this with Buck to make sure we don't interfere with something he might be working on. After all, the lodge fire involves arson and murder, so I don't want to jeopardize anything."

Bax left the room to call Buck, and Amber stood up, thanked the sheriff and headed for her office at the other end of the building.

Bax pulled out her phone and called Buck, who answered as soon as it started ringing. "Hey, Bax. Good news?" She lost focus as she watched Randy Stewart being escorted away, in handcuffs, to the county jail to be booked.

"Sorry, Buck. They just took Stewart over to the jail to book him. Listen, the DA is going to convene a grand jury tomorrow. She is hoping to indict Mark Richards on conspiracy charges, and she thinks we should ask him to come in voluntarily to answer some questions. I didn't want to fuck up anything you might be working on, so I told them I was checking with you first."

"Thanks, Bax. Can you hold off until I meet with the guy who says he has information on Mark Richards? I am meeting him in a couple of hours."

"I think I can make that happen. Oh, the DA is going to issue an arrest warrant for Hardy. Do you want me to bring him in, or do you want to handle it?"

"It's your case, and so far, other than being a part owner of the lodge, we have nothing on him on our end. Bring him in. Word of caution though. His lawyer may look like a little nerd, but he is incredibly sharp. Do everything by the book."

Buck took a few minutes to fill her in on the latest in the Jimmy Kwon murder investigation and about the letter and the tapes. Jess had called him back to tell him several DEA agents were on their way to Kwon's house to try to find the lockbox with the tapes in it. She would call as soon as she had something. Her bosses in Washington were interested in hearing what was on the tapes as well.

"Smart guy leaving an insurance policy. You think he knew he had been made?" she asked.

"I think he was covering his ass in case something happened. We may never know his motivation."

"You know, Buck, it seems like everything we have looked at in these two cases revolves around money. The illegal dumping, probably the fires, the lodge maybe, and the drugs. I can understand the little guys getting caught up in all that money, but what was in it for Mark Richards? He has more money than God."

"I don't know, Bax. Boredom maybe, or the fact he can get away with anything he wants because he has all that money. Guys like him usually have huge egos. It could all just be about power."

"Too weird. If I ever get that rich, please make sure you knock me down a peg or two now and then, will ya, Buck?"

"You got it, Bax. I need to run. I have one more stop to make before I meet Mr. Earp. We'll talk later."

CHAPTER FIFTY-ONE

Buck noticed the smoke in the air was a lot thicker, the wind had also been steadily picking up all afternoon and it was blowing towards Meeker. The air was heavy with moisture that had yet to turn into rain. His thoughts flashed on Cassie, and he hoped she was okay. Lucy would never forgive him if something happened to Cassie. He was the one who encouraged her when she told them she was quitting law school to become a firefighter.

He was focused on Cassie and almost missed the driveway on the right side of the highway. He turned in and followed the gravel drive past a small separate garage and parked in front of the house. He sat for a minute and admired the view. It was an old farmhouse with a big wraparound deck. The house was not quite dilapidated, though it needed some work, as did the surrounding yard, but what Buck admired most was the stretch of the White River that flowed for two hundred yards behind the house.

Buck could almost picture himself standing knee-deep in the middle of the river watching that tiny dry fly drift along in the lazy late summer current and hooking a nice-sized rainbow trout. He'd spent a lot of time on the river in the months after Lucy died. Fly-fishing was the outlet that got him through the worst moments, and it helped to clear his mind. He knew Lucy would be happy he used fishing as his release. She always loved sitting on the bank and watching him fish while she read a book or did needlepoint. He missed those days.

Buck shook off the melancholy moment and slid out of the car. Out of force of habit, he touched the pistol that was clipped to his belt. It was a habit developed over a lifetime of being a cop, and he didn't even think about it. He walked up the walkway, stepped onto the porch and rang the doorbell. He heard footsteps heading towards the door, and the door was pulled open.

Stephanie Street stood in the doorway wearing a pair of jeans, a University of Colorado sweatshirt, and bare feet. She did not look happy to see him.

"Agent Taylor, I thought I made myself clear the other day that you were not to harass my clients. What do you want?"

Buck looked at her and smiled. "I came to talk with your parents since they are the clients you tried to warn me off about. May I come in?"

Stephanie seemed a little taken aback that

Buck was aware who her clients were, but she shouldn't have been. She'd been told by everyone she contacted that Buck Taylor was incredibly thorough, and he was a dogged investigator. She hesitated for a minute like she was thinking about slamming the door in his face, but something about the way he asked seemed so unthreatening she decided to let him in.

Before she could open her mouth, Buck said, "Look, Ms. Street, I'm not here to harass your parents. I doubt your parents had anything to do with the fire at the lodge."

Sounding almost annoyed, she asked, "Why would you think that? They are well known in the international conservation movement and . . ."

"How long have they been sick?" he asked.

Stephanie stopped dead in her tracks and turned around. She was so close that for the first time, Buck could see the heavy lines under her eyes that she tried to hide with makeup. She fumbled for words.

"What are you talking about? My parents are fine. How dare you?"

Buck raised his hands in surrender. "Look, Ms. Street, it's obvious. This was once a beautiful house with what I am going to guess was a manicured lawn and flower beds, which have now fallen into disrepair. You are here cooking dinner. The roast smells awesome, by the way, and you have huge bags under your eyes from lack of sleep, which you try to cover up, but they are still there. There are also several unopened bags of pills sitting on the front table we walked past, which probably came in today's mail."

Tears started to roll down her cheeks, and she turned and walked towards the kitchen. Buck followed her and spotted a not so elderly woman sitting at the kitchen table. She was wearing a beautiful dress with a sweater, and her hair was combed and pulled back in a ponytail.

She had a crossword puzzle book sitting in front of her, upside down, and she was filling in the little squares with a black pen. She looked up as Buck entered and smiled. She then turned back to her puzzle.

Stephanie checked the roast in the oven and stirred the potatoes boiling on top of the stove. She used a kitchen towel to dry her eyes, and she leaned against the counter.

"My dad developed Alzheimer's first, about five years ago. He hardly ever gets out of bed anymore, and I have to feed him by hand. Mom developed it last year. She can still do some things when she has a lucid moment, but for the most part, her mind is shot. It's horrible. These two people were both college professors when they got into the conservation movement.

They were brilliant and were world-acclaimed, especially after we won the lawsuit.

"A year ago, I gave up my practice and moved in with them. Thank god they had the money from the lawsuit, or I'm not sure what we would have done. I don't want them in an institution. I promised I would care for them here in the house they have lived in for their entire lives. In the past, whenever there was an issue that put conservation in the limelight, they were the first ones to be questioned by the FBI or some other acronym. That's why I tried to warn you off. As you can see, they are no threat."

Buck listened to her story without comment. He said, "I know what it takes to care for someone, and I don't blame you for trying to protect them. When I said I didn't think they were involved, I meant it even before seeing them. From everything I read, it is not their style to set fires. They are more the academic type of fighters." Buck paused. "Do you know where your brother is?"

Stephanie looked surprised by the question. She thought about telling the same old family lie she always told, but she had a sense this cop was not going to buy it.

"We haven't seen my brother in several years. There was a very public split in the conservation and environmental movements while I was in college, and my brother and some of his friends headed in another direction. Mom and Dad did not agree with his choices. How did you know I had a brother?"

"There was a picture online of you and your parents celebrating the lawsuit victory in which you and your parents were named, but in the background was a young man who looked exactly like you. I assumed he must have been your brother."

"Yeah," she said. "That damn picture. We didn't even know he was at the courthouse until the picture came out in the newspaper."

"Stephanie, is your brother part of the NETF?"

"Honestly, Agent Taylor, I don't know for certain. He and his friends pulled some crazy shit, and I hope for my parents' sake he is not an arsonist, but if he is, at least they won't know about it. Now, if you'll excuse me, I need to get dinner on the table."

She walked him to the door, and as he stepped out onto the porch, he turned and said, "There are organizations that can help you take care of your parents."

"I know, but it's my job, and I wouldn't have it any other way. Thanks, Agent Taylor, for understanding." She closed the door, and Buck turned and headed for his car. He felt bad for Stephanie Street, but he also understood. He would never have called anyone to help with Lucy either. It was his job. He slid into his car and took one more look at the river. He started the car and turned around in the driveway. He had one more person to meet today.

CHAPTER FIFTY-TWO

Buck pulled into the parking lot of the Cozy Up and slid out of his car. He was about to open the back hatch to grab his backpack when a huge shadow loomed over him. He instinctively let his right hand drop down to the backstrap on his pistol, and he unsnapped the thumb break on his holster. He looked up as this mountain of a man stepped between the cars.

The man held up both his hands and said, "Whoa there. Didn't mean to startle you. Name's Morgan Earp." He lowered his hands.

Buck looked up at this man standing in front of him and kept his hand on his pistol. Morgan Earp was a giant of a man. Easily six foot six and 300 pounds if he weighed an ounce. He had short gray hair and a neatly trimmed gray beard, and wore a T-shirt that did nothing to hide his massive biceps or his incredibly flat stomach.

Earp reached his left hand into his front pocket and pulled out his ID. He handed it to Buck, who, keeping a wary eye on Earp, reached out and took the ID. He looked at the picture on the California private investigator's license and looked at Earp. The picture did not do him justice. Buck relaxed, handed back the ID and reached out his hand, which was lost in this giant's grip.

"Morgan Earp, huh? Any relationship?" Buck asked.

"No. No relationship as far as we know. Dad was a history buff, and he thought it was cute. He didn't realize what a pain in the ass it would be for me growing up."

"I was expecting to meet you inside. Would you like something to eat?"

"No, thanks. I'd rather do this out here. Too many pairs of ears in a bar like this. Can we talk out here?"

Buck nodded. Morgan Earp had spent twenty-five years with the Los Angeles County Sheriff's Department before retiring and going into private practice. His last ten years were as a homicide investigator. His practice, he told Buck, was very exclusive, and a lot of his clients had names Buck would recognize.

He explained to Buck that he had been hired by Veronica Richards, Mark Richards's wife, because she believed her husband was having an affair. Well, as it turned out, he was having many affairs, with many women, some famous and some not, which Morgan couldn't understand, because Mark Richards was about five foot eight and chubby and was starting to go bald. He was not a very pleasant man.

Veronica Richards, on the other hand, was five foot nine, drop-dead gorgeous, with an incredible body, and was a former swimsuit model. He guessed money made people do odd things. He pulled a folder out of a computer bag he had hanging over his left shoulder and handed it to Buck.

"I want you to understand I am violating a shitload of confidentiality rules I don't take lightly, but when I think the law is being broken, I can't sit by and do nothing."

"Why don't you tell me what you think is going on?"

"Mrs. Richards has known about the affairs for about a year and a half. She didn't react when I gave her the investigation package, like she already knew what was in it. She paid me the remainder of my fee without question, and I left. I guess curiosity got the better of me, and I parked my car down the street where I could see the front door and waited. A little while later, a brand-new Jag pulled into the driveway, and a good-looking guy stepped out and approached the door. He was met by Mrs. Richards before he reached the top step, and then they entered the house.

"When I got back to the office, I did a little digging, and I think the guy she was meeting with was her husband's attorney, Steve Fletcher. I let it go and went about my business, but a few months later, I started seeing the reports about the fires at the fracking sites. They began in California and then moved into Arizona, Utah and Colorado, and that was when Hardy Braxton called me. He asked me to investigate the fires.

"Mr. Braxton was sure the wells were being destroyed by an environmental group because of the fracking. The problem was nothing I discovered led me to that conclusion. When the lodge burned down the other night and ignited a massive wildfire, I felt certain it was not some ecoterrorist nutjobs. I couldn't put my finger on it, but the more I thought about it, the more it seemed like something else.

"I told Mr. Braxton I didn't believe it was the terrorists, but he didn't want to hear it. When I found out an official investigation had started, I decided to back off, but I thought you should know what I found out. I have a personal policy that once law enforcement gets involved, I'm finished. Call it professional courtesy. I reached out to a friend in the government, and he told me you were handling the investigation, and you could be trusted, so I reached out, and here we are."

Buck was now intrigued, and he opened the

file, looked through the pictures and then read the report Earp had given Mrs. Richards.

"You said you thought a crime was being committed. Care to elaborate?" Buck asked.

"I think Mrs. Richards is working with the attorney to destroy her husband. I don't have any proof, but thinking back on how she reacted when I gave her the report and what has happened since then, and the timing of when the fires started, I have a gut feeling she is behind a lot of this. After all those years as a cop, I always go with my gut."

Buck knew the feeling. He always followed his gut as well, so he knew how Earp was feeling. Buck thought about what Earp told him and sat down on the back bumper of his car. The little bug in his head was back, and he suddenly had some clarity.

He hadn't been able to figure out what the well fires and the burning lodge had in common other than Hardy Braxton and Mark Richards, and more important, he couldn't come up with a reason the lodge was so important that everyone wanted to burn it down. He also couldn't figure out how Jimmy Kwon's body ended up in the lodge. The bug was looking for an answer, and thanks to Earp, here it was. Revenge.

This wasn't about politics or money or even the environment; it was purely about revenge.

Could it be that simple? Mrs. Richards had been wronged by a cheating husband; she was going to get even, and she had the resources to do it. The problem was that the revenge had moved into criminal activity.

Another thought popped into Buck's head. Suppose Mrs. Richards found out her husband was going to ruin Jack Muldoon and have him put away for years just to protect his luxury fishing lodge? But why would that matter to her? Would she go as far as hiring someone to burn down the lodge? That still didn't tell him how Jimmy Kwon's death fit into the picture.

Buck looked at Earp. "Can I keep this?" He held up the file.

"Yeah. I don't like feeling like this woman used me to get more dirt on her husband, just to hurt him. You do whatever you need to with them."

Earp closed his computer bag, shook Buck's hand and disappeared between the cars. This case had taken a significant turn, and Buck needed to get someplace quiet to think. He was about to close up his car but instead pulled out his phone. He speed-dialed Bax.

"Hey, Buck. I was just going to call you."

Buck cut her off. "We may have been looking at all of this the wrong way. Can you get down to Meeker right away?"

"Sure, Buck. I'm on my way."

The quiet place would have to wait.

CHAPTER FIFTY-THREE

Buck had pulled into the parking lot when his phone rang. It was the main number for the CBI office in Grand Junction. Buck answered the call.

"Taylor."

"Hi, Buck, it's Paul Webber."

Paul had recently joined CBI after spending time with the Dallas Police Department. He was assigned to the Grand Junction office.

"Hey, Paul. What can I do for you?"

"The director asked me to do a background check on one James Robert Galvin, formerly of Lake County, Colorado. I just finished, and I'm not sure if this is the same guy you are looking for."

Paul explained there was no current record of a James Robert Galvin. No driver's license, no credit cards or bank accounts. Nothing. He did find a death certificate for Amanda Galvin, twenty-seven, and Sandra Galvin, seven years old, both at the same address, and both died in

1997. Cause of death was listed as homicide on both.

"I also found a death certificate on file in Lake County for a James Robert Galvin, forty-three, for later that same year. Cause of death is listed as suicide."

Buck stopped walking and asked Paul to repeat what he'd just said, which he did.

"Paul, the wife and daughter supposedly died of a rare form of brain cancer. Are you sure you have the right family?"

"That was my concern, so I double-checked and pulled their autopsies. Both the mother and the little girl did have similar forms of brain cancer, but that wasn't what killed them. I sent a request to Lake County but haven't heard back yet. This is really confusing."

"Paul, keep looking into their backgrounds. I need to make a call. I will get back to you."

Buck hung up and looked in his contact list. He found the number he wanted and dialed. The phone was answered on the second ring.

"Sheriff Whitmore, how may I help you?"

"Tom, it's Buck Taylor. How are you?"

"Well fuck, Buck, this is a surprise. I'm doing great; how about you? You hanging in there all right?"

Tom Whitmore had been a deputy in Lake County back in the late nineties. Today he was the sheriff of Lake County and had been since 2002. Buck figured if anyone could shed some light on this, it would be Tom, so he explained what he was looking for, and Tom responded in almost a reverent tone.

"Everyone here remembers that day. Amanda Galvin taught second and third grade at the county elementary school. She was one of the most popular teachers. A couple of months before she died, the family announced she would be leaving the school. Both she and her six-year-old daughter developed a rare form of brain cancer.

"I still remember the day we found them. It was one cold-ass January morning, and Amanda missed her doctor's appointment. The doctor asked us to do a welfare check because they weren't answering the phone, and Freddie Jameson and I drove out to their ranch to see what was up. We pulled into the yard, and it looked like the place was abandoned. There was no smoke coming from the chimney, and the windows were frosted over. We drew our weapons and pushed open the front door, which was unlocked, just like always.

"We found Amanda in her bed under a couple of quilts and blankets like she was trying to stay warm. At first, we thought maybe the heat went out, but then we noticed the bloodstain on the pillow. She had been shot behind her right ear with a small-caliber bullet.

"We searched the rest of the house and found Sandy in her room. She was also in bed and had almost the same wound. We didn't see any sign of Jim, so we called for forensics and put out an APB for James Robert Galvin. It was a sad day."

"Tom, we found a death certificate for James Galvin. What happened?"

"We got a call from one of their neighbors about four months later because she thought she saw a light moving around in the house. Thought it might be a ghost, so we responded. We found Jim hanging from the loft in the barn. He left a note on the kitchen table. I guess he couldn't stand to see them suffer anymore, so he shot them in their sleep, and then covered them up to keep them warm. Can you believe that? He killed them but didn't want them to get cold. Weird, huh? Anyway, he hid out in the mountains for a couple of months, couldn't live with what he'd done, so he went back to the ranch, wrote the note and hanged himself. We found him with one of Sandy's stuffed animals in his hand."

"Tom, any chance this was foul play made to look like a suicide?"

"Nah. The state troopers did a good job investigating, and your people even helped with the forensics. It was just what it looked like. Why are you interested?"

Buck explained what he and Bax had been involved with over the past couple of days, and Tom listened without comment. He told Tom about the guy Bax met who introduced himself as James Robert Galvin. Other information they'd gathered indicated his wife and daughter had gotten cancer from bad water on their farm.

"Well, Buck, either that's the damnedest coincidence with the names or someone's pulling your leg. I can assure you. He's been dead since ninety-seven."

Buck asked Tom if there were any incidents in the area involving chemical-tainted water. Tom told him that back around the same time, some of the county residents were complaining about a fracking company that supposedly polluted their wells, but it was never proven, and he hadn't heard a word since.

Buck thanked Tom and hung up. He would fill Bax in when she got to Meeker.

CHAPTER FIFTY-FOUR

J ack Muldoon stood on the front porch of his house in Buford and looked east. All day long, the flames had gotten closer and closer, and they could now see the tips of the flames above the treetops on the other side of Route 8. The long procession of cars evacuating the area and heading towards Meeker had slowed to almost nothing, and all they saw now were fire engines and emergency vehicles passing on the road.

The people of the town spent the day watering the lawns and watering down their houses. When the wind kicked up again, a couple of small spot fires started in the grass around town. The residents were able to put them out before they spread too far. He set up a fire watch as night approached.

Just before dark, another deputy came by and told them they needed to get out, but his security team ran him off like the last one. Some of the residents were starting to make noise about leaving, but Muldoon assured them they were completely safe. They had the underground bunker, and if they all worked together, they would prevail. He was not giving in to a government plot to take over his town. Besides, they still had shipments to receive and send out. About an hour before, he'd wondered why the delivery company hadn't come out to pick up the next load of boxes. He was hoping the government wasn't getting wise to his program.

Margaret Windsong stepped out onto the porch wearing a surgical mask against the smoke.

"Jack, you need to come in, the smoke is going to kill you."

Jack told her he was fine, and he needed to make the rounds of the town to make sure all was in order. He stepped off the porch, hopped onto his ATV and roared off towards the back of the town.

He swung by the warehouse to make sure the night shift was processing and packaging orders. He found out several of the team were not at their stations, and he intended to drive over to their houses and, if need be, drag them to work. As he sat back on his ATV, he noticed several shadows heading towards the back gate. He couldn't believe his people would abandon him. He fired up the ATV and roared towards the back gate, screaming orders into his headset for his security team as he went. By the time he got to the back gate, the damage was done and whoever had been trying to get away had managed to do just that.

He was tempted to drag everyone out of the bunker and their houses and find out who was gone. "Ungrateful SOBs," he thought to himself. He was going to make them rich, and they gave it all up because they couldn't stand a little smoke.

He turned his ATV around and headed back to town. The wind had died down a little, and the air was heavy with mist. Not a full-fledged rain, more like a fog, but hell, any moisture was a good thing if it knocked the smoke down. He had orders to get out, and the smoke was making that extremely difficult.

His security chief pulled up next to him, and Muldoon jumped his ass for not having a man stationed at the back gate. The chief promised to take care of it right away and roared off towards the front entrance. He would send one of those guys to the back entrance to secure it.

Since there were no other spot fires in the town, Muldoon headed for home. He needed a good stiff drink to clear the smoke out of his throat. As he sat there, his thoughts turned to the Asian Fed who had infiltrated their midst. He wondered, again, how much information Elliot Beech had passed on to the agent. He wished he hadn't been so quick to put an end to Beech's life.

He needed to know what the Feds knew. He hated looking over his shoulder.

CHAPTER FIFTY-FIVE

Buck pulled into the parking lot at the sheriff's office, grabbed his backpack and raced up the stairs. He presented his ID to the deputy on duty at the front desk and was buzzed in. The sheriff was walking out of his office with a coffee cup in his hand when he spotted Buck coming down the hallway.

Buck stopped and caught his breath. "Caleb, we may be looking at this all wrong. Bax is on her way down, so if you have time, I'd like to run through this again."

"I have a little time, but I need to head out to the fire command center. Damn thing blew up again. Let me get a refill, and I will meet you in the conference room."

Buck walked into the conference room, dropped his backpack on the table and grabbed a Coke out of the refrigerator. He walked back to the table and pulled the file Earp had given him out of the front pocket. He also pulled out the letter and package Jimmy Kwon had put together. He was spreading the papers out on the

292

table when his phone rang.

Buck answered. "Jess. Did they find the tapes?"

"Geez, Buck. I was at least hoping for a hello. Yes, they found the tapes right where Jimmy Kwon said they would be."

Jess went on to explain that Jimmy's office emailed the audio files to her, and she was calling to let him know they were also on his computer.

"Did you listen to them?" he asked.

"Yes. Right after I sent them to you. Jimmy was definitely working for Mark Richards. The first tape is Richards ranting and raving about the drug operation and how if his clients found out, they would never come to his lodge."

She told him that Richards had offered Jimmy one million dollars to put together an investigation package on Jack Muldoon. Richards was going to use it if Muldoon refused to cooperate and move his operation. He mentioned at one point on the tape that even though it was his money that set the whole thing up, he didn't have any of the business records they would need to prosecute Muldoon, and he wanted Jimmy to provide that stuff.

Buck was pulling out his laptop when the sheriff walked into the conference room with a full cup of coffee. Buck fired up his laptop and opened the email from Jess. He clicked on the attached audio files.

The first tape was what she said it was, so Buck clicked off it and played the next tape. This time it was Jimmy talking to Steve Fletcher. At one point, Jimmy asked why Richards wanted to crush this man so badly. The lawyer responded that Richards was concerned about the possibility of his lodge clients finding out he was involved with illegal prescription drugs. He figured if he could get rid of Muldoon, then he could give the business to his wife to run, and she could take the whole thing to California. She hated living in Colorado anyway, and this way, he killed two birds with one stone. Get rid of Muldoon and get rid of his wife as well.

The second tape was more planning, and the lawyer figuring out a timeline to send the information on Muldoon to the authorities. They wanted to move quickly once Jimmy's investigation was complete. The lodge was set to open soon.

Buck turned off the laptop and sat back in his chair. He still had Jess on speaker, and the sheriff was seated next to him, scratching his head.

"I will never understand rich people, I guess," said the sheriff. "A million bucks to run an investigation we could have run for free, and all to keep a lodge, which was miles away, from getting tainted by the town nearby that none of his guests would have even cared about. How weird is that?"

"Yeah, and to get rid of his wife," said Jess over the phone. "And it led to the death of a DEA agent, and even if he went rogue, he did it with the right intentions. I want these fuckers!"

Buck had to agree. This was a little bizarre, especially since he now knew Mrs. Richards was planning to destroy her husband and had been for quite some time.

"Maybe she wanted more than just the drug business. Maybe she wanted it all."

Buck and the sheriff turned to see Bax standing in the doorway. She stepped into the room, dropped her backpack on the table and pulled up a seat.

Jess's voice came over the phone. "Hey, Bax. You might be right. What do we know about the wife?"

Buck slid the file from Earp over to Bax. He filled them in on the conversation he'd had with Earp and that Earp was confident the wife was behind a lot of the problems the company had encountered lately, and she might be working with her husband's lawyer to bring down her husband.

"A woman scorned," said Jess, "and one with access to a lot of money. That's a bad combination."

Buck posed a question that just occurred to him. "Could she bring her husband down without destroying the hedge fund? That was where the big money was."

Bax was the first to respond. "We only know of two shady businesses Mark Richards is running under the hedge fund umbrella. Suppose he has a dozen businesses like this that are all self-sustaining. His wife would have more money than she could ever use, several times over, even without the hedge fund."

Everyone thought this made a good bit of sense, but it was still all speculation. All they had on the wife was a gut feeling from a private detective. Right now, they needed to deal with what they did know. Buck slid the package from Jimmy Kwon over to the sheriff, and Bax slid closer so they could both look at it together. Buck explained what was in the package so Jess could hear.

When he was finished, Jess suggested the next step was to arrest this Muldoon character. They all agreed. Buck told them he would walk the package over to the district attorney's office and see what they thought.

"Buck," said Jess. "I haven't gotten approval to run an investigation on this town, but if you are ready to move, you let me know. I have six agents and a helicopter ready to go."

Buck thanked her and clicked off his phone. Bax pulled together the files and stood up. Buck picked up his backpack, and they headed out the door.

CHAPTER FIFTY-SIX

On the walk over to the district attorney's office, Buck told Bax about the information he'd received from Paul Webber and Tom Whitmore. Bax stopped and looked at him.

"What the fuck, Buck? I didn't get shot at by a ghost. That guy was flesh and bones. What the hell is going on?"

"I'm not sure, Bax. All I can tell you is that Tom Whitmore was the first officer on the scene, and he knew the victims. If he says James Galvin is dead, then you can bet your last dollar that the guy is dead."

"Sounds like we have an impostor on our hands. It also drives me mad that we haven't had any sightings of his car, anywhere."

"Bax, this whole case is driving me nuts. Just when something starts to make sense, a new fact pops up that changes everything. I am having trouble keeping up. Just for shits and giggles, I would like to arrest someone. Let's see if the attorney can't help us with that."

Buck and Bax spent the next hour sitting with the Rio Blanco district attorney, Sylvia Garcia, reviewing all the information they'd collected from Jimmy Kwon's RV and from the package he left at the RV park. Sylvia looked through every picture and every document. Buck had worked with other attorneys who were careful, but Sylvia was cautious to the extreme. She made sure every *t* was crossed, and every *i* was dotted, and she had Bax rewrite the request for the warrant three times before she was comfortable. When they were finished, Sylvia sat back in her chair and looked at Buck and Bax.

"Okay, guys. I feel good about what we have here. This guy Kwon was a hell of an investigator. Let's call the judge and see if he is in."

Sylvia picked up her desk phone and dialed the number for County Court Judge Earl Flagg. The judge was just sitting down to dinner, but Sylvia was persuasive, and he finally relented and told her to send the two officers over with the evidence and he would look at it. She thanked the judge and hung up.

She picked up her pen, wrote the judge's address on a slip of paper and handed it to Buck.

"Good luck, guys, and be careful, okay?"

Buck thanked her, and they grabbed their pile of evidence, their backpacks and the warrant application and headed out the door. They loaded everything into Buck's car, and Buck pulled up the address on his phone. The judge lived a couple of blocks away, so they pulled out of the parking lot and headed north.

Three blocks later, they pulled up in front of a beautiful old Victorian-style home. Buck admired the craftsmanship as they parked and walked up the walk. Mrs. Flagg met them at the door and escorted them to her husband's office.

Judge Flagg was a lot younger than they'd envisioned when they saw the house. With dark brown hair and a brown mustache, the judge was distinguished looking. He looked up from the papers on his desk.

"Good evening, Agents, why don't you show me what you have."

Bax handed the judge the application, and Buck pulled out the files and laid them on his desk. Just like Sylvia, the judge reviewed every piece of evidence. He asked a lot of questions. When they were finished, he picked up the pen from his desk and signed the warrant.

He handed the warrant back to Bax and said, "Agents, get these people out of my county and be careful."

They thanked the judge and left his house. They needed to coordinate an arrest, one that was not going to be easy, since the person being arrested did not believe anyone had jurisdiction over him.

Buck pulled out his phone and called the director.

"Hey, Buck. What have you got?"

Buck told the director about the warrant and filled him in on his meeting with Earp and on the box Jimmy Kwon left. He ran through the approach he wanted to take with arresting Jack Muldoon, and the director offered a few suggestions. He also told him about the odd situation with James Galvin.

"So, this guy has been dead since ninety-seven. Does he have any family we know of who could be using his name? He'd be, what, about sixty-three now. I'll call Paul Webber and have him start looking."

The director told Buck to call if he needed any help and hung up, and Buck felt a little foolish. They were so busy he hadn't gotten back to Paul, so he never had a chance to ask the same question. Bax had heard the conversation and nodded.

"Makes sense, Buck. Maybe he had another kid who would be somewhere in his forties. The guy I spoke with appeared to be closer to sixty, but he might have been younger."

Buck pulled into the parking lot, and they grabbed their evidence and the warrant. Time to do some real police work.

CHAPTER FIFTY-SEVEN

Buck was sitting in the conference room, working his phone. He wanted to handle the arrest quietly, but the more he thought about it, the more he wished he had a platoon of army rangers available. He wanted to start by knocking on the front door, but he also wanted that platoon of rangers waiting in the wings in case the shit hit the fan. He knew he couldn't get rangers, but he could get the next best thing.

Buck called Sheriff Trujillo. Gil, besides being the sheriff of Moffat County, also ran the Northwest Colorado Interagency SWAT Team. Because most of the police agencies in the northwestern part of the state were relatively small, they'd banded together several years ago to create a mutual aid emergency response unit. Buck knew a lot of the officers and deputies who made up the SWAT team and had the utmost respect for them.

"Hey, Buck, what's going on?"

"Hey, Gil. I need you to call out the SWAT team

first thing in the morning."

He went on to explain his plan for the arrest of Jack Muldoon, and that he wanted to have the SWAT team available as backup if needed. Gil questioned Buck's approach.

"Sounds like you might be better off if we hit them hard and fast."

"I agree, but I don't want to get into a shoot-out, and we don't know Muldoon's state of mind. He might be a crazy survivalist, or he might still be the battle-hardened soldier the file says he is. We will go in easy at first."

"Whatever you need, Buck. Let me know at dawn where you want us, and we will be there."

Buck thanked Gil and dialed Jess Gonzales, who answered right away.

"Damn, Jess, are you ever away from your phone?"

"You know me better than that. What's up?"

Buck explained what he needed, and Jess was eager to help. She knew her team would be happy to get this Muldoon guy, and she hoped Buck would give her a few minutes alone with him, so she could get to the bottom of Jimmy Kwon's death. Of course, she knew Buck would never go along with that idea, but a girl could dream.

Buck thanked her and hung up.

Bax sat at the other end of the table coordinating the forensic team. She wanted them ready to go as soon as she called them after the arrest.

Buck looked at his watch and realized they'd missed dinner, so he told Bax to wrap up, and they headed out the door for the short drive to the Cozy Up.

They walked in the front door; as always, Buck noticed several male heads turn when Bax walked in, and like always, most of them turned back around when she took off her jacket and they could see the gun and badge on her belt. Bax had that effect on men, and Buck often wondered why some lucky guy hadn't taken her for his own, or vice versa. He wasn't the kind of man who thought a woman could only be whole if she was married, but as far as he could tell, Bax was a hell of a catch.

Sam walked around the bar and gave Buck a big hug, and Buck introduced her to Bax. The two hit it off right away, and after a few minutes, they were talking and laughing like they had known each other for years. Buck sat back and listened since he was the focus of most of the conversation.

Sam left to put in their order, and a few minutes later, a waitress returned with a Coke for Buck and a draft beer for Bax. They sat and looked around the bar, which was crowded with locals and tourists alike. The volume on the jukebox was up, and it made it difficult to talk, so they sat there and watched the people.

Most of the conversations seemed to revolve around the smoke in the air and the fire in the forest. Buck heard someone mention the fire was now up to four thousand acres, and there were almost a thousand firefighters on the line. Buck thought about Cassie, which made him think about his son Jason. He'd called Jason when he had first gone out to the lodge to see if he could get a set of blueprints, but Jason never called him back. It wasn't unusual for Jason not to call. Where Buck was close to Cassie and David, Jason seemed to gravitate towards Lucy, and he took it hard when she died. He made a mental note to call him later.

Dinner arrived, and Bax dug into her steak and salad like she hadn't eaten in a month. She looked over at Buck.

"Sam seems nice. Have you known her long?"

Buck nodded. "About twenty years, I guess."

"She's gorgeous. Are you sleeping with her?"

If Buck wore dentures, he would have swallowed his teeth. Instead, he felt his face get red, and he started to sweat. Bax smiled at him and laughed.

"Shit, Bax. What kind of question is that?"

"You can see by the way she looks at you that you mean something to her. I think you make a nice-looking couple."

Buck was getting redder in the face when his phone rang. He looked at the number and excused himself for a minute so he could go outside to hear.

"Hey, Caleb. What's up?"

"Hey, Buck. If you want to hit Buford tomorrow morning and pick up Muldoon, you might want to do it early. Pat says they are expecting strong winds to hit around nine, and he is afraid it might jump Route Eight. If it does, Buford is going to burn, and those idiots will not evacuate."

Pat took the phone from the sheriff. "Seriously, Buck. If the winds hit like we expect, and the rain doesn't come tonight, I'm afraid we might get overrun. I've got five hundred firefighters converging on the highway in front of Buford right now, and we are going to go like the hammers of hell to push back while we have the chance."

"Pat, is there anything I can do to help?"

"You don't happen to have a couple of bulldozers in your back pocket? State's resources are spread pretty thin with all the fires, and heavy equipment is not available, so we will do it the old-fashioned way."

Pat hung up, and Buck had started to walk back into the bar when he had a thought. He speed-dialed a number on his phone and waited.

"Hi, Buck. How are you holding up?"

"Hey, Rachel. I'm doing good. Is Hardy around?"

Buck waited while Rachel went to find Hardy. He knew what he was going to ask was a little out of line, but this was important.

"Hiya, Buck. What's up? Calling to warn me there's a warrant for my arrest in Moffat County? I already know that."

"I'm sorry, Hardy. I have been so busy today; I didn't know. Are you okay?"

"Yeah," said Hardy. "So, if that's not it, what can I do for you?"

"This may be a hard ask, but do you still have that road crew working outside White River City?"

Hardy said he did and asked why. Buck told him what he wanted, and he heard silence on the other end of the line.

"You got some balls, brother. I will give you that."

Buck waited quietly. He knew the old Hardy

would never refuse him, but with all that was going on, he wouldn't blame him if he did.

"When do you need them?"

"Now," Buck replied.

"Fuck, Buck. Let me make some calls."

Hardy hung up, and Buck walked back into the bar to finish his dinner. He hoped Hardy would come through.

CHAPTER FIFTY-EIGHT

Sunrise broke smoky, cold and damp, but the fire was still raging as Buck pulled over on the side of the road behind two SWAT vehicles. He wished they had time to scout out the area, but he was hoping with all the noise and confusion from the fire, they might catch Muldoon's people asleep at the switch. That's why he wanted to try the soft approach first.

He slid out of his car and opened the back hatch, pulled his ballistic vest out of the back and slipped it over his shoulders. He then checked the pistol on his hip, took his ankle holster out of the locked gun safe that was welded to the frame of the car and strapped it around his right ankle. He put his CBI nylon windbreaker on over the vest and put on his CBI cap.

Sheriff Trujillo had assembled his team, and they were looking at Google Earth on his laptop. They found a couple of ways to surround the town without being seen, and he was giving his team their assignments. Buck walked up and looked over the map.

"What do you think, Gil? Can we do this without getting anybody killed?"

"I think we can. My biggest worry is that fire. It's getting close to the road. If the firefighters can hold it back, we might have a chance."

Bax pulled in behind Buck and walked up to the group. She looked like she and Buck shopped at the same store. She was ready for action.

"Are we ready?" Buck asked.

"Yeah. What about the DEA? Are they ready?"

Buck had worked out the details with Jess while it was still dark out. They reconned the town and determined that one of the two big buildings was most likely the warehouse. The other building she wasn't sure about, so she positioned her guys between the two. The original plan was for them to chopper in and act as a diversion. The smoke from the fire put an end to that idea, so they came up with plan B.

Buck picked up his radio. "Jess. You guys ready?"

"Roger" came the response.

Buck looked at Bax. "You ready?"

"Let's go get him," she responded.

Buck shook hands with Sheriff Trujillo, and they headed for his car. He slid into his seat, pulled his pistol out of his holster and laid it on the seat between his legs. Bax pulled hers and held it down alongside the passenger seat. She held the arrest warrant in her hand.

Buck pulled off the shoulder and headed for the road into Buford. As he turned up the gravel road, he spotted the two sentries standing by the gate with their assault rifles at the ready. Buck pulled up to the gate and rolled down his window. He put his hand on the pistol on the seat.

"What do you want, cop? We told you guys before we ain't leaving, so back the fuck up and leave."

Buck studied the man holding the assault rifle. He waved him over to the car. The guy was hesitant at first, then he grew a pair and walked over.

Buck whispered, "We have a warrant to arrest Jack Muldoon."

The guy looked at him. His partner asked him what he said. He shrugged and stepped closer to the window and leaned in, a shade too close. Buck pushed his arm out the window, grabbed the strap on the assault rifle and pulled the guy towards the window at the same time he slid his pistol under the man's chin and told him not to move. His partner started to react, but two black-clad SWAT officers flew around the guard shack and dropped him to the ground.

Buck held his prisoner until the SWAT officers had FlexiCuffed his partner and then grabbed the guy Buck held and forced him to the ground. He was quickly incapacitated.

The sun, trying to shine through the smoke and the clouds, was clearing the trees as the SWAT officers opened the gate and Buck pulled through. He looked in his rearview mirror and saw the SWAT vehicles turn up the road. He keyed his mic and announced that the guards were down, and they were moving on the house. Buck drove down the main street and pulled to a stop in front of what they had determined was the largest house. According to the map Jimmy Kwon had made notes on, this house belonged to Jack "Fighting Red" Muldoon. Several members of the SWAT team raced down the street and moved behind the house.

Buck and Bax opened their doors and slid out of their seats. Buck could feel the wind starting to pick up. They walked onto the front porch and took up positions on either side of the door. Buck knocked, softly, like a neighbor might if she were coming to borrow some sugar. They waited and heard footsteps approaching the door.

The person on the other side opened the door without ever looking out the window. It was nice to see that survivalists were able to trust one another enough to think no one would bother them. As the door unlatched, Buck slammed his full weight into it, and the woman fell to the floor and screamed.

"Jack!"

Buck stepped over her and saw the blood streaming down her face from where the door hit her in the nose. Bax made fast work of rolling the woman over and cuffing her arms behind her back. She then put a piece of duct tape over her mouth.

"Jack Muldoon!" Buck yelled. "We have a warrant for your arrest."

They both moved cautiously with their guns pointed ahead of them. Buck was just thinking how quiet the house was when they heard the SWAT team smash in the back door.

"POLICE! WE HAVE A WARRANT!" came multiple yells as the SWAT team fanned out across the ground floor.

Buck pointed towards the woman on the ground, and the SWAT officers nodded. He pointed up the stairs and, following right on each other's backs, the three team members headed up the stairs. Buck moved towards the living room, which was off to the side of the entryway.

The SWAT team yelled that the upstairs was clear and started back down the stairs as a loud boom sounded behind a closed door, and a huge ragged hole appeared in the door. The first SWAT officer on the stairs took a couple of pieces of buckshot to his left arm, but he was able to return fire with his assault rifle.

Buck moved from the living room to the side of the door that was now destroyed and slammed his foot into it. The door pretty much fell off its hinges. The second blast from a shotgun took out a chunk of the doorframe to Buck's left, but he pulled back just in time to avoid getting peppered with buckshot.

The SWAT team was now standing on the other side, and one of them lobbed a flash-bang down the stairs, which exploded in a loud, blinding flash of light. When the sounds from the flash-bang cleared, they heard a door slam in the basement. Buck, with his gun pointing forward and his flashlight now in his other hand, peeked around the doorjamb.

Not seeing anyone at the bottom of the stairs, he advanced down the stairs, followed by the SWAT team. Buck panned his light around the basement and was amazed at the number of weapons that were stored in racks along the walls. This guy could have outfitted a small army. That was when he spotted the steel door that was built into the wall.

"He's got a bunker!" shouted Buck.

The SWAT team leader stepped up to the door and ran his hand over it and banged on it with the end of his Maglite. He turned to Buck.

"I doubt we can blow it. We can try."

Buck heard Bax call out. He told one of the SWAT officers to keep an eye on the bunker door, and he raced up the stairs.

CHAPTER FIFTY-NINE

Bax came running up the front steps and onto the porch as Buck came out the front door.

"The wind just blew up, and the fire is crossing the road." She pointed over her shoulder.

Buck stood there, stunned. What a little bit ago had been a wall of trees on the other side of Route 8 was now a wall of flames. Spot fires were popping up on their side of the road. The wind was howling, and they could feel the heat as the wind and the fire acted like a blast furnace.

Buck looked around and saw several of the black-clad security guys lying on the ground with their hands bound. A couple of people stood on the street and seemed unsure of what was happening. Buck told Bax to evacuate everyone as fast as possible. A gust of wind blew up, and as Buck watched, the roof of one of the houses at the outer edge of the town exploded in fire.

He keyed his mic. "Gil, we need firefighters and evac now!" He ran down the stairs before Bax could say a word and yelled for her to uncuff all the security people and get them all shovels.

Bax spotted Sheriff Trujillo racing up the street.

"Buck wants me to cut the security guys loose and get them shovels." She looked at the sheriff with doubt in her eyes. She rarely questioned anything Buck asked her, but these guys were under arrest, and she was worried about releasing them.

The sheriff looked over his shoulder. Flames had blown across Route 8 and were now racing across the field towards the town. Bax could see firefighters running from the flames and heading towards them. She knew this did not look good.

"Cut them loose, Bax. We are going to need everyone we can get to fight this monster."

Bax yelled over to the SWAT officer watching the guards to cut them loose and get them on the fire line.

Sheriff Trujillo keyed his mic. "Caleb. The fire has crossed the highway. We need everything you've got!"

"Hang in there, Gil," came the reply. "We are sending everyone we can."

The sheriff looked around. All eyes were on him. The noise from the firestorm sounded like a jet engine, and he could feel the heat on his face.

He started barking orders at the top of his voice. "Grab all the hoses you can find and start hosing down the grass between here and the road. If you don't have a hose, grab a shovel or a rake."

He grabbed one of the firefighters.

"You see that fence line?" The firefighter nodded. "We need a firebreak along that fence line, and we don't have a lot of time to get it done. Get everyone you can and start digging and clearing the brush. Also, get some of your guys and have them start putting out spot fires as fast as they can. Now move!"

"What about the people in the bunker?" someone shouted from the street.

Bax looked at the sheriff and at the civilians gathering around, who looked terrified. She grabbed a woman standing there with a shovel.

"What bunker?"

"The bunker under the warehouse. Muldoon locked the people who weren't working in the bunker after a couple of people fled the compound last night. They won't be able to breathe, and they will cook to death in there. You have to help them!" She ran off to join the others on the fire line.

The sheriff called over three of his guys. "Get into that building, find that bunker and get those people out!"

"What about Buck?" shouted Bax.

"Can't worry about him now. We have work to do." He handed her a shovel one of his guys found in a toolshed behind the house. Bax took the shovel and headed for the fire line.

She glanced across the field and saw Buck leading about a dozen firefighters towards the house that was burning. Buck was waving his hands and pointing as they ran, and then he did something she would never understand. She watched him kick open the door to the burning house and rush inside, followed by two firefighters. Her heart skipped a beat at that moment, and she wondered if she would ever see him again.

The two firefighters rushed out of the burning building dragging a woman behind them. "Where is Buck?" she thought. She was about to race towards the building when Buck ran out of the building carrying a dog in his arms. He fell to the ground coughing and laid the dog down. The last thing she saw before she raced off to join the fight was Buck getting licked by the dog.

The sheriff looked towards the fence line. There were hundreds of people scraping at the ground to get rid of the vegetation: both firefighters and civilians standing shoulder to shoulder. They were making a valiant effort, but as he looked across the field, he knew they would need a miracle to pull this off. He didn't have a plan B.

The first helicopters appeared over the tree line and started dumping their buckets of water on the fire that had crossed the road and was racing towards the town. As the helicopters left to pick up more water, several tanker planes flew over and dumped both water and fire retardant on the field between the town and the road.

The sound of an approaching airplane caused everyone to stop and look as a huge Boeing 747 flew past the town to the south, made a steep left turn to run parallel to the road and dropped a massive amount of water along the edge of the field. Bax was amazed by the accuracy and the daring of the pilots. She couldn't be sure, but she figured the plane was no more than two hundred feet off the ground.

The sound of the water hitting the ground reminded her of a flash flood she and her father had gotten caught in while hiking in the Canyonlands in Utah. She remembered the sound was deafening, and they had been barely able to climb to a ledge almost forty feet above the slot canyon they were hiking in. They spent two days sitting on that ledge until the water receded enough that they could walk out.

What scared Bax the most at this moment was

the silence after the planes and helicopter left the area. The only sound was the fire, and she realized she liked the sound of the aircraft a lot more.

The sheriff was standing next to Bax, clearing vegetation, when he stopped and looked up. Bax stopped too. The fire line was getting wider, but the flames were getting closer. They had no idea how long they had been at it, but they knew it had been several hours, and everyone around them looked exhausted, but they kept fighting. The airdrops were helping, but what everyone there wanted more than anything was rain.

Bax saw Buck several times, leading his intrepid band of firefighters from hot spot to hot spot, working along the edges of the fire. They were making a valiant effort to stay ahead of the flames, but she wasn't sure they were winning.

"Did you hear that?" the sheriff asked her. "Sounds like a tank."

Bax heard it too, but she didn't know what it was or where it was coming from. All she knew was it was getting louder. Several people along the fire line stopped to listen to the clanking metal sound.

A cheer rose and traveled along the fire line. Out of the smoke came three huge bright yellow bulldozers, followed by a couple of front-end loaders and three water trucks. The bulldozers rolled up towards the fence line pushing huge piles of dirt as they went. The water trucks followed behind, spraying the ground that was cleared, and then started working their way towards the town. And leading the fight, sitting atop the first bulldozer, was Hardy Braxton.

The sheriff tapped her on the shoulder and smiled. "Did you bring the arrest warrant? Looks like Mr. Braxton is coming to us." He let out a huge belly laugh and went back to shoveling.

Bax pointed towards the north, and the sheriff stopped and followed her gaze. Coming out of the smoke across the field, with what looked like a hundred firefighters, was Buck. He looked like a Civil War general leading the charge. The firefighters veered off and headed for the fire line, and Buck ran up to Bax and the sheriff. He was filthy from his head to his toes, and he was sweating up a storm. "I found a few guys to help," he said. "Pat is throwing everything he has at this spot right now."

A tanker plane flew over and dumped a load of retardant along the front edge of the fire line, followed by three helicopters. The fight was definitely on, and Pat was pushing his crews for a knockout.

It was amazing, because it looked like everyone got a second wind when the dozers and the new firefighters showed up, and now they were all working twice as hard to clear debris and vegetation. Many people raced off to help the firefighters put out spot fires, and a bunch more were hosing down the buildings.

CHAPTER SIXTY

Bax had no idea how much time had passed, but for the first time, as she looked around, she felt like maybe they were winning. The winds had started to die down about an hour ago, and the efforts of everyone on the line seemed to be paying off. She stopped to take a drink of water from a water bottle someone had thrown to her, and she looked around for Buck, who was nowhere to be found.

The sheriff looked towards the warehouse, and his SWAT team appeared at the door, followed by about a dozen men, women and children, many of whom were coughing and trying to breathe. The sheriff waved to his men. Jess Gonzales appeared at his side. He had no idea where she even came from. Her face was covered in soot.

"We've secured the warehouse as best we can. They have a massive amount of counterfeit prescription drugs here. We also put all the computers and file cabinets we could find into a room in the back of the warehouse. Hopefully, it will protect them from the fire."

"What happened to you guys? We haven't seen you all day," Bax asked as she walked up.

"Buck asked us to secure the warehouse and protect the evidence. The back wall caught on fire, but we were able to get it out before it spread. We needed to protect the evidence, but we ended up helping your guys get a bunch of people out of a bunker. The day got worse from there."

She looked at Bax. "Buck blew past us on an ATV a few minutes ago. Last we saw him he was headed for the tree line, and it looked like he was following someone on another ATV. What's going on?"

Bax keyed her mic. "Buck, can you hear me?"

A garbled message came back over the radio. All she was able to make out was "Muldoon" and "ATV." She asked him to repeat what he said, but she got nothing else. She looked at the sheriff and then at Jess.

"Do you think Muldoon had a back way out of his bunker?" the sheriff asked. "My guy reported a little while back that the door was still closed in the basement. Shit."

Suddenly, the sky opened up, and the rain came pouring down. Everyone on the fire line stopped and raised their faces towards the sky. The rain felt good, and the sheriff stood there and let the rain wash over him. He'd said they needed a miracle to survive this, and he got two.

The bulldozers that came out of nowhere, and now the rain. He turned around to talk to Jess and Bax, but they were nowhere to be seen. He looked across the field and spotted two ATVs racing off towards the west. "I wish I had those two women on my team," he said to no one in particular.

He was worried about Buck, so he keyed his mic and put out a call for his guys to meet on him. He was heading towards one of the SWAT vehicles when he spotted an SUV coming across the field. He raised his hand to keep the rain out of his eyes so he could see who it was.

Sheriff McCabe came bouncing across the field in his department SUV. He skirted around the fire and came in from the northwest. He pulled to a stop and spotted Sheriff Trujillo. He looked around at what looked like a war zone. He could not believe the number of people on the line still trying to push the fire back. The rain was making their jobs a lot easier.

"I can't believe you guys survived that firestorm! Absolutely incredible!" He saw the SWAT guys running towards them from all different directions.

"What's going on?" he asked.

"Looks like Muldoon got away, and Buck is in pursuit on an ATV. Bax and Jess Gonzales lit out after him," replied Sheriff Trujillo. "I was about to send my guys after them."

"Okay, Gil. You and a couple of your guys head out, and I will keep an eye on things here."

Sheriff Trujillo and three of his SWAT team officers jumped into the closest SWAT vehicle and headed out across the field on what earlier was a dirt road but now was a small river. The truck fishtailed in the mud, but the driver got some traction and they forged ahead.

Sheriff McCabe now took over the firefighting efforts and continued where Sheriff Trujillo let off, and he started moving civilians and firefighters around the town like pieces on a chessboard. There were still hot spots flaring up around the town, but the rain-soaked grass and dirt were killing most of the embers as they flew.

He knew the fight was not over, but the fight had left a lot of people on the line. All around the center of the town, firefighters and civilians were taking a breather from the fight. No one was looking for shelter from the rain since it felt too good to pass up.

More firefighters were joining the fight as time wore on, and he realized almost the entire firefighting force was now in the town. The water and retardant drops were continuing unabated, and it seemed like everything and everybody was covered in an orange tint. The rain was helping people look human again.

Most of the fire was now contained to the other side of Route 8, and the sheriff decided to risk bringing in some much-needed food and water. He called Pat on the radio and told him to open the north portion of the road from the command center to the town entrance, and he asked him to send in the supplies.

The small caravan of National Guard trucks pulled into the town about fifteen minutes later, and people started to line up. It reminded him of pictures he had seen of refugee camps. Everyone looked wiped out. He had been a part of many firefighting efforts in his role as sheriff, but the work these people had done today was unlike anything he had ever seen before. They had saved this small town and a lot of ranches beyond it.

CHAPTER SIXTY-ONE

Buck was working with the firefighters on one of the houses that caught fire when he spotted some movement in his peripheral vision. He turned and looked around. As he looked past Muldoon's house, he spotted someone running from the house to one of the two outbuildings that sat behind the house.

He squinted through the smoke to see who was running, and he realized it was the woman he had knocked down with the door when they entered the house to arrest Muldoon. He watched as she ducked behind the outbuilding.

"What the hell?" he thought.

He'd started walking up the street towards the house when a black ATV came roaring out from behind the outbuilding and headed west. The woman was sitting on the back of the ATV, but it was the driver he noticed. Well, it was the driver's red hair he noticed.

Jack Muldoon and the woman were trying to get away in all the confusion. Buck dropped his shovel on the ground and raced towards the house. One of the security ATVs was parked by the walkway to the front door. Buck looked around, trying to spot either Bax or the sheriff, but with everyone crowded together working the fire line, he couldn't locate them, so he ran up the street and jumped on the ATV.

Buck was an old hand at driving ATVs. He used to take the kids riding in the mountains behind Crested Butte ski area. There were several small streams and lakes he used to love to fish, and an ATV was the only way to get there. He turned the key, and the engine roared to life, so he kicked it into gear and headed after Muldoon.

By the time Buck cleared the town, Muldoon was about a mile ahead, and the visibility was terrible. Buck was not wearing a helmet or goggles, and the ash in the smoke stung his eyes as he picked up speed. He could barely see the tree line, but he knew Muldoon had entered the forest, so he bore down on the throttle. The bouncing jarred his teeth, and he felt like his head was going to explode as he raced up the dirt trail.

The sky opened up, and the rain filled his vision. He was glad the rain was washing the dust out of his eyes, but now he had raindrops stinging his eyes and clouding his vision. He also noticed the trail was getting slick, and he felt out of control as he raced towards the woods.

He heard his radio crackle, and a muffled voice asked, "Buck, can you hear me?"

He keyed the mic that was clipped to his jacket, but the bouncing made it hard to speak. "Bax, Muldoon is trying to get away on an ATV. Need backup."

The ATV started to slip sideways on the slick mud, and he let go of the mic so he could grab the other handlebar. It took everything he had not to flip the ATV, but he pushed the throttle as far as it would go.

Out of the smoke, he saw the trees, and by sheer luck, he stayed on the trail and flew into the forest. He could see Muldoon's tracks in the mud, and he knew he should back off the speed, but he needed to stop Muldoon.

About a half mile into the forest, Buck came around a corner and cranked down hard on the brakes as the ATV spun sideways and slid in the mud, stopping at the edge of the gulley. He jumped off the ATV, wiped the dirt and mud out of his eyes, unsnapped the thumb break on his holster and pulled his pistol.

He pocketed the ATV key and stepped towards the gulley. The ATV Muldoon had been driving was smashed against the far bank of the gulley and had buried itself in the mud. The dry creek bed at the bottom of the gulley was beginning to fill with water. Buck scanned the area with his pistol and then slid down the slope into the water.

He knew as soon as he saw the position of her head that the woman who had been riding with Muldoon was dead—her neck had obviously broken when the ATV hit the gulley—but even though she appeared to be dead, Buck had learned a long time ago not to take anything for granted. He reached down and checked her neck for a pulse. The woman was dead. Looking around, he noticed a small spot of blood on a rock. The rain was causing the blood to spread out and run off the rock into the now-rushing water below.

Muldoon had been hurt when he drove into the gulley. Buck had no way of knowing how bad, so keeping his pistol pointed ahead and using his left hand for leverage, he pulled himself up the bank and scanned the area. He could make out footprints in the wet undergrowth, so cautiously, he moved forward.

He hadn't walked far when Muldoon charged from behind a tree and slammed into him. The gun flew out of his hand, and they both tumbled into another gulley that was full of mud.

Buck had been hit hard while playing football in his youth, but this was a whole new experience. Muldoon, a seasoned combat veteran, grabbed Buck's jacket and flipped Buck over his head as he fell. Buck landed hard on his back and gasped for air. The mud in the bottom of the gulley absorbed some of the pressure, but it still hurt like hell, and he knew he was in trouble.

Muldoon was on his feet and dove at Buck, who was able to move just enough that Muldoon was only able to catch him with one of his arms. It helped that Muldoon couldn't get any traction in the mud and slid as he dove.

Still gasping for air, Buck grabbed Muldoon's arm and rolled over him, twisting his arm behind his back in an unnatural position. Muldoon let out a yell and slammed his fist into the side of Buck's head. Buck saw stars, but he knew he was in the fight of his life, so he scrambled back up the side of the gulley and then launched, feet first, and hit Muldoon in the chest as he was starting to stand up.

Buck picked himself up off the ground and charged Muldoon again as he stood up. Muldoon hit the ground hard with Buck on top of him. He was able to get in a couple of lucky shots that staggered Buck, but Buck was able to hang on and counter punch. They rolled around in the gulley, and Muldoon pushed Buck off and tried to stand but slid in the mud.

By this time, Buck had had enough. He was feeling dizzy, and he was afraid he might pass out. He needed to end this and fast. Muldoon, who had both height and weight on him, was trying to stand up, and Buck knew if he did, this fight might be over. He dug deep, and five months of holding back the anger of losing Lucy exploded out of him like a volcano. He jumped off the bank and, in one swift move, kicked Muldoon in the side of the head.

Muldoon flopped down in the mud, and Buck attacked with everything he had. The fight had gone out of Muldoon, who was now moving slowly, but Buck wasn't finished. He grabbed Muldoon by his collar, jerked his head up and pounded his face with his fist until his knuckles started to bleed. Blood poured out of Muldoon's nose and mouth, spraying all over Buck as the blows continued to find their mark. Somewhere during the beating, Muldoon lost consciousness, but Buck wasn't finished yet. He had a lot more anger to get out of his system.

He reared his right hand back, and as he started to drive forward, something grabbed his arm.

"Buck, that's enough!"

He spun his head around; standing behind him, soaking wet and covered in mud, was Jess Gonzales. She let go of his arm and wrapped her arms around him.

"It's okay," she said in a soft, calming voice.

"You got him."

Buck, looking half-dazed, looked at Jess and then at Muldoon. He climbed off Muldoon's chest, fell back against the bank and looked up at Jess, who had slid over to the opposite bank. He looked down at Muldoon and stared for a minute. Dazed and bleeding, he tried to stand up but had trouble keeping his balance, so Jess stood up, grabbed his arm and helped him up. He shook off the dizziness and wiped the mud and blood out of his eyes.

"Fuck, Buck. Looks like we missed a hell of a fight."

The voice came from Sheriff Trujillo, who was standing on solid ground above Buck, along with Bax and two of his SWAT officers. Buck just smiled.

CHAPTER SIXTY-TWO

Buck was able to walk under his own power back to the ATV; of course, Jess and Bax walked on either side of him, just in case. They were okay with him walking, but they drew the line at him driving the ATV back to the town. The sheriff called for two of the ambulances that were stationed at the fire command center, and then he and Bax walked back to where Muldoon was still lying, handcuffed and unconscious, guarded by one of the SWAT officers. With the rain coming down, it was difficult to get good pictures, but Bax documented the scenes as best she could.

The light was beginning to fade as the EMTs carried the bodies of Margaret Windsong and Jack Muldoon out of the woods to the waiting ambulances. Windsong's body would be heading to the forensic pathologist in Grand Junction, while Muldoon was heading to the small hospital in Meeker, accompanied by two SWAT officers.

Buck was checked over by the EMT, who bandaged his right hand, cleaned up the cuts on his face and arms and told him he needed to rest. He told Buck to stop by the hospital and get his head checked since he more than likely had a concussion. Buck said he would, and then he downed a handful of ibuprofen and climbed into the front seat of the SWAT vehicle.

The SWAT vehicle headed back towards the town, and Buck put his head back and closed his eyes. The bouncing, as they hit water-filled potholes on the trail, made the pain in his head unbearable. He had to grit his teeth after one pothole because he wanted to scream to make the pain stop. The driver, noting the look of anguish on Buck's face, slowed down and tried to miss as many potholes as he could. The rain made seeing difficult.

They'd passed the outer edge of the town when Buck's radio crackled. He opened his eyes and turned up the volume.

"Buck, come in."

He keyed his mic. "Go ahead, Caleb."

"Did you guys pass a concrete block building at the far end of the town?"

Buck said they hadn't, and the sheriff explained that one of the security guards was willing to make a deal in exchange for immunity. In good faith, he'd told him to get someone to look in the old pump house by the tree line.

Buck hated the idea of turning around and

driving around looking for a pump house since his head was throbbing, but he told the sheriff they would take a look, so he asked the driver to turn around and head back the way they came.

Now that the smoke had started to clear out of the air from the rain, and the fire seemed to be on its last legs, the visibility improved significantly. They made it back to the edge of the woods and then started driving northwards along the tree line. Bax, sitting in the back seat, was the first one to spot an old building in the distance, and she shouted over the engine noise for the driver to head towards it.

The driver stopped a couple of yards away from the building, and everyone stepped out of the vehicle and looked around cautiously. They had no idea if this was some kind of ambush, so everyone had guns drawn as they approached the building.

Buck pointed towards the side of the building, and Sheriff Trujillo and one SWAT officer headed around to the back of the building. Buck and Bax took up positions on either side of the old rusted metal door. The building was not large, maybe one hundred square feet with concrete block walls and a metal roof.

The sheriff and the SWAT officer came back around the building and joined Buck and Bax at the door. They reported there was no back door and no windows. Everyone tensed as Buck grabbed the doorknob and turned.

They knew it was going to be bad when Buck pushed the door open and they rushed in and fanned their guns around. The space was pitch black, but the smell was overwhelming. The smell of urine and the coppery smell of blood invaded their nostrils and mouths, but it was the smell of decomposition that was the worst. Buck, already queasy from the head blows, and not having eaten anything all day, had to step back outside. Bax came out behind him and helped him lean over. He rested his hands on his knees and tried to breathe. She stood by him until the sheriff and the SWAT officer stepped back outside, and the SWAT officer vomited. The sheriff looked a little green himself, but he was able to keep it inside.

"We have a body," he said. "Looks like it's been here a couple of days." He keyed his mic and called Sheriff McCabe and explained what they had found in the pump house.

Buck stood up, took a deep breath and pulled out his phone. "Buck Taylor, how's my favorite cop?" said Max Clinton as she answered her phone.

Buck told her he was doing good, and then he explained what they'd found. He asked her to send the forensic team from Grand Junction back up. Bax would be waiting for them.

Max told him not to worry, and then she ended the call as always. "You're a good man, Buck Taylor. God will watch over you."

Bax, Sheriff Trujillo and Buck got back in the SWAT vehicle, while the SWAT officer remained behind to secure the scene. They drove in silence back to the town.

The sheriff came to a stop in front of Muldoon's house. It was still raining, but not as hard, and it looked like the last rays of sunlight were trying to break through the clouds as they exited the vehicle.

Buck looked up to see Hardy standing next to Sheriff McCabe. He walked up, shook hands and said, "You really came through, Hardy. Thanks for the equipment, but I was surprised to see you here."

Hardy, soaking wet like everyone else and dog-tired, smiled. "I couldn't ask my people to charge into hell unless I was willing to go with them."

He looked at Bax. "Young lady, I understand you have a warrant for my arrest. If you can promise me some dry clothes and some food, I am ready when you are."

Bax looked at Buck and then at both sheriffs. Buck nodded, and she pulled her handcuffs out of the pouch on her belt.

"Hardy Braxton, you are under arrest. You have the right to remain silent . . ."

When Bax finished, she asked Hardy to put his hands behind his back, and she applied the cuffs. Sheriff McCabe called over one of his officers and asked him to take Hardy back to Meeker and place him in the holding cell until they could get back to town. He also told him to get him a dry prison jumpsuit and to have someone run over and get him a steak at the Cozy Up.

Sheriff McCabe looked at Buck, who looked like he wanted to pass out, and he told him to get in the passenger side of his car. He would have one of his deputies drive him to the hospital in Meeker.

Buck asked Bax if she was good, and she told him to go on. She would be okay. Buck headed for his car with the help of the deputy. It had been a hell of a day.

CHAPTER SIXTY-THREE

Buck woke up in his dark hotel room with a start. He had a headache and ringing in his ears until he realized the ringing was his cell phone, which was sitting on the bedside table. He reached over and picked it up.

"Taylor."

"Hi, Buck. It's Paul Webber. Do you have time to talk?"

Buck, who was now sitting on the side of the bed with his head propped against his hands, told him to go ahead. Paul explained that he'd continued to research James Robert Galvin and found something he thought might be important. Buck sat up straight and listened to what Paul had to say.

"James Robert Galvin had a son from a previous marriage. I had to scour the country, but I found a birth certificate in Enid, Oklahoma, that had Galvin listed as the father. I can only assume Galvin had little to do with the kid because he was raised by his mother and stepfather, and he had the stepfather's name."

"What's the son's name?" Buck asked.

"His name is Steven Fletcher. The mother's name was Regina Keller. Stepfather is Harold Fletcher."

"Can you background Steven Fletcher?"

Paul explained he already had. "Fletcher grew up in Enid. In high school, he lettered in football, track and sharpshooting. He went to the University of Oklahoma and Harvard for law school. Here is where it gets interesting. His current employer is listed as the International Heritage Fund. He is . . ."

"Mark Richards's attorney," said Buck, "and he was a sharpshooter in high school. Shit, Paul, nice work."

Buck hung up and checked his phone. He had four missed calls. He had no idea what time it was, but when he opened the curtains, the sun almost blinded him. He jumped in the shower and was getting dressed when his phone rang.

"Buck, are you okay? I called you four times and no answer."

"I'm good, Bax. How long was I out?"

"You've been out about thirty-six hours. You sure you're okay?"

"Yeah, so what's up?"

She told him that Jack Muldoon was awake and

on his way to the Rio Blanco Sheriff's Office, and Hardy's attorney was requesting a meeting for this afternoon at two.

Buck said he was on his way. He grabbed his gun and badge and clipped them to his belt, grabbed his backpack and ran out the door.

He pulled into the parking lot, grabbed his backpack, walked into the building, presented his ID to the deputy at the desk and headed back to the conference room.

"Looky there," said Sheriff McCabe. "He is alive. You don't look too worse for wear." The sheriff laughed because Buck looked as bad as he felt. He had assorted cuts and bruises, a black eye, bandages on his knuckles and a concussion. Even with that, Buck was glad to be alive.

Buck smiled and set his backpack down on the desk, and he grabbed a donut from the box on the desk and a bottle of Coke from the refrigerator. He was starving.

While he ate, he filled everyone in on the phone call he'd had with Paul Webber.

"You think this is the guy who shot at me? But the guy the sheriff and I talked to was much older than this guy would be."

"Here's what I'm thinking in my very sore brain. Suppose there was something to Galvin's wife and daughter dying from chemicals that one of Mark Richards's companies dumped near their ranch. Now, let's assume for a minute that Fletcher found out Galvin was his real father and then found out he killed himself because of their deaths. He could have decided to get revenge, and what better way to do that than from inside the company?"

"Jesus, Buck. That's a lot of assumptions," said Bax. "How would he know he would get a job with Mark Richards? No way that's a coincidence."

Buck wasn't sure how to answer. Bax was right. This was all conjecture, and they had no proof of any of this, but the more he thought about it, the more he felt he was close. Bax sat down at the table and did an internet search of Steven Fletcher. Buck pulled out his phone and dialed a number.

Tom Whitmore answered on the third ring. "Buck Taylor, twice in one week. To what do I owe the pleasure?"

"Tom, have you ever heard the name Steven Fletcher?"

"Sure, we all knew Steven."

Tom explained that Steven had contacted Jim Galvin a couple of years before his wife and daughter died. Steven had been raised by his mom and stepdad and had no contact with his father until out of the blue he called one day.

He wanted to connect. Jim was hesitant at first, but they met and hit it off. He came for a visit and ended up staying for a long time. The family grew close. Steven was a young attorney and tried to convince Jim to sue, but Jim wasn't interested.

Buck interrupted. "Sue, about what?"

"Jim had used a new fertilizer on the ranch, mostly on their vegetables. A few months later, the first signs of the tumors occurred. If I remember right, a couple of cows died as well. Jim blamed the fertilizer for the cancer. Jim was a meat eater; his wife was a vegetarian, and that was how they were raising their daughter."

Tom continued, explaining that Steven tried to get the fertilizer company to cover their medical expenses and he got laughed at, so he tried to get Jim to file a lawsuit. By then, it was too late for his wife and daughter. He tried to file a lawsuit after Jim died, but the suit was dismissed.

"Steven was heartbroken when Jim killed them. He was back in Oklahoma, helping his mom with some legal matters. When he heard the news, he rushed back here and helped with the search for Jim. He took care of all the funeral expenses.

"When Jim killed himself, Steven went off the deep end—ranting about getting even with those

SOBs. Not sure where he is now, but last I heard he went to work at some big financial company his stepdad had worked for. Why you askin'?"

Buck didn't answer. Instead, he asked, "Do you remember the name of the fertilizer company, and do you know what kind of cars the family drove?"

"Sure. Jim drove an old Chevy pickup truck, and his wife drove an old yellow Ford station wagon. The company was Gardner or something like that. Buck, what's going on?"

"Tom, the car may have been involved in a shooting in Moffat County."

"The one involving one of your agents? Saw the APB, but the plate and the description of the driver didn't match their car or anyone I knew."

"Can you have someone run out to the ranch and see if the car is around there someplace and have them take along a fingerprint tech?"

Buck hung up and looked at Bax and the sheriff. Bax was clicking away on the keys on her laptop, and suddenly she stopped. "Guardian Agricultural Products."

Buck and the sheriff looked at her, waiting for more.

"Guardian Agricultural Products was started in the nineteen forties. It struggled along until it was purchased by a young entrepreneur in nineteen ninety-eight. The buyer was Mark Richards. The company filed for bankruptcy after allegations came out about one of its fertilizer products killing animals. Mark Richards turned the company around. This was the first company he bought after establishing a mutual fund company. Today it is valued at forty billion dollars."

The sheriff let out a low whistle.

She clicked on another page. "Steven Fletcher, according to everything I could find, has worked for Mark Richards's company for about ten years. Two years ago, he became Mark's personal attorney. I looked up Harold Fletcher as well. Harold worked as a CPA for the company in the nineties and early two thousands before he retired."

"Would Steven Fletcher try to sue a company his father worked for?" asked the sheriff.

"Maybe he didn't know and only found out after his stepdad retired. Interestingly, he became Mark's attorney two years ago, and that was about when the fires started," replied Bax.

"I know one thing," said Buck. "We need to talk to Fletcher."

CHAPTER SIXTY-FOUR

Fletcher would have to wait. Muldoon had been brought into interrogation room one, and Buck needed some answers. Buck opened the door to the interrogation room, walked in and sat down. He looked across the table at a man whose nose was bandaged; he had a split lip, two black eyes and assorted cuts and bruises. Since Buck didn't look much better, he had no sympathy for the damage he caused.

Buck laid a file folder on the table and sat back. He wondered how Muldoon would react to questioning. After all, he had been in the military a long time, and when Buck reviewed his file, he noticed Muldoon had received a great deal of evasion training, as well as training in how to deal with interrogation. Muldoon had been subjected to some of the most severe interrogation techniques in the anti-terrorist playbook. He had been waterboarded, he'd had electrodes connected to his body, and he had been subjected to physical and emotional attacks. His record indicated a man who did not crack easily.

"I'm sorry about Margaret Windsong," he said.

Muldoon shrugged, but Buck could see a tear form in the corner of his eye.

"I'll say one thing, Jack; may I call you Jack? You are one tough SOB."

"I should have killed you," Muldoon replied unapologetically.

"You certainly tried. I never fought that hard in my life," said Buck. He sat back and looked at Muldoon.

For the next two hours, Buck didn't say a word. So far, he hadn't asked for an attorney, so Buck decided to play it patiently. He needed answers, and he didn't want Muldoon to clam up. So, he sat there quietly.

Buck could see Muldoon was getting anxious. He started fidgeting in his chair, looking around the room and sweating. Though Muldoon had been subjected to numerous interrogation techniques during his military training, the one thing Buck couldn't find in his file was that he had been tortured with silence, and Buck was good at silence.

Buck felt Muldoon was ready, so he opened the file and took out the picture of the charred body of Jimmy Kwon. He looked at it for a minute and slid it across the table. Muldoon tried to stay stone-faced, but Buck noticed a small micro reaction in his eyes.

"Why did Jimmy Kwon have to die?" he asked.

Muldoon stared at the picture. Buck slid another picture out of the folder and looked at it. He slid it towards Muldoon, and this one got a definite reaction. Muldoon looked at the picture of Elliot Beech, still sitting in the chair in the old pump house. The hole behind his ear was quite visible in the photo.

"Shit" was all he said, but Buck noticed a lot more sweat on his brow, and his hands fidgeted enough to jangle the handcuffs.

Buck waited a few more minutes, letting the photos sink in. Then he pulled out another picture and slid it across the table. The image of Margaret Windsong lying in the gulley with her head hanging at an unnatural angle was more than he could bear, and the tough old fighting-guy façade broke in a million pieces. Muldoon hung his head in his hands and cried like a baby. Buck sat back and didn't say another word.

Muldoon looked up and, with tears in his eyes, said, "What do you want from me?"

Buck slid several reports out of the folder, which he'd asked Bax to print off for him from the investigation file. He spread them out on the table. A lot had happened during the thirty-six hours he had been asleep.

"Look, Jack, here's the deal. We have you for the murder of Jimmy Kwon and the murder of Elliot Beech. The witnesses and the forensics nail that down. We have the gun you used to kill them both, which we found in your house. We have Kwon's fingerprints in your house and on the arm of the chair in the pump house. Those two charges alone will get you the death penalty in Colorado. You killed a federal agent, which will get you a federal death sentence, and, so you know, those guys want you bad. We have you for running an illegal prescription drug distribution network. We have you for kidnapping for the townspeople you locked in the bunker, flight to avoid prosecution, resisting arrest, assaulting a law enforcement officer and a whole mess of other crimes, plus the Feds want you for the murder and the drug distribution. The list goes on. With all that, if the state or the Feds don't kill you, you will spend the rest of your life in jail."

Buck let all that sink in. He'd had only one question when he walked into the room, and he was holding that for the right moment. Muldoon turned an interesting pale color and looked like he was going to be sick.

"Oh, I almost forgot about the arson charges for starting the fire at the lodge and causing the wildfire."

He sat back in his chair and waited.

Muldoon sat there, and Buck could see the gears turning in his head. He hoped Muldoon was suffering from the same headache he was right now.

"I may have done all those other things, but I didn't set that fire," Muldoon said.

Buck slid a white pad across the table along with a fine-tipped felt marker and told Muldoon to write his story. Two hours later, Muldoon slid the pad back to Buck, sat back and closed his eyes.

Buck read the twenty pages Muldoon had written. He explained that he discovered Kwon was a Fed and Elliot had been the one to contact him, and how he dealt with both of them. He laid out the whole drug distribution setup, including the names of some of his principal players. He wrote about finding out that Mark Richards, who had been the one who purchased the ground the town was built on, and who financed the entire operation, turned on him and was going to ruin him and send him to jail, all because of a stupid lodge.

Buck was no psychologist, but as he read the statement, he could see the paranoia creeping in. Muldoon was probably brilliant when he first put the whole plan together, but some of his decision-making was questionable. He put down the statement.

"How did you get involved with Mark Richards

in the first place?"

The question caught Muldoon off guard, and he glared at Buck.

"You leave her out of this!" he yelled.

"Leave who out of this, Jack? I have no idea who you're talking about."

"Bullshit! All she did was tell me Richards had sent a Fed into my town. That's it. I will take full blame for everything." He pointed at the pad. "But you stay away from her!" he screamed.

Buck thought Muldoon was going to have a heart attack, he was so red in the face as he strained against the handcuffs.

Buck had his answer. "Veronica Richards is your daughter?" he asked.

Muldoon sank into the chair. His face got soft, and his voice got low. "Please, sir. You have my statement. Please don't hurt my little girl. She had nothing to do with any of this, I swear." Tears rolled down his face.

"Okay, Jack. I understand, but I need to know who started the fire at the lodge."

Jack looked up and wiped the tears away. "I have no idea. We put the body in the lodge to embarrass Richards when his first guests arrived. I thought the government started the forest fire to force us out of our town so they could get the drugs. I didn't even know the lodge was the cause until you told me. Thought it was the forest fire that burned the lodge."

Buck thanked him for his honesty, gathered up his papers and Jack's statement and left the room. In the hallway, he met the sheriff and the DA. He handed the papers to the DA and walked away. He needed a handful of aspirin.

CHAPTER SIXTY-FIVE

They found Buck sitting in the conference room with his head back and his eyes closed.

"Buck, you okay?" asked the sheriff.

Buck opened his eyes. "Yeah, I'm fine. Just trying to shake this headache."

Muldoon was being processed into the county jail, and the DA was holding a paper in her hand. She handed it to Buck.

"That's a warrant for Veronica Richards. She is being charged with conspiracy and as an accessory to murder before the fact. From Muldoon's statement, her telling him about the investigation her husband was running on the town directly led to the deaths of Jimmy Kwon and Elliot Beech. She's as responsible as he is," said the DA.

Buck couldn't agree more, and it was the opening he needed to get to Mark Richards and Steven Fletcher. He still wasn't sure how this all would play out, but he had a working theory.

He knew Mark Richards had some shady deals working, and he had little direct evidence to convict him. He could use the same charges as they had for Veronica. Mark Richards's investigation into Muldoon had also directly led to the deaths of both men. They also had the testimony of Randy Stewart. The picture from the wall in his office was enough to prove a connection between Mark Richards and the illegal dumping.

He knew Steven Fletcher had set up and executed an elaborate plan to hurt Mark Richards and had most likely either set the oil well fires or hired someone to do it. He was probably the one who told Veronica about the investigation to ruin Muldoon, not knowing she was his daughter. Logic said he had something to do with the fire at the lodge, but Buck still didn't know who had actually torched the lodge.

He finished explaining what they knew, and the sheriff asked, "Why did you believe Muldoon when he said he didn't set the fire?"

One thing Buck knew about career soldiers was that honor was a huge part of their lives. Muldoon had accepted his involvement in all the crimes Buck listed.

"Accepting the crimes he committed was the honorable thing to do, but he was not going to accept being charged for a crime he didn't commit. Call it vanity, call it honor or call it something else, but either way, it violated his personal code."

The DA smiled. "Buck, you have an amazing gift for reading people. I am glad you're on our side."

Realizing he had eaten only a donut in the last forty-some hours, Buck decided to walk across the street to the diner and fill up. He pulled out his phone and dialed Pat Sutton at the fire command center.

"Hi, Buck. You doing okay? Heard you got into a hell of a fight."

"Yeah, I'm okay, Pat, and you heard correct."

Buck asked him how the fire was doing. He noticed the smoke and haze seemed to be gone from the air over Meeker. Pat told him the fire was about 90 percent contained. He was starting to send some of the firefighters off to other fires around the west. The rain had helped, but Pat had some more to say.

"I owe you a lot, Buck. Getting that heavy equipment and helping lead those townspeople to fight the fire was amazing. At first, I was pissed when we got word what you guys were doing in the town. I figured against that firestorm, there was no way you could come out ahead, and I was worried we would end up burying a lot of people. We understood you had no choice but to stay and fight, but that still took a lot of balls. The wind shift caught us all off guard, and I feared for your safety."

Pat continued. "When we heard a bunch of the hotshot teams had to converge on your location because of the wall of flames, we decided it was time to make a stand, so we threw everything we had at that location. It was winner takes all, and to be honest, I had no idea how it was going to turn out. It might have been the biggest mistake of my career, but I had to protect all of you. Once it started raining, I knew we had broken her back. At that point, it was all-hands-on-deck and balls to the walls. I still can't believe how long and hard everyone worked. I owe you one. You ever need anything, you can count on me."

Buck thanked Pat and hung up. He still hadn't heard from Cassie, but he hoped her team was one of the ones being pulled off the line.

Just before he stepped into the diner, Buck looked down the street. The white pickup truck that had been shadowing him since he arrived was no longer there. He wondered if his visit to Stephanie Street had something to do with his no longer being shadowed. He also wondered if one of the two guys in the truck might have been her brother.

Buck had been toying with the idea that the NETF had targeted the lodge for destruction to make another big statement. He wondered if that was why the gas cans were found outside the building. That thought made him think something happened to scare them off.

Could that something have been another fire? That led him back to Steven Fletcher. Did Fletcher set the fire in the lodge to take away one of Richards's prize possessions, without knowing Muldoon had put a body in the lodge to embarrass Richards? He couldn't wait to get Fletcher and the Richardses into an interrogation room.

Buck grabbed a quick lunch at the counter and then headed back to the sheriff's office. It was almost time to meet with Hardy.

CHAPTER SIXTY-SIX

Hardy Braxton and Irv Tuttleman were seated at the table in the conference room opposite Sheriff McCabe, Sheriff Trujillo and Bax when Buck walked into the room. Bax gave Buck a confused look, wondering why they were all there. He shook his head.

Buck took the seat next to Sheriff McCabe and looked at Hardy. Sheriff McCabe told him they were waiting for a representative from the U.S. attorney's office. As they were talking, Bill Unger stepped into the room and took a seat.

Buck was watching Hardy the entire time, and he thought Hardy looked remarkably calm. He also noticed the bags under his eyes. He was betting Hardy hadn't slept much in the past couple of days. Jail would do that to a person.

Buck was about to ask Hardy how he was holding up when a tall, statuesque Black woman walked into the conference room, followed by a young man with a briefcase and a young woman pulling a small suitcase on wheels.

"Good evening, folks, don't get up. I'm

Assistant U.S. Attorney Olivia Rivera." She pointed towards the young man. "This is James Worthington, my associate, and the young woman setting up in the corner is Angie Jackman. Angie is a court reporter and will be making a transcript of everything we say here today. Does anyone have any objection to a written transcript as well as a recorded transcript?" She placed a small digital recorder in the center of the table.

She asked each person around the table to introduce themselves and state the organization they represented. Once that was completed, she sat down and opened a black leather-bound notebook. Buck had never worked with this woman before, so he decided to listen to what she had to say.

Ms. Rivera looked at Hardy and then at Tuttleman. "Mr. Tuttleman, you pulled a lot of strings to get this meeting, so why don't you tell us why we are all here?"

Tuttleman opened a folder he had sitting in front of him and slid a document across the table to Ms. Rivera, who picked it up and read through the three pages. She slid the papers over to Buck, and he and the sheriffs each read through the document. He then passed it to Bax and Bill Unger.

"For the record, the document we received

from Mr. Tuttleman is a statement alleging certain facts as they pertain to the illegal dumping of hazardous chemicals, as well as a proposal for how to remedy those allegations in what Mr. Tuttleman believes is a fair and equitable way. Is that correct, Mr. Tuttleman?"

"That is correct."

She waved her hand to indicate he should continue. Irv Tuttleman explained that his client, Mr. Braxton, had entered into an agreement with Mark Richards to develop several oil fields, and Mark Richards violated that agreement by getting involved in the dumping of illegal chemicals. He said Hardy was unaware of the dumping. He pulled a piece of paper out of his briefcase and slid it across the table.

"This is a signed and notarized statement from the drilling contractor who was hired at the request of Mark Richards. He states that he falsified the drilling reports and inventory reports at Mark Richards's direction."

He went on to state that even though Hardy was unaware of the situation, he was willing to take responsibility for the dumping since the wells belonged to his company, provided he was given complete immunity in exchange for testifying against Mark Richards. He also agreed to deposit five million dollars into an account that would be used to clean up the three well sites under his name and to help anyone in the county impacted by the dumping, as long as they could provide proof the contamination was a result of the dumping of the chemicals in the wells.

He reached down and picked up a box off the floor. "This box is one of several containing information we believe could be used to prosecute Mark Richards for numerous crimes. Mr. Braxton and Mr. Richards are involved in several companies besides energy development, and after a careful review, we are concerned about possible illegal activities that may be taking place at some of those businesses. We will surrender these boxes to agents of the federal government once we have reached an immunity agreement."

Ms. Rivera asked Hardy and his attorney to wait in the hall while they discussed the matter. They rose from their seats and left the room. She turned her attention to the folks in the room.

"This is a complicated situation that I am going to make more complicated. The U.S. Justice Department has been running a yearlong investigation into Mark Richards's business dealings, and before I ask you to agree with this immunity deal, you need to know the U.S. Attorney General and the governor of Colorado both signed off on the deal. It seems Mr. Braxton has friends in high places."

CHUCKMORGAN

Everyone at the table looked surprised, except Buck. He knew Hardy's political connections ran deep. He was surprised, however, that the director hadn't called him to fill him in, but sometimes that was the way things went. Buck would have been inclined to go along with the deal anyway, and not because of family loyalty.

It was unlikely Hardy would have received jail time anyway. He was an upstanding member of the community, and he had been taken advantage of by Mark Richards, like everyone else he dealt with, but more important, Hardy came through when they needed him, and he came through in a big way.

Ms. Rivera went on to explain that several small development companies had come to them with complaints detailing the way Mark Richards did business. She told them these companies, like Hardy's company, were caught in one crime or another, and they had little in the way of records to implicate Mark Richards.

"A sample of the information Mr. Tuttleman has offered to provide was reviewed by subject matter experts at the Justice Department last night, and they believe this may be the first time we have a chance to penetrate Mark Richards's world. We have spoken with the district attorneys in each of your respective counties, and they are willing to go along with whatever decision you make. If you decide to pursue this on your own, we will not interfere, but understand that we can do a lot of things you can't do or don't have the resources to do.

"We have asked you all here because many of the crimes in question are still considered to be local crimes, and we are asking you, on behalf of the United States government, to allow us to take jurisdiction over those crimes. We can now discuss this if you wish."

"It sounds like the decision has already been made, way above us, so why even ask?" asked Bax.

Everyone around the table nodded, except Buck. He looked around the table.

"Bax and I were sent here to help you guys solve a couple of what we thought were unrelated crimes, which are part of what we all now believe to be a larger criminal enterprise. I, as much as anyone in this room, would like to get my hands on Mark Richards and his associates and prosecute the shit out of them, but the truth is, the evidence we have against him is mostly conjecture. We all know what he has done; we just can't prove most of it. Ms. Rivera is correct. They have the resources, meaning money, and the infrastructure to run this investigation much better than we can. I believe the information they are offering can be better utilized by the federal government. That said, we will also go along with whatever decision you make."

Both sheriffs stood up and walked to the back of the conference room. Everyone else watched as they calmly discussed their options. Bax looked like she was ready to explode until he gave her a look that said, "Let it go for now."

The sheriffs stepped back to the table and sat down. Sheriff Trujillo asked the only question they had decided on. "We understand that Hardy Braxton gets a pass, but per this agreement, Mark Richards, his wife and his attorney are out of our reach, correct? What happens if you can't prosecute?"

"You are correct. If we fail to prosecute at the federal level, then these people are fair game." Both sheriffs nodded their agreement.

CHAPTER SIXTY-SEVEN

Bax was not happy and hadn't been since Ms. Rivera left, along with copies of all their files. They were sitting on a bench outside the sheriff's office. Well, Buck was seated; Bax was pacing back and forth.

"It's not fair. We worked our asses off trying to solve these crimes, and the Feds are going to waltz in here and take all of our work. I was shot at, Buck. I want the son of a bitch who did that."

Buck let her get it out of her system, and when she calmed down, he said, "You heard what the director said. The governor is going to be all over the Justice Department to make sure they don't let this drop. You know Governor Kennedy as well as I do; he is not going to let this go."

Bax knew he was right; she just hated to admit it. Prosecuting someone like Richards was going to cost a fortune, and the state could not bear that cost all alone; besides, the crimes being investigated covered violations of federal laws as well as laws in multiple states. This investigation and eventual trial would go on for years.

"Look at it this way," he said. "We stopped a potential environmental crisis here and alerted several other states so they could begin fixing the problem with the help of the EPA. We broke up a major international prescription drug ring and solved two murders, including the murder of a federal agent, and we helped put out a monster forest fire. Not bad for less than a week's worth of work."

"But we still don't know who shot at me, and we don't know who burned the lodge down. I hate walking away and leaving the job unfinished."

"Look, Bax, we can't solve them all. All we can do is the best we can do. You did great work on this, and I am proud to have been able to work with you, so go back to the hotel, close out your investigation report and head home tomorrow. We will never run out of crimes to solve."

"Thanks, Buck, it was a real pleasure working with you again."

She hugged him and headed for her car. Buck sat there for a few minutes and enjoyed the silence. He was about to get up when his phone rang. He looked at the number and smiled.

"Hey, Jason. I thought you fell off the ends of the earth. Where you been?"

Jason explained he had gone on a fly-fishing trip to Alaska with some of the guys from his architecture firm. He only got home that afternoon and was stunned by everything that had happened while he was gone. Buck filled him in on some of the events that had unfolded and then suggested they get together the following weekend, and he would tell him and his wife the whole story. Jason told him to come to Boulder and they would do a barbecue, and Buck agreed. He hung up the phone as the rain started. It wasn't heavy, just a nice, gentle rain, and Buck decided to do something he hadn't done in a long time.

He walked down the street in the rain to a little mom-and-pop ice cream parlor. When the kids were younger and they did a lot of family camping, one of their family traditions was to go out for ice cream. The only stipulation was it had to be when it was raining. They used to all pile in the car, drive to the nearest place where they could get ice cream and then stand under an overhang of some kind and eat their ice cream and listen to the rain. Even after the kids were grown, Buck and Lucy continued the tradition. He hadn't done it since Lucy died.

Buck stepped out of the ice cream parlor, walked to the building next door and stood under the awning, his thoughts turning to Lucy and how much he missed her. Tears formed in his eyes, and he stared at the street, lost in thought.

At first, he didn't notice someone had walked up and stood next to him. When he looked over, the first thing he saw was the yellow firefighter shirt and the green suspenders. Cassie stood there, eating an ice cream cone. She reached over and wiped a tear from his cheek, then she laid her head against his chest, and he reached around, put his arm around her shoulders and pulled her tighter. With tears in her eyes, she softly said, "Mom would have loved this."

EPILOGUE

Steven Fletcher had been told by an anonymous source in the Justice Department that they were all being investigated for various crimes, and he filled Mark Richards and his wife in on what he'd discovered. He knew Mark and Veronica were safe for now, since they were on their private island and had no fear of extradition. He would join them after he cleared up some legal matters, and then they would come up with a plan to squash the investigations. A lot of politicians owed their careers to Mark and his money, so he was confident they could end this before it even got started. At least that was the story he told Mark.

So here they were, Mark and Veronica, on a beautiful white sand beach in a quiet cove on their private island. Veronica was lying naked on a blanket and looked like a Greek goddess with her blond hair and incredible body.

Mark didn't even notice. He was too busy walking up and down the same hundred feet of beach, screaming into his cell phone. Veronica had no idea who he was yelling at, but it was a heated conversation.

Mark turned and was walking back in her direction when he stopped and stared out towards the breakwater. He clicked off his phone, shoved it into the pocket of his shorts, stepped closer to the water's edge and raised his hand to shield his eyes.

"Who the fuck does this guy think he is?" he was yelling.

He turned to Veronica and started pointing.

"This is my fucking island, what the fuck? Can't he read the goddamn signs?"

Veronica sat up on the blanket and looked towards the end of the secluded bay. A small boat was coming through the channel that cut through the coral reef that protected this little bit of heaven. Mark watched as the boat seemed to slow down. It was almost a half mile across the bay, so he was having trouble making out who was steering it, but he would find out, and this guy was going to have all the trouble he could handle.

He stepped into the water and placed his hands on his hips, looking defiantly towards the little boat. The bullet hit him square in the chest, fragmented and blew his spine out through his back. Mark Richards fell over onto the beach. His death occurred without a sound.

The little boat started moving again and headed for the beach, where it plowed into the sand and stopped. An older man with gray hair and a slight beard jumped out of the boat and looked at the body lying in the sand. He still carried his rifle with the unusual-looking silencer.

"I do need to thank the welder. This thing works perfectly," he said to no one in particular.

He looked over at the still-naked Veronica sitting on the blanket and headed in her direction. Veronica, at that moment, was now the wealthiest woman in the world, and that thought made her smile. The guy stopped at the foot of her blanket, and they looked at each other. Steven Fletcher laid the rifle down next to the blanket and pulled off his gray wig and beard. He stripped off his shirt and shorts as Veronica lay back on the blanket and spread her legs.

Steven knelt on the edge of the blanket and then lay down on top of Veronica. She was lying there listening to his grunts and groans, but she was thinking about the fact she could have anything or anyone she wanted.

Steven turned his head towards her left shoulder. She put her right hand under the blanket, dug down in the sand a couple of inches and pulled out a six-inch stiletto.

Acknowledgments

A special thank-you to my daughter Christina J. Morgan, my unofficial editor in chief. She devoted a significant amount of time making sure the book was presented as perfectly as possible. Any mistakes the reader may find are solely the responsibility of the author.

Also, I would like to thank my family for all of their encouragement. I have been telling them stories since they were little, and I always told them someone should be writing this stuff down. I finally decided to write it down myself.

A special thanks to my other daughter Stephanie Morgan for being my beta reader and offering some great comments as we went through the process.

I want to thank my closest friend, Trish Moakler-Herud. She has been encouraging me for years to write my stories down. I hope this will make her proud.

Finally, a very special thanks to my late wife, Jane. She pushed me for years to become a writer, and my biggest regret is she didn't live long enough to see it happen. I love her with all my heart and miss her every day. I think she would be pleased.

About the Author

Chuck Morgan attended Seton Hall University and Regis College and spent thirty-five years as a construction project manager. He is an avid outdoorsman, an Eagle Scout and a licensed private pilot. He enjoys camping, hiking, mountain biking and especially fly-fishing.

He is the author of the Crime series, featuring Colorado Bureau of Investigation Agent Buck Taylor. The series includes *Crime Interrupted* and *Crime Delayed.*

He is also the author of *Her Name Was Jane*, a memoir about his late wife's nine-year battle with breast cancer. He has three children, three grandchildren and two dogs. He resides in Lone Tree, Colorado.

Other Books by the Author

"*Crime Interrupted: A Buck Taylor Novel* by Chuck Morgan is a gripping, edge-of-the-seat novel. Right from page one, the action kicks off and never stops, gaining pace as each chapter passes." Reviewed by Anne-Marie Reynolds for Readers' Favorite.

"This crime novel reads like a great thriller. The writing is atmospheric, laced with vivid descriptions that capture the setting in great detail while allowing readers to follow the intensity of the action and the emotional and psychological depth of the story." Reviewed by Divine Zape for Readers' Favorite.

Made in the USA
Las Vegas, NV
23 June 2024

91354171R00229